"You are only a duty child, Murdoc. Though mark me true, I have never made the less of you in this house because of that. And no one can say that I have!"

A duty child—one of those embryos shipped from a populous world to a frontier planet in order to vary the stock, by law assigned to some family to be raised and nurtured as their own. It did not greatly matter to me that I was not of her blood. But that I was not a son of Hywel—I hated that! I think she read this in my eyes for she shrank from me. But she need not have feared any trouble, for I turned and went from that room, and that house, and later from Angkor. All I took with me was my heritage—*the ring out of space....*

THE ZERO STONE

THE
ZERO STONE

ANDRE NORTON

SF
ace books
A Division of Charter Communications Inc.
A GROSSET & DUNLAP COMPANY
51 Madison Avenue
New York, New York 10010

THE ZERO STONE

Copyright ©, 1968, by Andre Norton

An Ace Book, by arrangement with The Viking Press, Inc.

All Rights Reserved.

For A. M. LIGHTNER,
who was the "Godmother" for EET

This Ace printing: August 1981

4 6 8 0 9 7 5
Manufactured in the United States of America

ONE

The dark was so thick in this stinking alley that a man might well put out his hand and catch shadows, pull them here or there, as if they were curtain stuff. Yet I could not quarrel with the fact that this world had no moon and that only its stars spotted the night sky, nor that the men of Koonga City did not set torch-lights on any but the main ways of that den of disaster.

Here the acrid smells were almost as thick and strong as the dark, and under my boots the slime coating the uneven stone pavement was a further risk. While my fear urged me to run, prudence argued that I take only careful step after step, pausing to feel out the way before me. My only guide was an uncertain memory of a city I had known for only ten days, and those not dedicated to the study of geography. Somewhere ahead, if I was lucky, very, very lucky, there was a door. And on that door was set the head of a godling known to the men of this planet. In the night the eyes of that head would blaze with welcoming light, because behind the door were torches, carefully tended to burn the night through. And if a man being hunted through these streets and lanes for any reason, even fresh blood spilt before half the city for witness, could lay hand upon the latch below those blazing eyes, lift it, to enter the hall beyond, he had sanctuary from all hunters.

My outstretched fingers to the left slid along sweating stone, picking up a foul burden of stickiness as they passed. I had the laser in my right hand. It might buy me moments, a few of them, if I were cornered here, but only a few. And I was panting with the effort that had brought me so far, bewildered by the beginning of this nightmare which had certainly not been of my making, nor of Vondar's.

Vondar—resolutely I squeezed him from my thoughts. There had been no chance for him, not from the moment the four Green Robes had walked so quietly into the taproom, set up their spin wheel (all men there going white or gray of face as they watched those quiet, assured movements), and touched the wheel into life. The deadly arrow which tipped it whirled fatefully to point out, when it came to rest, he who would be an acceptable sacrifice to the demon they so propitiated.

We had sat there as if bound—which indeed we had been, in a sense, by the customs of this damnable world. Any man striving to withdraw after that arrow moved would have died, quickly, at the hands of his nearest neighbor. For there was no escape from this lottery. So we had sat there, but not in any fear, as it was not usual that an off-worlder be chosen by the Green Robes. They were not minded to have difficulty thereafter from the Patrol, or from powers beyond their own skies, being shrewd enough to know that a god may be great on his own world, and nothing under the weight of an unbeliever's iron fist, when that fist swung down from the stars.

Vondar had even leaned forward a little, studying the faces of those about us with that curiosity of his. He was as satisfied as he ever was, having done good business that day, filled himself with as fine a dinner as these barbarians knew how to prepare, and having gained a lead to a new source of lalor crystals.

Also, had he not unmasked the tricks of Hamzar, who had tried to foist on us a lalor of six carats weight but with a heart flaw? Vondar had triangulated the gem neatly and then pointed that such damage could not be polished out, and that the crystal which might have made Hamzar's fortune with a less expert buyer was an

6

inferior stone in truth, worth only the price of an extra laser charge.

A laser charge— My fingers crooked tighter about my weapon. I would willingly exchange now a whole bag of lalors for another charge waiting at my belt. A man's life is ever worth, at least to him, more than the fabled Treasure of Jaccard.

So Vondar had watched the natives in the tavern, and they had watched the spinning arrow of death. Then that arrow had wavered to a halt—pointing at no man directly, but to the narrow space which existed between Vondar's shoulder and mine as we sat side by side. And Vondar had smiled then, saying:

"It would seem that their demon is somewhat undecided this night, Murdoc." He spoke in Basic, but there were probably those there who understood his words. Even then he did not fear, or reach for a weapon— though I had never known Vondar to be less than alert. No man can follow the life of a gem buyer from planet to planet without having eyes all around his head, a ready laser, and a nose ever sniffing for the taint of danger.

If the demon had been undecided, his followers were not. They came for us. From the long sleeves of their robes suddenly appeared the bind cords used on prisoners they dragged to their lord's lair. I took the first of those Green Robes, beaming across the table top, which left the wood scorched and smoking. Vondar moved, but a fraction too late. As the Free Traders say, his luck spaced, for the man to his left sprang at him, slamming him back against the wall, pinning his hand out of reach of his weapon. They were all yammering at us now, the Green Robes halting, content to let others take the risk in pulling us down.

I caught a second man reaching for Vondar. But the one already struggling with him I dared not ray, lest I get my master too. Then I heard Vondar cry out, the sound speedily smothered in a rush of blood from his lips. We had been forced apart in the struggle and now, as I slipped along the wall, trying to get

7

beam sight on the Green Robes, my shoulders met no solid surface. I stumbled back and out, through a side door into the street.

It was then that I ran, heedlessly at first, then dodging into a deep doorway for a moment. I could hear the hunt behind me. From such hunting there was little hope of escape, for they were between me and the space port. For a long moment I huddled in that doorway, seeing no possible future beyond a fight to the end.

What fleeting scrap of memory was triggered then, I did not know. But I thought of the sanctuary past which Hamzar had taken us, three—four—days earlier. His story concerning it flashed into my mind, though at that instant I could not be sure in which direction that very thin hope of safety might lie.

I tried to push panic to the back of my mind, picture instead the street before me and how it ran in relation to the city. Training has saved many a man in such straits, and training came to my aid now. For memory had been fostered in me by stiff schooling. I was not the son and pupil of Hywel Jern for naught.

Thus and thus—I recalled the running of the streets, and thought I had some faint chance of following them. There was this, also—those who hunted me would deem they had all the advantages, that they need only keep between me and the space port and I would be easy prey, caught deep in the maze of their unfamiliar city.

I slipped from the shadow of the door and began a weaving which took me, not in the direction they would believe I would be desperately seeking, but veering from it north and west. And so I had come into this alley, slipping and scraping through its noisome muck.

My only guides were two, and to see one I had to look back to the tower of the port. Its light was strong and clear across this dark-skyed world. Keeping it ever at my right, I took it for a reverse signal. The other I could only catch glimpses of now and again as I scuttled from one shadowed space to the next. It

8

was the watchtower of Koonga, standing tall to give warning against the sudden attacks of the barbarian sea rovers who raided down from the north in the lean seasons of the Great Cold.

The alley ended in a wall. I leaped to catch its crest, my laser held between my teeth. On the top I perched, looking about me, until I decided that the wall would now form my path. It continued to run along behind the buildings, offering none too wide a footing, but keeping me well above ground level. There were dim lights in the back windows of these upper stories, and from one to the next, they served me as beacons.

When I paused now and then to listen, I could hear the murmur of the hunters. They were spreading out from the main streets, into some of the alleys. But they did so cautiously, and I believed they did not face too happily a quarry who might be ready to loose a laser beam from the dark. Time was on their side, for with the coming of dawn, were I still away from the sanctuary, I could be readily picked out of any native gathering by my clothing alone. I wore a modified form of crew dress, suited to the seasoned space traveler, designed for ease on many different worlds, though not keeping to the uniform coloring of a crewman.

Vondar had favored a dull olive-green for our overtunics, the breast of his worked with the device of a master gemologist. Mine had the same, modified by an apprentice's two bars. Our boots were magnet-plated for ship wear, and our under garment was of one piece, like a working crewman's. In this world of long, fringed overrobes and twisted, colored headdresses, I would be very noticeable indeed. There was one small change I could make; I did so now, balancing precariously on my wall perch, once more holding the laser between my teeth as I loosed the seam seal and pulled off my overtunic with its bold blazoning. I rammed it into as small a ball as I could and teetered dangerously over a scrap of garden to push it into a fork

9

of branches on a thorn bush. Then I crept along the wall top for the distance of four more houses until I came to the end at the rise of another building. From there I had a choice of leaps—down to a garden, or into the maw of another alley. I would have chosen the alley had I not frozen tight against the house wall at a sound from its depths. Something moved there, but certainly no number of men.

There was the sucking sound of a foot, or feet, lifted out of the slime, and I even thought I could hear the hiss of breathing. Whoever crept there was not moving with the openness of those who quested on my trail.

My hands had been braced against the house wall and now my fingers fell into holes there. I explored by touch and knew that I had come upon one of those geometric patterns which decorated the walls of more important buildings, some parts being intaglio and others projecting. As I felt above me, higher and higher, I began to believe that the pattern might extend clear to the roof and offer me a third way out.

Once more I crouched and this time I unsealed my boots, fastening them to the back of my belt. Then I climbed, after pausing for a long moment to listen to sounds below. They were farther away now, near the mouth of the alley.

Again my schooling came to my aid and I pulled myself up those sharply etched hand and toe holds until I swung over an ornamental parapet, past bold encrustations of demon faces set to frighten off the evil powers of natural forces.

The roof onto which I dropped sloped inward to a middle opening which gave down three floors to a center court with a core pool, into which rain water would feed during the spring storms. It was purposely smoothed to aid in that transfer of rain to reservoir, so I crept beside the parapet, my hands anchoring me from one spike of the wall to the next. But I did so with speed, for even in the dark I could see that now I was only a little away from my goal.

From this height I could see also the space port.

There were two ships there, one a passenger-cum-trader, on which that very morning Vondar had taken passage for us. It was as far from me now as if half the Dark Dragon curled between. They would know that we had bought passage on it and would keep it cordoned. The other, farther away, was a Free Trader. And, while no one normally interfered with one of those or its crew, I could make no claim on it for protection. Even if I reached sanctuary, what further hope would I have? I pushed aside that fear and turned to examine the immediate prospect of getting to the doorway. Now I would have to descend the outer face of the building into a lighted street. There were more bands of decoration and I had little doubt they would make me a ladder, if I could go unsighted. However, torches flamed in brackets along that way, and compared with the back streets through which I had fled, this was as light as a concourse on one of the inner planets.

Few men were abroad so late with legal reason. And I heard no sounds to suggest that the hunt had spread this far. They must rather be patrolling near the field. I had come this far; there was no retreat now. Giving a last searching glance below, I slipped between two of the ornaments and began the descent.

From hold to hold, feeling for those below, trusting to the strength in my fingers and wrists, I worked my way down. I had passed the top story when I came upon a window, my feet thudding home on its jutting sill. I balanced there, my hands on either side, my face to the dark interior. And then I was near startled into letting go my grasp by a shrill scream from within.

I was not conscious of making the first few drops of my continued flight down the wall. There was a second scream and a third. How soon would the household be aroused, or attention raised in the street? Finally I let go, fell in a roll. Then, not even stopping to put on my boots, I ran as I had not run before, without looking back to see what fury I had roused.

Along the house walls, sprinting from one patch of

11

shadow to the next, I dashed. Now I could hear cries behind. At the least, the screamer had aroused members of her own household. But there came a street corner and—memory had served me right! I could sight the bright eyes of the godling on the door. I ran with open mouth, sucking in quick breaths, my boots still fastened to my belt and knocking against my hips, the laser in my hand. On and on—and always I feared to see someone step into the open between me and the face with the blazing eyes. But there was no halting and with a last burst of speed I hit against the portal, my fingers scrabbling for the ring below the head. With a jerk I pulled it. For a second or two the door, contrary to promise, seemed to resist my efforts. Then it gave, and I stumbled into a hall where stood the torches which gave light to the beacon eyes.

I had forgotten the door as I wavered on, intent only on getting inside, away from the rising clamor in the street. Then I tripped and fell forward on my knees. Somehow I squirmed around, the laser ready. Already the door was swinging shut, shutting off a scene of running men, light gleaming on the bared blades they held.

Breathing hard, I watched the door shut by itself, and then was content to sit there for a space. I had not realized how great the strain of my flight had been until this island of safety held me. It was good simply to sit on the floor of that passage and know I need not run.

Finally I roused enough to draw my boots on and look about me. Hamzar's tale of sanctuary had not gone beyond the few facts of the face on the door and the guarantee that no malefactor could be taken from within. I had expected some type of temple to lie behind such a story. But I was not in the court of any fane now, only in a narrow hall with no doors. Very close to me stood a stone rack in which were set two oil-soaked torches, blazing steadily to form the beacon of the door eyes.

I got to my feet and rounded that barrier, waiting

for a challenge from whoever tended those night lights. With my back to their flames I saw only more corridor, unbroken, shadows at its far end which could veil anything. With some caution I advanced.

Unlike the glimpses I had had into the various other temples of Koonga, these walls were unpainted, being only the native yellow stone such as cobbled the wider streets. The same stone formed the wide blocks of the floor, and as far as I could see, the ceiling as well.

They were worn in places underfoot, as if from centuries of use. Also here and there on the floor were dark splotches following no pattern, which suggested unpleasantly that some of those who had come this way earlier might have suffered hurts during their flight, and that there had been no effort to clean away such traces.

I reached the end of the corridor and discovered it made a sharp turn to the right, one which was not visible until one reached it. To the left was only wall. That new way, being out of the path of the torches, was almost as dark as the alleys. I tried to pierce its dusk, wishing I had a beamer. Finally I turned the laser on lowest energy, sending a white pencil which scored the stained blocks of the flooring, but gave me light.

The new passage was only about four paces long. Then I was in a square box of a room and the laser beam touched upon an unlighted torch in the wall bracket. That blazed and I switched off the weapon, blinking. I might have been in a room furnished by one of the cheaper inns. Against the far wall was a basin of stone, into which trickled a small runnel of water, the overflow channeled back into the surface of the wall again.

There was a bedframe fitted with a netting of cords, a matting of dried and faintly aromatic leaves laid over it. Not a comfortable bed, but enough to keep one's bones from aching too much. There were two stools, a small guesting table set between them. They bore none of the customary carving, but were plain, however smoothed by long use.

13

In the wall opposite the bed was a niche in which sat a flagon of dull metal, a small basket, and a bell. But there were no doors to the room. And I could see no other exit save the corridor along which I had come. It began to impress me that this vaunted sanctuary was close to a prison, if the trapped dare not venture forth again.

I forced the torch out of its wall hold and carried it about, searching the walls, the ceiling, the floor, to find no break. At last I wedged it back into place. The bell by the flagon next held my attention and I picked it up. A bell suggested signaling. Perhaps it would bring me an explainer—or an explanation. I rang it with as much force as I could get into a snap of the wrist. For so large a bell, it gave forth a very muted tinkle, though I tried it several times, waiting between each for an answer. that did not come, until at last I slammed it back into the niche and went to sit on the bed.

When the delayed answer to my impatient summons came, it was startling enough to bring me to my feet, laser drawn. For a voice spoke out of the air seemingly only a few feet away.

"To Noskald you have come, in His Shadow abide—for the waning of four torches."

It was a moment before I realized that that voice had not used the lisping speech of Koonga, but Basic. Then they must know me for an off-worlder!

"Who are you?" My own words echoed hollowly as that voice had not. "Let me see you!"

Silence only. I spoke again, first promising awards if my plight was told at the port, or if they would give me help in reaching it. Then I threatened, speaking of ill which came when off-worlders were harmed—though I guessed that perhaps they were shrewd enough to know how hollow those threats were. There was no answer—no sign I was even heard. It could have been a recording which addressed me. And who the guardians here were I did not know either—a priesthood? Then they might be akin to the Green Robes and so would do me no favors, save those forced upon them by custom.

14

At last I curled into the bed and slept—and dreamed—very vivid dreams which were not fancies spun by the unconscious mind, but memories out of the past. So, as it is said a dying man sometimes does, I relived much of my life, which had not been so long in years.

My beginnings were overshadowed by another—Hywel Jern—who, in his time, had had a name to be reckoned with on more than one planet—and who could speak with authority in places where even the Patrol must walk with cat-soft feet, fearing to start what would take death and blood to finish.

My father had a past as murky as the shallow inlets of Hawaki after autumn storms. I do not think that any man save himself knew the whole of it; certainly we did not. For years after his death I still came across hints, bits and pieces, which each time opened another door, to show me yet another Hywel Jern. Even when I was young, at times when a coup of more than ordinary cleverness warmed whatever organ served him as a heart, he launched into a tale which was perhaps born out of his own adventuring, though he spoke always of some other man as the actor in it. Always this story was a lesson aimed at impressing upon his listeners some point of bargaining, or of action in crisis. And all his tales made more of things than of people, who were only incidental, being the owners or obtainers of objects of beauty or rarity.

Until he was close to fifty planet years old, he was prime assessor to the Veep Estampha, a sector boss of the Thieves' Guild. My father never tried to hide this association; in fact it was a matter of pride to him. Since he seemed to have an inborn talent, which he fostered by constant study, for the valuing of unusual loot, he was a valuable man, ranking well above the general core of that illegal combine. However, he appeared to have lacked ambition to climb higher, or else he simply had an astute desire to remain alive and not a target of the ambition of others.

Then Estampha met a rootless Borer plant, which someone *with* ambition secreted in his private collection of exotic blooms, and came to an abrupt finish. My father withdrew prudently and at once from the resulting scramble for power. Instead he bought out of the Guild and migrated to Angkor.

For a while, I believe, he lived very quietly. But during that period he was studying both the planet and the openings for a lucrative business. It was a sparsely settled world on the pioneer level, not one which at that time attracted the attention of those with wealth, nor of the Guild. But perhaps my father had already heard rumors of what was to come.

Within a space of time he paid court to a native woman whose father operated a small hock-lock for pawning, as well as a trading post, near the only space port. Shortly after his marriage the father-in-law died of an off-world fever, a plague ship having made a crash landing before it could be warned off. The fever also decimated most of the port authorities. But Hywel Jern and his wife proved immune and carried on some of the official duties at this time, which entrenched them firmly when the plague had run its course and the government was restored.

Then, some five years later, the Vultorian star cluster was brought into cross-stellar trade by the Fortuna Combine, and Angkor suddenly came to life as a shipping port of exchange. My father's business prospered, though he did not expand the original hock-lock.

With his many off-world contacts, both legal and illegal, he did well, but to outward appearances, only in a modest way. All spacers sooner or later lay hands on portable treasures or curiosities. To have a buyer who asked no questions and paid promptly was all they wanted at any port where the gaming tables and other planetside amusements separated them too fast from flight pay.

This quiet prosperity lasted for years, and appeared to be all my father wanted.

TWO

If Hywel Jern had contracted his marriage for reasons of convenience, it was a stable one. There were children, myself, Faskel, and Darina. My father took little interest in his daughter, but he early bent more than a little energy to the training of Faskel and me; not that Faskel showed any great promise along the lines Hywel Jern thought important.

It was the custom for us to assemble at a large table in an inner room (we lived over and behind the shop) for the evening meal. And at that time my father would bring out and pass around some item from his stock, first asking an opinion of it—its value, age, nature. Gems were a passion with him and we were forced to learn them as other children might scan book tapes for general knowledge. To my father's satisfaction I proved an apt pupil. In time he centered most of his instruction on me, since Faskel, either because he could not, or because he stubbornly would not learn, again and again made some mistake which sent our father into one of his cold and silent withdrawals.

I never saw Hywel Jern lose his temper, but his cold displeasure was not to be courted. It was not so much that I feared such censure as that I was really fascinated and interested in what he had to teach. Before I was out of childhood I was allowed to judge the pledges in the shop. And whenever one of the gem merchants who visited my father from time to time came, I was displayed as a star pupil.

So through the years our house became one divided, my mother, Faskel, and Darina on one side, my father and I on the other. And our contact—or mine—with other children of the port was limited, my father drawing me more and more into the shop to learn his old trade of valuing. Some strange and beautiful things passed through our hands in those days. Part were sold openly, others remained in his lockboxes, to be offered in private transactions, and of those I did not see all.

There were things from alien ruins and tombs, made before the time that our species burst into space; there were pieces looted from empires which had vanished into the dust of history so long past that even their planets had been buried. And there were others new from the workshops of the inner systems, where all the creative art of a jeweler is unleashed to catch the eye of a Veep with a bottomless purse.

My father liked the old pieces the most. Sometimes he would hold a necklet, or a bracelet (which by its form had never been meant to encircle a human wrist) and speculate about who had worn it and the civilization from which it had come. And he demanded of those who brought him such trinkets as clear a history of their discovery as he could obtain, putting on tapes all he could learn.

I think that these tapes in themselves might have proven a rich treasure house for seekers of strange knowledge, and I have wondered since if Faskel ever suspected their worth and used them so. Perhaps he did, for in some ways he proved to be more shrewd than my father.

In one of our round-table meetings after an evening meal my father produced such an alien curiosity. He did not pass it from hand to hand as was his wont, but laid it on the well-polished board of dead-black creel wood and sat staring at it as if he were one of the fakirs from the dry lands seeking to read a housewife's future in a polished seed pod.

It was a ring, or at least it followed that form. But the band must have been made for a finger close to the size of two of ours laid together. The metal was dull, pitted, as if from great age.

18

Its claw setting held a stone bigger than my thumb-nail, in proper proportion to the band. And it was as dull and unappealing as the metal, colorless, no sparkle or hint of life in it. Also, the longer one studied it, the more the idea grew in mind that this was the corpse of something which might have once had life and beauty but was long since dead. I had, at that first viewing, a disinclination to touch it, though I was always avid to examine these bits and pieces my father used for our instruction.

"Out of another tomb? I wish you would not bring these corpse ornaments to the table!" My mother spoke more sharply than was usual. At that time it struck me odd that she, whom I thought immune to imaginative fancies, had also so quickly associated the ring with death.

My father did not raise his eyes from the ring. Rather he spoke to Faskel in the voice he used when he would be answered, and at once.

"What make you of this?"

My brother put out his hand as if to touch the ring and then jerked it back again. "A ring—too large to wear. Maybe a temple offering."

To that my father made no comment. Instead he said to Darina:

"And you see what?"

"It is cold—so cold—" My sister's thin voice trailed off, and then she pushed away from the table. "I do not like it."

"And you?" My father turned to me at last.

Temple offering it might have been, fashioned larger than life to fit on the finger of some god or goddess. I had seen such things pass through my father's hands before. And some of them had had that about them which gave one a queasy feeling upon touching. But if any god had worn this— No, I did not believe it had been made for such a purpose. Darina was also right. It evoked a sensation of cold, as well as of death. However, the more I studied it, the more it fascinated me. I wanted to touch, yet I feared. And it seemed to me that my feeling reflected something about the ring which made it more than any other gem I had seen, though it was now but age-pitted metal set with a lifeless stone.

"I do not know—save that it is—or was—a thing of power!" And my certainty of that fact was such that I spoke more loudly than I had meant to, so my final word rang through the room.

"Where did it come from?" Faskel asked quickly, hunching forward again and putting out his hand as if to lay it over ring and stone, though his fingers only hovered above it. In that moment I had the thought that he who did take it firmly would be following the custom of gem dealers: to close hand about a jewel was to accept an offered bargain. But if that were so, Faskel did not quite dare to accept such a challenge, for he drew back his hand a second time.

"From space," my father returned.

There *are* gems out of space—primitive peoples pay high sums to own them. What forms them we are not quite sure even yet. The accepted theory is that they are produced when bits of meteor of the proper metallic composition pass through the blaze of a planet's atmosphere. It was the fad for a while to make space Captains' rings out of these tektites. I have seen several such, centuries old, which must have been worn by the first space venturers. But this gem, if gem it really was, bore no resemblance to those, for it was not dark green, black, or brown, but a colorless crystal, dulled as if sand had pitted the surface deeply.

"It does not look like a tektite—" I ventured.

My father shook his head. "It was not formed in space, not that I know of—it was found there." He leaned back in his chair and took up his cup of folgar tea, sipping absent-mindedly as he continued to stare at the ring. "A curious tale—"

"We expect Councilor Sands and his lady—" my mother interrupted abruptly, as if she knew the tale and wanted not to hear it again. "The hour grows late." She

20

started to gather our cups, then raised her hands to clap for Staffla, our serving maid.

"A curious tale," my father repeated as if he had not heard her at all. And such was his hold over his household that she did not summon Staffla, but sat, moving a little uneasily, plainly unhappy.

"But a true one—of that I am sure," my father continued. "This was brought in today by the first officer of the Astra. They had a grid failure in mid-passage and had to come out of hyper for repairs. Their luck continued bad, for they had a holing from a meteor pebble. It was necessary then to patch the hull as well." He was telling this badly, not as he usually spun such stories, but more as one who would keep strictly to facts, and those were meager. "Kjor was doing the patch job when he saw it—a floater— He beamed out on his stay line and brought it in—a body in a suit. Not"—my father hesitated—"of any species he knew. And it had been there a long time. It wore this over its suit glove." He pointed to the ring.

Over the glove of a space suit—the strangeness of that indeed made one wonder. The gloves are supple enough; they have to be if a man wears them in outer space for ship repair, or while exploring a planet deadly to his species. But why would anyone want to wear an ornament over such a glove? I must have asked that aloud for my father answered:

"Why indeed? Certainly not for any reason of show. Therefore—this had importance, vast importance to him who wore it. Enough that I would like to know it better."

"There are tests," Faskel observed.

"This is a gem stone, unknown to me, and twelve on the Mohs scale—"

"A diamond is ten—"

"And a Javsite eleven," my father returned. "Heretofore that was the measuring rod. This is something beyond our present knowledge."

"The Institute—" began my mother, but my father put out his hand and cupped the ring in it, hiding it

21

from sight. So hidden, he restored it to a small bag and slipped that into his inner tunic pocket.

"This is not to be spoken of!" he ordered sharply. And from that moment on we would not speak of it as he well knew. He had trained us very well. But neither did he send it to the Institute, nor, I was sure, did he seek any other official information concerning it. But that he studied and tested it by all methods known, and they were not a few, that I also learned.

I became used to seeing him in his small laboratory, at his desk, the ring on a square of black cloth before him, staring down at it as if by the very strength of his will he would extract its secret. If it had ever had any beauty, time and the drift through space had destroyed that, and what was left was an enigma but no blazing treasure.

The mystery haunted me also, and from time to time my father would speak of various theories he had formed concerning it. He was firmly convinced that it was not meant to be an ornament, but that it had served its wearer in some manner. And he kept its possession a secret.

From the day my father had taken over the shop, he had set into its walls various hiding places. And later, upon enlarging the rooms, he had built in more such pockets. The majority of these were known to the whole family, and would answer to hand pressure from any of us. But there were a few he showed only to me. And one of these, in the laboratory, held the ring. My father altered the seal there to answer only to our two thumbs, and he had me seal and unseal it several times before he was satisfied.

Then he waved me to sit down opposite him.

"Vondar Ustle arrives tomorrow," he began abruptly. "He will bring an apprentice warrant with him. When he leaves, you go with him—"

I could not believe my hearing. As eldest son, apprenticeship, save to my father, was not for me. If anyone went to serve another master it would be Faskel. But

22

before I could raise a question, my father went on with as much explanation as I was ever to get from him.

"Vondar is a master gemologist, though he chooses to travel rather than set up an establishment on any one planet. There is no better teacher in the galaxy. I have good reason to be sure of that. Listen well, Murdoc—this shop is not for you. You have a talent, and a man who does not develop his talent is a man who ever eats dry oat-cake while before him sits a rich meat dish, a man who chooses a zircon when he need only reach out his hand to pick up a diamond. Leave this shop to Faskel—"

"But he—"

My father smiled thinly. "No, he is not one who has a great eye for what is to be seen, beyond a fat purse and the value in credits. A shopkeeper is a shopkeeper, and you are not meant for such. I have waited a long time for a man such as Ustle, one on whom I can depend to be the teacher you must have. In my day I was known as a master at valuing, but I served in murky ways. You must walk free of such ties, and you can gain such freedom only by cutting loose now from the very name you carry on Angkor. Also—you must see more than one world, walk other planets, if you are to be all that you can be. It is known that planetary magnetic fields can influence human behavior, some ebb and flow in them producing changes in the brain. Alertness and sensibility are stimulated by these changes; memory can be fostered the brighter, ideas incited. I want what you can learn from Ustle during the next five planet years."

"Something to do with the space stone—?"

He nodded. "I can no longer go seeking knowledge, but you who have a mind link unto mine are not rooted. Before I die I want to know what that ring holds, and what it did or can do for the man who wears it!"

Once more he got up and brought out the ring bag, removed the band with its dull stone, and turned it about in his fingers.

There was an old superstition once believed in by our species," he said slowly, "that we left impressions of

23

ourselves on material things we had owned, providing those objects were closely tied into our destinies. Here—" Of a sudden he tossed the ring at me. I was unprepared, but I caught it, almost on reflex, out of the air. For all the months we had had it under this roof, that was the first time I had held it.

The metal was cold, with a gritty surface. And it seemed to me, as it rested in my palm, the cold grew stronger, so that my skin tingled with it. But I lifted it to eye level and peered at the stone. The clouded surface was as gritty as the band. If it had ever held fire in its heart, that was long since quenched or clouded over. I wondered briefly if it could be detached from that rough setting and recut, to regain the life it had lost. But knew also that my father would never attempt to do that. Nor, I decided, could I. As it was, the mystery was all. It was not the ring itself but what lay behind it that was of importance. And now my father's plans for me also made sense—I would be the seeker for a solution to our mystery.

So I became Ustle's apprentice. And my father proved right; such an instructor is seldom found. My master might have made several fortunes had he wished to root on one of the luxury worlds, set up as a designer and merchant. But to him the quest for the perfect stone was far more meaningful than selling it. He did design—usually during our voyages his mind and his fingers were busy, turning out patterns which other, less talented men were eager to buy when he wanted to offer them. But his passion was exploration of the secrets of new-found worlds, doing his own bargaining with natives for uncut stones not far from where they were first unearthed.

He laughed at the frauds he uncovered—the lesser stones soaked in herbs or chemicals to make them more resemble the precious, the gems treated by heat to change their color. He taught me odd ways to impress native sellers so that they respected one's wisdom and brought out the better rather than the worse. Such things as that a human hair stretched across real jade will not burn, even though you set match to it.

24

Planet time is reckoned in years, space time less easily. A man who makes many voyages does not age as quickly as the earth-bound. I do not know how old Vondar was, but if he were judged by his store of knowledge, he must have outstripped my father. We went far from Angkor, but in time we returned to it. Only I had no crumb, not even infinitesimally small, to offer my father on the history of the space ring.

I had not been more than a day under our own roof when I knew that all was not well there. Faskel was older. When I looked upon him and then upon my own face in my mother's well-polished mirror, I would have said he was the elder by birth. Also he was more assertive, taking over the role of my father's assistant, making decisions even within my father's hearing. And Hywel Jern did not lift even an eyebrow in correction of his presumption.

My sister was married. Her dowry had been enough to bring her the son of a Councilor, to my mother's great content. Though she had vanished from the house as if she had never lived, "my daughter, the Councilor's son's lady" was so ever on my mother's lips as to make of my sister a haunting ghost.

Of this household I was no longer a well-fitting part. Though Faskel masked for the most part his displeasure at my return, he became more and more officious in conducting the business when I was present—though I did nothing to confirm his suspicions that I had returned to supersede him. Once I had thought the shop all important, but off world so many doors had opened to me that now it seemed a very dull way to spend one's days, and I wondered that my father could have chosen it.

He roused himself to ask questions about my journeying, so I spent most of my time in his inner office retailing, not without some satisfaction, all I had learned. Though now and then a crisp comment reduced my self-esteem and sent me into confusion, for he made it clear that much of this he already knew.

However, after my first burst of enthusiasm, it became increasingly clear that if my father listened, he heard, or strove to hear, more than my spate of words. Behind his interest—and it was interest; in that I was not deceived—lurked some preoccupation which was not concerned with me or my discoveries. Nor did he mention the space ring, and I too had a strange reluctance to introduce the subject. Not once did he bring out that treasure to brood over it as he had in the past.

It was not until I had been four days home—that the shadow which I sensed on the household drew closer. Like all shops, we would remain closed during the festival. It was customary for families to entertain kinfolk and friends, making up parties to go from home to home. My mother spoke pridefully at the table that night of our going to Darina's and being included with them in the Councilor's own group for a pleasure cruise on the river in his own barge.

But when she had done, my father shook his head. He would, he announced, stay home. I had never seen my mother, though of late years she might have grown more assertive, stand against my father's pronouncements. But this time her anger exploded, and she stated that that choice might be his, but that the rest of us should go. To this he nodded and so I found that indeed I was absorbed in what seemed to me a very boring party. My mother beamed and nursed another dream, for Faskel was ever by the side of the Councilor's niece—though it appeared to me that that lady shared her smiles with several young men and that the portion of them which fell to my brother were not particularly warm. As for me, I escorted my mother, and perhaps pleasured her a little by the fact that I was traveled and that once or twice the Councilor singled me out to ask of off-world matters.

As the barge slipped down the river, there grew a kind of impatience in me, and I kept thinking of my father and who he might be seeing in the locked shop. For he had hinted to me that he stayed there, not only because of boredom, but because he had a definite

26

reason for wishing the house to be empty that day so that he might meet with someone.

There had always been visitors whom my father had not made known to his family, some of them using darkness for a cloak, entering and leaving without their faces being seen. That he trafficked in things of uncertain history must have been known to the authorities. But no man ever spoke out against him. For the Thieves' Guild has a long arm and they move to protect one who is of service to them. My father may have outwardly retired from their Veep councils, but did a man *ever* retire from the Guild? Rumor said no.

Only there had been something in my father's attitude this time which made me uneasy, as if he both wished for and feared whatever meeting was to take place. And the more I thought on his manner, the more I decided that fear—if one could term it fear—had been uppermost. Perhaps, as my father had suggested, my travel had heightened in me a sensitivity which the rest of the family did not share.

At any rate I excused myself before sunset with the lame explanation that I must meet with Vondar, though my mother did not believe me. And I summoned one of the small boats for hire, ordering the oarsman to make good time back to port. Only so thronged were the waterways that our speed was no more than a weary crawl, and I discovered myself sitting tensely, willing us forward, my hands gripped tightly together.

Again, on landing, I found the streets crowded, and worked my way with impatient thrusting, which earned me some harsh words, splashes of scented water. The shop front was closed even as we had left it, and I went through the narrow garden at the back.

As my hand fell upon the door lock, the thumb against the print which would release it, I felt, as a blow, the full force of all the unease which had plagued me. It was dark and cool in the family rooms. I stopped by the door which gave upon the shop to listen, thinking that if my father still entertained his mysterious caller, he would not thank me to burst in upon them. But there was no sound, and when I rapped upon the door to the office, it echoed holowly.

When I pushed, the door gave only a little, and I was forced to exert pressure of shoulder to force my way in. Then I heard the rasp of wood against stone, and saw that my father's desk, overturned, blocked my entrance. I thrust desperately and was in a wildly upset room.

In his chair sat my father, the ropes which held him upright stained with his blood. His eyes glared at me fiercely in denial of what had come to him. But that denial was the glare of a dead man. All else was over-turned, some boxes smashed to bits as if the searcher, not finding what he sought, had wrecked the inanimate in his temper.

There are many beliefs in many worlds concerning the end of life and what may lie thereafter. How can any man deny that some of them may be true? We have no proof one way or another. My father was dead when I came to him, and dead by violence. But perhaps it was his will, his need for revenge, or to communicate, which hung on in that room. For I knew, as if he had indeed spoken, what lay at the roots of this.

So I passed him and found that inconspicuous bit of carving on the wall. To that I set my thumb as he had taught me. The small space opened, but not easily; it might have been some time since it was last bared. I took out the bag, feeling through it the form of the ring. That I drew forth and held before my father as if he could still see and know that I had it. And I promised him that what he had sought, I would seek too, and that perhaps so I would find those who had slain him. For this I was sure of, that the ring held the key to his death.

But this was not the last of the shocks and losses which were to come to me on Angkor. For after the authorities had come and the family had gathered and been questioned, she whom I had always called mother turned on me and said, in a high, fast voice, as if she dared not be interrupted:

"Faskel is master here. For he is blood and bone of me, heir to my father who was lord here before Hywel Jern came. And so will I swear before the Council."

That she favored Faskel I had always known but there was a chill in her words now that I did not understand. She continued, making the reason plain.

"You are only a duty child, Murdoc. Though mark me true, I have never made the less of you in this house because of that. And no one can say that I have!"

A duty child—one of those embryos shipped from a populous world to a frontier planet in order to vary the stock, by law assigned to some family to be raised and nurtured as their own. There were many such in the early settlement of any world. But I had never thought much about them. It did not greatly matter to me that I was not of her blood. But that I was not the son of Hywel—that I hated! I think she read this in my eyes, for she shrank from me. But she need not have feared any trouble, for I turned and went from that room, and that house, and later from Angkor. All I took with me was my heritage—the ring out of space.

THREE

The torch which had been in the room of the sanctuary when first I entered was sputtering to the end as I woke. What had the voice said? For the space of four torches I could shelter there. I looked at the floor. There were three more torches lying ready. Now I got up to force the dying one from its hold, light another in its place.

But after four torches—what? Would I be thrust out into the streets of Koonga again? At intervals I questioned the walls of the room, but no answer came. Twice I searched again, seeking some cunningly hidden exit. There was a building frustration within me. I had passed part of a night here, by my timekeeper, and some of the day thereafter. The four torches, I calculated roughly, would cover perhaps three days. But long before that the ship on which Vondar and I had passage would lift. Nor would its Captain worry if we did not claim those passages. Once planetside, passengers were strictly on their own. A Captain would take steps to rescue a member of his closely knit crew, for the ship unit became as tightly welded as a family or clan, but strangers he would not aid.

What chance had I left? Was I under observation? How would the keepers of this place know when their torches were exhausted? Or had they through the years fallen into such routine that they could judge approximately? And what was their purpose? What did they get out of this service? A temple would accept a gift for a god. And to me this sanctuary continued to suggest a religious establishment.

I lay down again on the bed, rolled so that I faced the wall and that my breast was hidden from the room. My hands moved stealthily, for I had to believe that there was a watcher. If I could not hold to that hope, I had nothing left. Two pockets in my safe-belt. Between thumb and forefinger rolled the sleekness of the gems I carried. I palmed them and lay still, letting them believe I slept.

Vondar had had the best of our stock already locked in the safe of the ship. Eventually those should reach the storehouse of the jeweler to whom they had been consigned, there to wait for one who would never claim them.

What I carried were inferior stones, or so reckoned on inner planets. Only here two of them might well present a temptation to any watcher. Both were fruits of my own trading—one a carved crystal in the form of a small demonic head, with rubies inset for eyes, fang teeth of yellow sapphires, a weird, small curiosity. The very force of the carving might make it attractive on this world. The other was a thumb-sized "soothing stone" of red jade, one of those pieces the men of Gambool carry to finger while they talk business. There is a sensuous satisfaction in the handling of such a piece, and perhaps they are wise in their choice of this tension relaxer.

How much is a life worth? I could empty my safe-belt—but I knew I must reserve a second payment if my plan was to succeed. And I had chosen as best I could. Now I rolled over and sat up. The light of the new torch was brighter than the old.

The guesting table—I looked at it. Then I crossed the room to sit on one of its flanking stools, lay the stones on its surface. I did not raise my voice in any demand this time but tried to be as one bargaining in the market place.

"It is said that for all things there is a price," I began as if I spoke to someone who sat on the other stool to my right. "There are those who sell, and those who wish to buy. I am a stranger in your land, upon your world of Tanth. By no fault of my own I find myself a hunted man. My friend and master is dead, slain also for no fault—for since when have the Green Robes ever before chosen one not of their belief to satisfy their master? Is it not said the unwilling sacrifice is the lesser one and not pleasing to the power to which it is sped?

"It is true that I have killed, but only to defend myself. I am willing to offer blood price if that is required of me. But—remember, I am from off world, and so cannot be bound by the laws of your land unless I willfully and willingly break them by intent—answering only to my own authority for all else."

Did anyone hear me? Was Tanth so removed from the civilized worlds that the Confederation's authority could be flouted? What would priests of a local god care for a rule based light-years away? Nor could I flatter myself that Vondar's death would set any fleets in motion to demand answers from Tanth's inhabitants. Like the Free Traders, we accepted risks when we traveled the far star lanes.

"Blood price will I pay," I repeated, fighting my mounting tension, willing my voice to remain even and low. I opened my hand and allowed the fingering piece to lie in the open. "This is a gem of virtue. He who holds it while thinking of or speaking on matters of import will discover his temper remains calm, his mind clear—" I wrapped my tongue in the rolling formality of the native speech, using the wording common to men of substance. In such little things sometimes there is great influence.

"To this gem of power"—I allowed the carved crystal to be seen now, the leering face uppermost—"I will add this talisman. As one can see, it bears the face of Umphal—" (Which it did not, having come from another world, where that nightmare demon was unknown. But it was enough like the effigies of Umphal I had seen here to pass.) "Set such on a frontlet and what fear need a man longer have of the grimace of the red-eyed power. For seeing his *own* face, Umphal will flee—is that not so? Thus doubly do I pay blood price, with a stone which gives men wisdom, and one which promises protection from that which rides the night north winds."

Trying to keep out of mind the thought that I might be speaking only to unhearing walls, that there were no eyes which watched, I spoke again:

"There is a Free Trader planeted at your port. For my blood price I ask only speech with her Captain."

Then I sat in silence, watching the two gems on the table, straining to hear the slightest sound which might reveal I did have a listener. I could not believe that after a period of time within this room sanctuary ended and that the desperate souls who came here had no other recourse.

I could not be sure—a click—had I heard a click? Dared I believe that I had heard such a sound? It had come from behind me. I waited a long moment and then arose and went to the niche, as if to drink from the flagon there. In the small basket beside that lay something which had not been there before—a flat cake. Once more I picked up that tantalizing bell and was about to ring it when the basket caught my attention. It had been shoved forward, leaving marks in the dust. By the look of those the stone behind it had slid out.

Certainly I had not been mistaken in my hearing of that click. There *was* an opening in the wall and I had been observed through it. They had furnished me with food. The cake was crumbly and smelled of coarse cheese, as it had been split open and smeared with that. To off-world taste it was unpleasant, but I ate it. Hunger can conquer much.

Waiting is the hardest test to which one can be put and waiting was now mine. The torch had burned down and I was about to set another in its place when, without warning, a man appeared in the doorway through which I had first come. Though I went for my laser, he had me covered before my hand touched its butt.

"Steady on!" He spoke Basic, coming a step or two farther into the room. I saw a ship's tunic with the insignia of Cargo Master on the collar. "Keep your hands in plain sight."

He was an off-worlder, and his uniform was that of a Free Trader. I drew a deep breath. In so much had my plea carried.

"You have a proposition—" he eyed me narrowly, with little cordiality. "Speak your piece." There was a snap of urgency to that as if he were there against his will with danger breathing hot upon him.

"I want passage out." I cut my answer to that bare statement.

He had backed around so that his shoulders were at the wall—and faced me warily. A Cargo Master of a Free Trader needs must be more than a merchant. He does not grow fat and sleek, and slow of reflex, no matter if he is not a fighting man—officially—but a trader.

"With half the city to tear you down should you step upon the street?" he countered. Still his laser was aimed at my middle. There was no softening for my plight to be read on his face. The Free Traders are clansmen, with their ship their home. I was not of his brood.

"Tell me, Cargo Master"—I did not approach him, and now I must be a master bargainer indeed if I was to win my life—"what have you heard of me?"

"That you spat upon one priest, slew another—"

"I am a gem trader, late apprentice to Vondar Ustle—you have heard that name?"

"I have heard. He travels far. What of it? Does that make your crime the less here in Koonga?"

"There was no crime." How could I make the truth so plain he would believe me? "Do you think a man thrusts a rod into a yaeger-wasp nest and turns it deliberately, when he is in his right mind? We were in a tavern—the Sign of the Mottled Corby. Our business here was done, we had passage on the *Voyringer*. Then the Green Robes came in and set up that infernal spinning arrow of theirs. We thought we were in no danger, being off-worlders. When it stopped I swear it pointed between the two of us. Then the Robes moved in to take us—"

34

"Why?" I saw the disbelief in his eyes. "They do not play such games with off-worlders."

"As we thought also, Cargo Master. Yet they did. And Vondar was knifed down when he tried to resist. I burned a priest and was near enough to the door to get free. I had heard of this sanctuary—so—"

"Tell me—what was Vondar Ustle's hallmark? And it I have seen, I warn you." That shot from his lips as a ray might have from his laser.

"A half-moon wrought in opal with the signet, between its horns, a Gryphon's head in firestones." I made prompt reply, though I wondered what this Free Trader would know of a master gemologist's mark, which he would display for identification only to an equal in rank.

He nodded and slipped his laser into its holster. "What enemy did Ustle make here?"

That thought had plagued me also since I had had the time within this hole to think. For it was reasonable that, were a desire for revenge strong enough, my master might have been set up for such a kill. Though their demon was supposed to select his prey by chance alone, without aid from his servant priests, rumor suggested that he sometimes had assistance of mortal means, that a suitable gift to his shrine could produce a sacrifice which would please more than just the Green Robes and their lord. But there had been no clash with any local power. We had visited Hamzar, inspected his wares and purchased what Vondar thought good, exchanged trade gossip with him. There had been one visit to the nomads' market and some dickering for uncut crystals out of the salt deserts, but both sides had been pleased with the deal. I could see no local tie-up with any trouble. And now, though I would have given much to be able to produce such a neat solution, I had to admit the truth.

"It need not have been of Tanth at all," the Cargo Master replied. And he watched me as if I could then supply name and reason. A moment later, he continued. "Some strokes are aimed from longer distances. But—if you wish to take knife-oath for your master later, that is your affair. Always supposing you do come out alive. Now, what do you want of us? You say passage off-world—how?"

"How would you do it?" I countered. "I will pay well to lift in your ship, and for passage to the nearest planet with a second-stage port. And do not tell me"—now I dared push a little; I could lose nothing by it, for my whole chance hung on the slenderest of threads—"that you cannot get me forth if you wish. The will of the Free Traders is too well known."

"We care for our own. You are not one of us."

"You care for your cargo also. Then accept me as cargo—a profitable cargo."

He suddenly smiled. "Cargo, is it?" Then his smile vanished and his eyes narrowed as he regarded me, as if by that gaze he could indeed transform me into a box or bale, to be stored in the hold of his ship. "You talk of profit?" he began, brisk again. "What sort of profit and how much?"

I turned away and sought my safe-belt. Then I showed him what I held and it took fire in the torchlight. Profit of a half year's careful trading on my own—two of them matched as closely as anyone could hope to find—Eyes of Kelem. They were gold, and scarlet, with flecks of green deep in them. And if you looked upon them long, the color flowed. Not a fortune, no. But, offered in the proper market, worth a whole voyage for a trader who was only average lucky most of the time. They were my best and I knew he guessed that.

He did not try to bargain, or belittle my offering. Whether he did indeed have some half sympathy for my plight, I do not know. But he looked at the stones and then to me, nodding, holding forth his hand and closing it over them in a manner which showed that he knew the rules of our trade also. Free Traders are alert to any cargo and deal in many things.

"Come!"

I followed him out of that room, leaving my offering behind me on the guesting table. For I was satisfied that they had kept their part of the bargain. We were again in the hall where the torches blazed behind the face, but these were now quenched and I saw through the holes the light of day. The Cargo Master stooped and picked up a bundle lying there, shaking it out to show me a worn uniform tunic and the cap of a crewman.

"Put them on."

I laughed, feeling a little lightheaded. "It would seem you came prepared," I said as I pulled the tunic over my head and shoulders, sealed it at collar and belt. It was small for me, but not too much so.

"I was—" He hesitated. "The news is loud. Ustle was known to our Captain. When the message came through he was enough interested to send me."

The set of his jaw told me that that was all I would get out of him on the subject. But I was the more heartened by this evidence that he had come prepared to get me out—though I would still have liked to go through the door weapon in hand.

We were not, however, to go that way, for the Free Trader walked briskly to the wall on our left, slapped his hand against it. Though that touch could not have moved the heavy stone, it swung inward, disclosing another narrow way, and he stepped confidently into that, leaving me to follow. When the stone swung back behind us, we were left in a thick dark, reminding me unpleasantly of the alleys through which I had earlier fled.

It was a very narrow passage, our shoulders brushing wall on either side. I bumped into my guide, who had stopped short. There was a click and then a blaze of bright light.

"Come!" He reached out a hand to pull me after him. I blinked and screwed up my eyes against the assault of that brilliant sun. We were in another alley, piled along the wall with containers of refuse. Things scuttled in the slime under our boots and my guide swore roundly as he kicked out at something which hissed at him. Six strides, as long and fast as we could make them, brought us into another and much cleaner byway. I had to fight my desire to run, or to look about me for attackers. It was necessary to put on the cloak of unconcern and match my pace to the Cargo Master's.

Then we were through the gates of the port. As I had thought, the *Voyringer* had lifted and only the trader remained, fins down, on the blast-scorched ground. The Cargo Master caught at my sleeve.

"Trouble—maybe—"

But I had already sighted that blaze of bright robes around the ship. There was a reception committee waiting. Perhaps just on the general principle that a hunted off-worlder would make for the only ship left.

"Drunk—you're an off-ship drunk!" The Cargo Master hissed at me in a sound much like that made by the alley scavenger. "This ought to do it !" I saw the blow coming, but I was totally unprepared to dodge it. A blast of pain spread from my jaw, and I must have gone down and out in the same moment, for there my memories of Tanth come to an abrupt stop.

There was a tap-tapping of jeweler's hammers in my skull, setting tighter and tighter a brazen band about my brain. I could not lift a hand to stop that torment. Then liquid splashed over me and I drew a choking gasp of air, which seemed to subdue for the moment the worst of the hammering. I opened my eyes.

A face hung over me, two faces, one very close, the other blurry and at a greater distance. The close one was furred, with pricked, tassled ears, green-gold eyes. It opened a black-lipped mouth and I looked into a wedge-shaped space set with fangs, and a curling, rough-surfaced tongue. It was a small face—

Now the larger approached and I tried to focus on it. Space-tanned, with close-cropped hair, for the rest the face of any crewman, ageless and now expression-less.

I heard words—"Well, so you are back with us—"

Back? Back where? Memory stirred sluggishly—back in the cell of the sanctuary? No! I tried to sit up and my head whirled so that I was sick. But as ungentle hands thrust me flat again, I felt something else which could never have vibrated through Koongan walls—I was not only aboard a ship, but we were in flight. And the vast flood of relief which followed that realization carried me back into a limbo which was half unconsciousness, half sleep.

So I found myself aboard the *Vestris*, though the first days in her were not the usual spent by a passenger. The Cargo Master had indeed knocked me out to carry me aboard as his drunken assistant. But it would seem I was of less hardy structure than those his fists had dealt with heretofore, and I continued semiconscious for a longer space than the medico liked. When I was again fully aware of my surroundings, I lay in a cramped cubby off the medico's cabin, used by the seriously ill. It was some time before I had my interview with Captain Isuran. Like all Free Traders, he was ship-born, ship-bred, of a type growing more and more apart from planet-orientated men. All the Free Traders I had known before had been only casual acquaintances, and I found myself oddly ill at ease with these in such close quarters. I told him my story and he listened. And he asked who had wanted Vondar Ustle dead, but that I could not tell him. That there had been some tie in the past between my master and this Captain, I was sure. But Isuran did not explain and I dared not ask questions. It was enough that he would take me to another world, one on which I could contact sources who had known me as Vondar's assistant.

I had some time to meditate upon the future, for space travel is sheer monotony once one is off world. The crewmen develop hobbies to occupy mind and hand. For me there was nothing but my thoughts. And they were not so pleasant I cared to dwell long upon them.

Ustle had had contacts on many worlds, and I thought one or two might be willing to give me a chance at a planetside job. But, though I knew gems as a buyer, I was no designer, nor did I want a settled existence. I had tasted too deeply of Vondar's way of life. My

39

safe-belt was very light now. And I would have to reach a second-stage port to tap past resources for expense money. Also—my savings were limited. I could not keep on as we had done alone. And there were very few, if any, Vondar Ustles in search of apprentices.

Also—what had been behind Vondar's death? That it was planned and not by the Green Robes alone, I had come to accept. But, though I tried—sifting memories— I could not bring to mind a single happening which would plant so deep a reason for someone to wish him dead. And perhaps not only him, for the Green Robes had moved in on both of us.

This was the second time death had abruptly come so close to me. I thought again of my father, or of him I would always think of as my father, for he had treated me as of his own flesh and blood and had settled for me (knowing as he must have how matters would go after his death) a future he thought would be the best. Who had been his visitor that day? And the space ring—my hand sought the last and deepest pocket of my safe-belt. I did not unseal it, only felt through it the shape of the band and that lusterless stone. Was I right that this was what my father's killer had sought? If so—could it also be—? I did not see how this could have followed us to Tanth. All the property on the bodies of their victims belonged to the Green Robes and were offered to their dead demon. No one but their order would have had the ring had I fallen prey to them.

I had a handful of facts and could go on endlessly building many surmises, without ever being sure that any were close to the truth. Although in the meanwhile I must seek some way of earning my living, I would, in time, have to learn what lay behind Vondar's killing. For I had such ties with him as would indeed demand the equivalent of the Free Traders' knife-oath.

But I was still far from the solution of my twin problems when the *Vestris* prepared for a landing, not on the planet at which I aimed, but on a lesser world. Cargo Master Ostrend briefed me as to their reasons for the landfall. It was a lushly overgrown land, over-warm, too, to our tastes, with a nonhuman, batrachian-evolved native race. What those had to barter was a substance strained and fermented from certain plants, medicinal in nature. What the *Vestris* gave in return was seed shellfish, to be loosed in beds, considered a great delicacy.

"You might be interested in these." Ostrend took from his lockbox three objects and set them out on the top of his swing desk.

They were a pinkish purple in shade, and each was a tiny figure. I brought out my jeweler's lens to study them closer. Figures they were, as weirdly grotesque as any of the demons dreamed up by the imaginations of the artists of Tanth. They seemed to be fashioned of nacre, though not carved. I had not seen their like before. They were oddities which might appeal to collectors of the curious.

"There is a planter of shellfish beds—Salmscar. He has been experimenting with some of the mutated crustaceans. That's what keeps our trade going here; the things mutate so quickly that they cannot be bred true past about the second year. He plants tiny metallic 'seeds' in the mutants and in about three or four years gets these. Just a hobby with him. But you might do a spot of trading if you are interested."

I knew the Free Traders and their jealously guarded sources of items. If the mutant pearls had any value, Ostrend would not have made that suggestion. Unless, of course, he was either testing me or setting a trap—now I saw dangers standing to right and left. It was almost as if he were urging me to break their ship law. But I would not tell him so. A very small third mystery to add to the others. I expressed interest, which I did not have to feign, and did wonder what I had that I could offer for some of the things—not that I could use my few assets on a gamble, nor would I attempt any trade without full consent of my present shipmates.

FOUR

Since the ingrown community of the Free Traders was
a closed clan and an outsider remained that, I was left
very much to my own company, save for one member
of the crew. The furry face which had hung so close
to mine at my first awakening was one I was to see
again and again. For Valcyr, the ship's cat, apparently
decided that I was an object of interest second to none,
and spent long periods of time crouched on bunk or
floor of the cabin allotted to me, simply staring.

I was not used to companionship with animals and
at first her attentions irked me, for I could not throw
off the absurd feeling that behind those round, seldom-
blinking eyes was a mind which marked my every move,
sifting and assessing me and all I did. Yet in time I came
to tolerate her, and finally, when it became apparent
that the crew were not inclined, beyond a distant civility,
to friendliness, I found myself talking to her for want
of other conversation. For among themselves the Traders
spoke a language of their own, unintelligible to me so
that any attempt to follow their speech was fruitless.

After my interview with Ostrend I returned to my
cubby to discover Valcyr stretched on my berth taking
her ease. She was a lithe and beautiful creature, her
fur short and very thick, of a uniform silver-gray, save
for her tail, where there were dark rings. She had
moments when she displayed affection, and now she
raised her head to rub against my hand, while from her
throat rumbled a purr. Since such favors were rare, I
was flattered enough to continue to stroke her while I
considered the Cargo Master's suggestion.

We would planet on this world shortly, near a trading post where the men of the *Vestris* had been before. There were no cities, the natives being nomads by inclination, wandering in family-clan groups along the rivers from one marshy spot to the next. A few more civilized and enterprising clans had staked out semi-permanent settlements near places where crustacean beds could be fostered. But these were no more than collections of flimsy reed-and-mud huts.

What I had brought to the *Vestris* had been carried on my person. Now I took inventory of my scanty possessions to see if I had anything at all which could serve as a trade item. The few small stones still in my safe-belt were not to be touched. Not that it was likely they would interest Salmscar. I regretted the packs abandoned at the inn on Tanth, the luggage gone with the freighter. But if one permitted regret for little, one might as well remember all the rest lost on Tanth. I had nothing to risk here. I said as much to Valcyr, and she yawned widely and set her teeth gently upon my hand to suggest she was no longer interested in being petted.

However, when we set down, I was ready enough to go planetside. The chance to get firm earth under one's feet is always acceptable to any traveler, unless he is as wedded to space as a crewman—and even crewmen must earth now and then.

What greeted our noses as we went down the outflung landing ramp was more than the scorch of burning from our fin-down—it was a stink of chemicals, enough to make one hold one's nose. Ostrend said the natives favored this section of hot springs and volcanic action, and now we could see rocks, water- and steam-worn into strange shapes. At intervals steam and vile smells burst through holes in the ground.

Beyond this tormented land was the bluish foliage of the marshes, while the various overflows from the caldron lands lapped on to feed a yellow river. The heat from the steam was almost stiffling, the more so when combined with the chemical stench. We coughed and sputtered as we picked our way along a path, to find, on the banks of the river, the village we sought.

Ostrend stood there, his trade board between arm and hip, looking about in open puzzlement. After his description I had not expected to see much in the way of buildings. But certainly we looked now on what was not even the most primitive attempt at providing shelter, but rather an area of ruin and decay.

Mounds of ill-smelling reed stuff, with dried mud flaking off in great chunks, humped here and there. Among this litter nothing moved until a thing which was more leather-winged lizard than bird arose with a squawk and flapped awkwardly across the river. None of the traders pressed past Ostrend, but their heads swung from left to right and back again as if they were men suddenly suspicious of a trap.

The Cargo Master took from his belt a slender metal rod. Under his fingers it expanded longer and longer until he had a pole of double his own height. To the tip end he affixed a small pennon of bright yellow before he planted it fast in the soft mud of the riverbank. From comments, I gathered that, the village being deserted for some time by the signs, we could do no more than wait for the return of the natives—always providing that they were able to return. But since the visits of the *Vestris* were regular this could be expected to occur, again always excepting the fact that sóme disaster had not put an end to the established custom.

Captain Isuran, philosophical as a Free Trader must learn to be, was not happy. While his ship did not run on a tight schedule, yet time did set some barriers on each planeting. We could not wait too long before taking off. However, a failure to trade here would upset all plans and make necessary rearrangements to cover the losses caused by such an abortive stop.

Ostrend was in conference with the Captain for the hours that followed, while the rest of the crew speculated as to what might have happened, taking turns at sentry duty by the pennon. Since I was excluded from that, I allowed my own curiosity rein and explored, though not outside the limit wherein I could sight the sky-pointing nose of the ship.

Save for the novelty of the hot springs, and those soon palled, their heat and smell being more than anyone could take for long, there were few sights worth seeing. The flying thing which had fled our entrance into the deserted village was the only living creature I had sighted. Even insect life here either was remarkably sparse, or for some reason shunned the vicinity of the ship. At last I squatted down by the side of one of the small streams which issued out of the section of hot pots and gushers, inspecting it for gravel. The gem hunter's preoccupation could grip me even here. But I saw northing in the mess I scooped out and washed which held any promise.

There were some bits of a curiously dull black, which had the look of no mineral or the like, but of a kind of fuzzy burr. Yet when I separated them from the sand and stones with a stick, I discovered them to be extremely hard. Even pounding with a stone did not crush them, or even mar their velvety-seeming surface. I did not believe them seeds, or vegetable refuse, and my interest in them grew, until I had about a dozen laid in a row in the sun, being cautious at first not to touch them with my fingers. Nature provides some nasty traps on many planets. They had no beauty, and I did not think any value. But the contrast between their suggestion of softness to the eye, and their real hardness of surface was odd enough to make me gather up three for future examination. There are gems which must be "peeled," worked down in layers from their unattractive outer coatings or shells. One of little worth may so be turned into something of value. And I had some vague ideas that perhaps these might hide a surprise under that fuzzy surface, though I had neither the tools nor the skill needed for such a task.

As I knotted my choice into a square of seal-foam, Valcyr came walking, with that particular sure-footed daintiness of her species, along the bank of the small runlet. She progressed with nose to earth, almost as

45

might a hound on a warm trail, and she was manifestly sniffing something which absorbed her attention.

Then she reached my line of rejected ovoids and nosed each avidly. To my limited human nostrils they had no scent, but it was plain they did for the cat. Squatting down, she began to lick the largest, having sniffed them all. Fearing for her, I tried to knock it out of reach, but a lightning swift slash from unsheathed claws, ears flattened to skull, and a low growl warned me off. Sucking my bloodied fingers, I withdrew. It was plain that Valcyr guarded what she considered a treasure of price and was not minded to have any interference.

Once I had withdrawn, she went back to her licking. Now and again she picked it up in her mouth to retreat a little way before she squatted down to return to her tongue-rasping exploration of the find.

"Any luck?" Ostrend's young assistant threw a long shadow past me as he came up.

"What are these? Have you seen them before?" I pointed to the fuzzy stones scattered about by Valcyr as she had made her examination and choice.

Chiswit sat on his heels to study them. "Never saw them before. In fact"—he looked up and about—"this whole stream is new here. Maybe one of the big mudholes blew its top. Wait! Do you suppose that was what happened and there was gas? That could have driven out the Toads. They like the stink and the heat, but maybe they could not stand up to gas."

"Could be." But guesses about the disappearance of the natives, interesting as that might be, were not what I sought. I wanted information concerning the stones. If stones they were not, that was all I could term them. "You say you have never seen these. Was Valcyr with you when you planeted here last?"

"Yes. She has been ship's cat for a long time."

"And you never saw her do that before?" I pointed to where she now lay, the stone between her outstretched forepaws, her tongue working over and around it with absorbed concentration.

Chiswit stared. "No—what is she doing? Why, she's licking one of these things! Why did you let her—?" He scrambled to his feet and took two strides. Valcyr might not have seen him coming, but she seemed to sense a danger to her find. With it in her jaws, she was gone in a bound, heading away from the ship, weaving in and out among the twisted rocks.

We ran after her, but it was no use; she had disappeared—doubtless into some crevice where she could enjoy her find in peace. Chiswit turned on me with a demand as to why I had not earlier separated her from it. I showed him my bleeding hand and reported my failure. But the crewman was obviously upset and hunted through the rocky outcrops, calling and coaxing.

I did not believe that Valcyr was going to appear until she was ready, the independence of cats being their marked characteristic. But I trailed him, peering into each shallow, cavelike hole, rounding rocks in search.

We found her at last, lying on a small ledge under a deep overhang. Had it not been for the motion of her head as she swept the stone back and forth with her tongue, we might have missed her altogether, so close in color was her fur to the porous stone on which she lay. As Chiswit, speaking in a coaxing voice, went to his knees and held out his hand to her, she flattened her ears to her skull, hissed, and then gulped, and the stone vanished!

She could not have swallowed it! The one she had chosen had been the largest of those I had fished out of the stream, and it had been an ovoid far too big to descend her gullet. Only the fact remained that that was what had happened and we both had seen it. She crawled out of her crevice and sat licking her lips like a cat who has dined well. When Chiswit reached for her, she suffered him to pick her up, kneading paws on his arm as he carried her, purring loudly, her eyes helf shut, with no signs that the swallowing of her find had done her harm, or choked her. Chiswit started at a swift trot for the ship, while I knelt to look at the ledge, still hoping that the stone might have rolled somewhere, unable to believe it was now inside Valcyr.

The gray rock of the ledge was bare. And had the stone rolled, it would lie now somewhere directly before me. But it did not. I even sifted the gravely sand through my fingers, to produce nothing. Then I ran a forefinger over the ledge. There was a faint dampness, perhaps from Valcyr's saliva. But, in addition, something else, a tingling, almost a shock as I touched one point. The second time I put tip of finger to the same spot there was nothing but the damp, and that was drying fast.

"We saw her, I tell you! She swallowed a stone, a queer black stone—" Chiswit's voice rang down the corridor as I came along to the medico's quarters.

"You saw the ray report—nothing in her throat. She cannot have swallowed it, man. It probably rolled away and—"

"It did not, I looked," I said quietly as I came to the doorway.

Valcyr was in the medico's arms, purring ecstatically, her claws working in and out. She had the appearance of a cat very well pleased with herself and the world.

"Then it was not a stone, but something able to dissolve," he answered me assuredly.

I took out my improvised bag. "What do you call these? They are the same things she swallowed. I picked them out of a stream bed."

He placed Valcyr gently on the bunk and motioned me to lay the bag on his small laboratory table. In the ship's light the fuzziness of the stones was even more marked. He picked up a small instrument and touched the surface of the largest, then tried to scrape away some of the velvet. But the point of the knife slipped across the stone.

"I want a look at these." He was staring as intently as Valcyr had done.

"Why not?" He might not have the tools of a gemologist, but at least he could give me some report on their substance. His interest was triggered and I thought he

48

would work to get to the bottom of the mystery. Then I looked at Valcyr. The surface of the table on which the stones lay was very close to her. Would she be as attracted to another as she had to her first choice? Instead, she drowsily stretched out full length, her purring growing fainter, as if she were already half asleep.

Since the size of the medico's quarters did not allow for spectators, Chiswit and I left him to his tests. But in the corridor the assistant Cargo Master asked:

"How big was that thing when she first picked it up?"

I measured off a space between two fingers. "They are all oval. She took the biggest one."

"But she could not have swallowed it, not if it was that size!"

"Then what happened to it?" I asked, trying to remember those few instants when we had last seen the stone. Had it been as large as I thought? Perhaps she had only nosed the one I believed she had picked, and had taken another. But I did not distrust my eyes that much. I was trained to know stones and their sizes. An apprentice to such a master as Vondar could judge a stone's size without taking it into his hand at all. True, this was something new. I had tried to crush one of those things between two rocks with no results.

"She licked it smaller," Chiswit continued. "It is a seed or some hardened gum—and she just kept licking at it—so finally it melted."

A reasonable explanation, but one my own tests would not allow me to accept. So—I had a paradox—Valcyr had swallowed what seemed to me a gemhard stone, and one far too large to pass her gullet. Perhaps the medico would come up with an answer. I would have to wait for that.

On the second day the Captain broke out a small scout flitter, a one-man affair, but with range enough to explore the surrounding district. We could go on waiting here fruitlessly for months and he did not want to waste the time.

Ostrend took off in it and was gone two days. He

returned with the disappointing news that not only had he not found the villagers, but that he had seen no natives at all. And that there appeared to be an unusual scarcity of all life along the river and its tributaries. A few of the flying things such as we had disturbed on the first day, and which were eaters of carrion, were all he sighted. For the rest, the planet, as far as his cruising range, was as bare as if any higher forms of life had never existed at all.

At that report the Free Traders held a conference, to which I was not a party, and it was decided that they would dump their now worthless cargo of crustaceans into the usual river pens, as a sign of good faith should the natives ever return. They would also leave their trade flag flying as a symbol of their visit. But they would have to vary their future route in order to make up for the loss of trade here.

Which meant, I was curtly informed by Ostrend, that I was to continue my voyage on the *Vestris* for longer than planned. My first possible exit port had been that for which their medicinal cargo had been destined, and it would not now be visited. By space law I could not be summarily dumped on just any world, not when I had paid my passage, but must be carried to at least a second-stage port from which there was regular service. Now I would have to wait in boredom and impatience until we touched at such a place. And when that would be depended upon Ostrend's luck in picking up a cargo. He was continually with the Captain, going over taped trade reports, trying to find a way to make up for this failure.

As far as could be observed, Valcyr was none the worse for her extraordinary meal—not at first. And the medico's efforts to solve the mystery of the stones continued, until at last he came to the mess cabin, fatigue's dark shadows under his eyes, wearing a bewildered expression. He drew a half cup of boiling water, added a caff pill, and watched it bubble and brown in an absent way that suggested he saw something very different from that ordinary shipboard drink.

50

"A break-through, medico?" I asked.

His eyes focused as if he saw me for the first time. "I do not know. But—that thing is alive!"

"But—"

He nodded. "Yes—but— The reading is very low—resembling hibernation level. Nothing I have can open its shell, or whatever holds that germ of life. I'll tell you something else—" He paused to drink the full contents of his cup in one intake of liquid. "Valcyr is going to have kittens—or something—"

"The stone? But how—"

He shrugged. "Do not ask me. I know it is against all nature as I know it. She ate that thing, you both say she did. And now she is going to have a kitten—or something—"

"I'll tell you something else," he added as he drew a second portion of water. "I have rayed those stones into ash. And maybe I ought to do the same to the cat—"

"Why?"

This time he dropped two pills into the steaming cup. "Because if what I think is true, it is no kitten she is carrying. In fact it may be nothing we want aboard. I will keep an eye on her from now on. When her time comes—well, I can do what is best then." He took the second cup in a couple of gulps. When he left the mess cabin I saw that he turned to climb to the Captain's quarters.

One of the dreads of a trading ship is an unnatural life form loose on board. There are all kinds of horror tales about what has happened to ships unfortunate enough to pick up stowaways which later turned them into drifting charnel houses. That was the very reason Valcyr and her kind had their secure position on board ship. There were other safeguards, irradiation of suspect cargo by immunization rays and the like. But still, in spite of all precautions, sometimes the alien slipped in. If it was harmless it could prove a nuisance or even a new and amusing pet. But the chances were great that such uninvited guests would be inimical.

Traders are mainly immune to diseases of planets other than their native ones. Parallel but different roads of evolution performed this essential service. But they are not always immune to bites, stings, and attack from living creatures.

Now it seemed that Valcyr, meant to be the sentry at the gate, might well have unwittingly betrayed our fortress. She was kept in an improvised cage in the small sick bay. But the medico reported she did not protest imprisonment as she might have done normally. Instead she slept much of the time, rousing only to eat and drink. She did not resent his handling of her, but seemed happy and content. We all visited her, and speculation concerning the nature of what she was about to introduce among us was rife.

Ship time differs from planet time; we reckon it only artificially in days and nights because for so many centuries our species did live by sunrise and sunset and the flow of days. We were perhaps four weeks of such arbitrary time off the marsh planet when the medico broke into the off-watch rest cabin with the news that Valcyr had disappeared. In spite of his initial uneasiness, she had been so lethargic since we had upshipped that he had come to believe she would not fight confinement. Nor had she. But the fact remained that when he had taken her food and water, he had found the door swinging free and the occupant gone.

A ship's interior is limited, and one would think that there would be few places where a cat, small as she was, could hide. But when we started a search from the control room down to the sealed cargo hatches and then, mentally accusing one another of having been careless, retraced the same way in pairs, even in threes, we found no trace of our quarry.

We were in the corridor outside the mess cabin when Chiswit and Staffin, the junior engineer, both turned on the medico and accused him of doing away with Valcyr. Tempers were out of control by then and I had never realized how much the cat meant to these space voyagers until I heard the hot flow of anger in their tones. The medico denied their accusation just as vehemently, saying that he was well prepared to take measure for anything she might deliver, but that Valcyr would be safe. It was he who turned them all on me, snarling that I had allowed her to eat the stone in the first place, had even brought more of them on board.

What might have happened I do not know. But the Captain swung down the ladder and snapped orders. I was sent to my cabin, to remove temptation from his men, I suppose. And at that moment I was willing enough to go. In fact, when I closed the door behind me I thumbed the lock. For I had discovered in the last few minutes that that wild night of flight through Koonga City had left its mark—and that when I heard that note in the voices of the crewmen, I had instinctively reached for a weapon I did not wear.

I turned toward my bunk and froze. By the medico's reckoning Valcyr was still some time from the moment when she was to solve the mystery. Yet she lay now on my bunk. Where had she been during the search? I had looked in here twice, the others at least once, yet now she lay there as if she had rested for hours. And she was licking again—a thing which lay limply by her side.

Though I was not familiar with kittens, I was sure that what Valcyr now cared for was not the normal young of her kind. It lay supine at its greatest length, head and tail outstretched. I could see the rise and fall of its side as it breathed with fast, fluttering breaths, so it was alive. But otherwise it looked dead. The body was covered with a black fuzz, close in appearance to the outward coating of the "stone." This was wiry and did not yield much to Valcyr's caressing tongue.

The neck was long, out of proportion, the head sharper of muzzle than seemed right, while the ears were only indicated by tiny upstanding tufts of hair. The legs were short, the tail again long, the underside and tip furless, rather as if it were covered with dark, tough skin. The paws, which it had drawn up and curled against its belly, were also furless, those in front resembling hands more than beast's paws.

No, I did not believe it was a kitten. But it looked very helpless as it lay there panting. And Valcyr's pride and concern for her strange child were very apparent. It was my duty to go and call the medico. But instead I sat down on the side of the bunk, leaving Valcyr good room, and watched her energetic washing of the changeling. What she had given birth to I could not guess, but somehow I thought it worth saving. And that was my first meeting with Eet.

FIVE

I found it increasingly hard to think of betraying Valcyr and her offspring to the crew. Because that was the feeling which I finally identified—that a disclosure of their presence would be a betrayal. And I who had never felt any strong emotion for an animal knew one now. I questioned myself, trying to discover why, and found no answer. But the fact remained that I could not call anyone, no more than if I were chained to the bunk, silenced by a gag.

The small creature stirred at last, raising its narrow head and turning it back and forth as if seeking something. But it did so blindly, for its eye slits were closed. Valcyr, purring, put out a foreleg and fondly drew it closer. But that head had swung around to face me, and I thought that, though the thing was so young, blind, and helpless, yet somehow it was aware of me, not in fear, but for a purpose. I tried to laugh at that.

Disturbed, I got up from the bunk and went to sit on a wall seat, my back half turned to those two. I strove to concentrate on my own difficulties. Since I could not hope now for an early release from the *Vestris,* or even be sure on which planet I would land, I must be prepared for a dubious future. Once more I ran my hand along my safe-belt, fingering each of the pitifully few bulges left in it. The last one of all —the space ring—

Hywel Jern had been killed for it; of that I was as certain as if I had witnessed the act. But—had our disaster on Tanth also stemmed from its possession? Why Vonder and not me, if that were true? Or was it necessary to make sure of us both, so that no awkward questions could later be raised by a survivor? Why—who—?

My father had had close ties with the Thieves' Guild, in spite of his retirement from their company. Any man in those ranks could and did make powerful enemies. But, I believed, his services had continued in part even after his settlement on Angkor.

I continued to rub the ring's shape through the stuff of the belt and my thoughts went round and round, presenting me with no solution. I do not know when it was that I had begun to notice an unusual degree of heat in the cabin. I had opened the sealing of my coverall, and felt the trickle of sweat drops down my cheek and chin. Now I raised my hand to swab those away and my eyes lit upon the skin across the back and fingers. Rising on that once-smooth surface were purplish blotches, swelling as might water-filled blisters.

I tried to rise, only to discover that my body was no longer under my control. And I was shivering. The extreme heat of moments earlier was now an inner cold. I knew a tearing nausea, but I could not vomit. I clawed open my clothing and saw that the blisters were thick also across my chest and upper arms.

"Help—" Had I croaked that, or only thought I had? Somehow I lurched up and pushed around the wall of the cabin, using its support to make my way to the small com on the wall. There I shook and wavered as I tried to press the alert button.

It was getting hard to see—in fact a thick fog curled up about me as if I were back in that world of geysers and steam. Had I been able to press the button? I leaned my forehead against the wall so that my lips were not too far from the com as I croaked my plea:

"Help—sick—"

I could no longer stay on my feet. Aiming myself at the bunk, I tottered forward, completely forgetting Valcyr. But as I crashed down I encountered no furry bodies. The bunk was empty and I lay on it shuddering.

Now I was back in the dank steam of the deserted planet, and that wreathed in scalding curls about me, so that I cried out in torment. Across seamed and stinking mud I ran, unable to sight my pursuers but knowing I was hunted. Once the mists parted and I saw them for an instant. They came laser in hand and all wore the same face, that of the medico Velos. But still I kept my stumbling feet and fled.

"They will kill—kill—kill—" The words rang across this evil world in a vast thundering. "They will kill you—you—you!"

I was lying once more on my bunk, shivering again. But the mist had disappeared and my sight was clear. And not only my sight but my mind. There was a whistling whisper—it came from the wall—out of the wall. Once before I had heard words out of a wall—or the air. But that had been on Tanth in the sanctuary. And I was not there—but in a cabin on a Free Trader. In me was a vast urgency, a need to hear more of that whispering.

As I pulled myself up my covering slipped away. I was no longer clothed and my body was covered with purple blotches which were dried in scabs. Hideous! I was lightheaded when I moved, but somehow I got to the wall and the com set there. The light below it was on—it was open—and somewhere in the ship people were talking, close enough to the mike so that some of their speech was broadcast, though slurred. I tried to hear—

"—danger—seal up—cannot even space him—seal door —set down on moon—burn out the cabin—"

"—deliver him to—"

"No chance." The first speaker must have moved closer, for I heard him more clearly. "He is dead, or near enough not to matter. We are lucky so far, and we can take no chance of the infection spreading. Get rid of the plague evidence before we planet on any port. Do you want to be proclaimed a plague ship?"

"—held responsible—"

"Return their fee. Show them the picture tape from the cabin; one look at that ought to convince them that he was of no use. As for searching him—do you want the plague?"

"—not people to be easily satisfied—"

"Show them the tapes!" It was the medico talking, I was sure now. "Do not even open that cabin again until we can burn it out, and we go suited when we do that. On a dead moon where the infection cannot spread. Then we keep our mouths shut, and tightly. No one but *those* will be asking for him. As far as the rest, he is still back on Tanth, or dead there. And there will be no questions asked for some time anyway—if ever. *Those* will see that his trail is muddled. We cannot deliver him now—we have a body and a sealed cabin—plague—"

That they were discussing me I had no doubts. Now that I was on my feet, the first giddiness had gone and I could think. Velos termed me dead, or near so, but at the moment I felt very much alive. And I had no mind to fall victim to the fate the speakers had in mind for me. If Velos had his way my cabin door would be welded closed from the outside, not to be opened again for fear of contagion. They would shut off the ventilation, all outlets, to confine the disease, and I would have a hard and lingering death. On the other hand it would appear that I had not engineered my own escape from Tanth. Why had I not been suspicious at how easily it had worked? I had been taken to be delivered elsewhere. And I nursed no doubts as to the nature of those to whom I would have been presented as if I were a piece of cargo.

What escape was left me?

"Outside—"

I turned my head too quickly and had to clutch at the frame of the bunk as my vertigo returned. There was a small dark patch there and it moved. I stared stupidly for a moment, until I could focus on it.

The creature I had last seen curled by Valcyr hunched

58

beside my pillow. Now it seemed twice the size it had been at birth. Its eyes were well open and it looked at me intently. Seeing me stare in return, it reared its head, its long neck moving with reptilian sinuosity.

"Outside." Again that word formed in my mind, and I could only connect it with the animal. Somehow in my weak state of health such communication did not make me wonder.

"Outside, where?" I asked in a whisper, and then squeezed around to shut off the com. I had no desire to reveal my partial recovery to any possible listener.

"That—was—well—done. Outside—the—ship—" returned the thing backed against my rumpled pillow.

"That is open space—" I continued to carry on the conversation, convinced now that it was part of my fever. Perhaps the other words I had heard over the mike were also fever dreams—

"Not—so. You heard—they will kill—you. Smell their fear—it is a bad smell—all through this ship—" The narrow head raised higher and higher and I saw the nostrils expand as if the creature were indeed scenting the unusual in the flat air. "Go outside—quick—before they seal—the door. Take a suit—"

Wear a space suit—through the lock? I might live then as long as the air in the suit lasted. But that would only prolong life for a short time.

"They will search—not find—then come back—hide—" persisted my strange cabin mate.

A very wild plan with practically no chance of succeeding. But such is our clinging to life that I was ready to consider it. My cabin was not too far from the space lock, and the cubby storing the suits. On the other hand, the opening of that compartment would be instantly signaled to the bridge—and suppose we were in hyper—?

"Not so," cut in my companion. "Feel—"

It was right. The hum of a ship in hyper was absent. Rather I felt the vibration of a ship cruising in normal space.

"They seek—moon—dead world—to hide plague—or perhaps to meet others."

I pulled open a storage compartment. A coverall hung inside and I jerked it out, put it on. Wherever the fabric touched my scaling blotches they itched, but that was a minor discomfort when I had so much else to worry about. As I sealed the front opening, the creature on the bunk hunched together, quivered, leaped —landing on a small railed shelf level with my shoulder. I flinched and blinked.

Now that it was closer I could see it in detail. And it was indeed a weird mixture. Its fur was still the wiry black fuzz. The paws were naked skin. They were gray, white on the undersurfaces, and the fore ones were very like tiny hands. The head was reminiscent of a feline's, as was the body, except the limbs were too short in comparison with the length of the frame. Stiff whiskers bristled from the upper lip, but the ears were smaller than a cat's. The eyes were also out of proportion, being large and showing no pupils at all, only dark, slightly protruding orbs.

The whiplike tail was furred for its length in a ridge along the upper surface, but the tip and underparts were bare. Strange as it looked, it was not in any way repulsive, only different.

It stepped from the shelf to my body, settling itself around my neck, its hand-paws clinging to my right shoulder, so that its head was not far from my ear, its hind claws driven into the fabric over my upper left arm.

"Go—they come."

It was as sharp as an order and I found myself obeying. But before I left the cabin I received one more instruction.

"The air duct—feel inside."

The screen across it gave way easily to my first tug. I was so bemused now I followed instructions without question. Inside I found my safe-belt, which had been laid in the center of that tube, concealed from without. Automatically I searched its pockets by touch. My small resources were still mine.

"Quick!" That was reinforced with a sharp pinch from the hind claws.

I inched open the cabin door. The faint glow of the passage showed me it was empty. But I could hear the ring of boot plates on a ladder not too far away. I lurched for the suit locker. Suddenly it seemed my very thin chance was better than no chance at all!

The dreamlike quality of my actions continued to hold. I no longer, even with a small part of my brain, questioned the need to flee the interior of the ship, or whether any of this wild plan was feasible.

I regained a measure of strength and the more I walked the steadier I became. There was a fleeting satisfaction in disappointing Velos, who claimed I was dead or close to it.

The latch of the suit locker yielded to my tug and I slipped inside, pulling the door shut behind me. In one way I was favored, I saw as I glanced around that dim interior. The *Vestris* followed the general pattern of an exploring vessel—which was only logical, since a Free Trader often did discover new worlds.

There was another opening at the end of this space, giving entrance directly to the lock, saving time when one must suit or unsuit in leaving or entering the ship. I ran my hand along the rack of suits, striving to find one enough my size to be, if not comfortable, usable. Free Traders are now of a general physical type, slight of build. Had I not myself been thin and under height, I could not have squeezed into their protective covering. As it was, I was going to have a tight fit—a very tight one—so much so that I could not even buckle the safe-belt about my middle. Well, perhaps it could go over, if not under, the suit.

When we entered the locker my small companion swung down from its perch on my shoulders, and seemed almost to flow across the floor. It stopped before a clear-sided box and sat up on its haunches, using those hand-paws to feel along one edge in a

61

way which argued intelligent purpose. Then the front of the box sprang open and it flashed in, to curl up. Mystified, I watched.

"Close this!" The imperative command ringing in my head brought me down on one knee, the suit making me clumsy.

I was not quite sure what the box was. Its clear front, metal sides and back were both protective and designed to give one visibility of the contents. There were hooks at the back, as if it were meant to hang from a support. I guessed that it had been fashioned to bring back specimens from a new-found world.

"Close it—hurry—they come! You will take me—so!" The bright eyes turned up to mine, willing me. Yes, I could feel the force of the will. Again I obeyed.

My safe-belt could not be hooked over the suit. I hurriedly unsealed its pockets and shoveled their contents into a belt pouch—all save the space ring. That wide band of metal had once fitted over a space glove; perhaps it could again. And it did—snugly.

I strapped on the rest of the equipment, dimly aware of the suicidal folly of my plan. But the fact remained that were I to appear now anywhere in the ship I would probably be burned down without mercy. There is no fear quite like that of plague. With the carrying case containing my self-appointed company under my arm, I opened the door into the lock. My issuing out of the ship would activate alarms. But would they immediately believe that their quarry was seeking such a way out? Velos had reported me comotose. And I hoped they would cling to that thought.

The door of the hatch rolled back into place and I dogged it shut. Why not stay just where I was? Because there were inner controls and that door could still be opened from the corridor. They need only open it and beam a hole in my protective suit, then thrust me into space. A clean death as far as they were concerned, with little chance of my contaminating my slayers.

Even as I thought all this my hands were busy

thumbing the release of the outer hatch, almost as if they worked independently of my orders. Then the warn light flashed and there was a rushing of air. I edged through, planting the magnetic plates of my boots on the surface skin of the ship.

I had traveled spacers for years. However, my acquaintance with such had been limited to the activities of a passenger. But now I had sense enough to keep my eyes on the ship under my feet, resolutely away from the void it sailed. I had fastened the box by a safety cord to my harness and that swung out, tugging at me, but not with force enough to break my magnetic hold on the ship.

Shuffling, not daring to break contact with the surface, I moved away from the hatch. I thought it would not be long before I was followed and the folly of what I had done struck me like a blow, breaking that dream state which had held me since the creature had first thrown its thoughts at my receptive mind.

If that *was* all real and not some fever dream, I had received telepathically those suggestions and orders. No man can laugh at the idea of esper powers, as the so-called enlightened once did. It has been established that they exist, but do so rarely, and erratically. However, I had never had any contact with such before, and was certain I had no "wild talent."

"Move!" That order rang as sharply in my head as the first communication had done. "Move—toward the nose—"

For the first time since our association had begun, I balked. In fact I could not have moved in any direction at that moment. I was frozen in such wild terror as I had never believed a man could experience and not go mad. For I had lost all prudence and looked away from the ship under me, out and up.

Words hammered in my mind, but I did not understand them. I knew nothing, saw nothing but that emptiness. Something jerked and tore at my harness. The creature was plunging about in its box. I could see its mouth open and close, its eyes no longer shining beads but fiery and bright. But I watched it with detachment, the terror of space holding me fast.

But it was while I watched the creature's frenzied movements inside that box that I also saw the closing of the hatch I had left open. And I think I screamed inside my helmet, the shrilling of my own voice deafening me. I was locked out here now, alone with nothingness!

Did I go a little mad? I am sure now that I did. I must get to the door, I must— I have no true recollection—did I hurl myself? What happened in those seconds of raw, mind-shattering panic? I have never known. But I was no longer rooted—the ship was there, and I was turning over and over, away from it, without any hope of aid—floating out into the eternal dark.

I think I fainted then—because there are blank spaces in my memory. True consciousness only returned with the sensation of being pulled, drawn. I had a moment or two of heartfelt relief. They had roped me, I was going back to the *Vestris*. Even if that meant I was going to certain death, I did not care. Quick death was an end to be sought in preference to this spinning in the void forever.

My shoulder, my arm, pain—a pulling pain which grew stronger. My right arm was stretched straight ahead of my body as if I pointed to some unseen goal. And on the glove blazed light, a light which fluctuated as if it were fed by energy which came in spurts. I followed that outstretched arm as a diver's body follows his upheld, water-cutting arms, and there was the strong, sinew-tormenting pull, as if my arm had become a rope drawing me to an anchorage.

Nor could I move my arm, or even my legs. I was frozen into this position—a human arrow aimed for a target which I could not guess. That I was aimed I did not doubt. There was no rope on me—no, I was swinging through the void following that light on my glove. My glove? No! The space ring on my finger!

That once-clouded stone was the beacon of light pulling me on and on. I could turn my head a little and see in the reflected glory of that light that I still towed the box with its furry occupant. But the creature was curled in a tight ball which rolled helplessly and I thought it was probably dead.

Where the *Vestris* might be I had no idea. There was a sense of speed about my present passage. And I could not turn my head very far to see what lay behind, above, or below.

Time ceased to have any meaning. I wavered back and forth between consciousness and black non-being. Only gradually did I become aware of approaching something. At last I could make out the outline of what once might have been a ship; at least the inner portion of that drifting mass might have been a ship. About it, like tiny satellites about a planet, were crowding bits of debris, grinding now and then against the hull, swinging out, but not to break away. And the ring was pulling me straight into that grinding! Caught by even a small fragment of that and I would be as dead as if a laser had cut me down.

Yet try to fight the pull as I did, I had no chance against the force drawing me on. My arm was numb, the joints seemingly locked in that position. I had ceased to be a man; I was only a means for the ring to reach whatever target it must find.

Inside the suit, my helpless body, that which was the thinking, feeling part of me, cowered and whimpered. I shut my eyes, unable to look upon what lay before me, and then was forced to open them again because hope refused to die. We were very close to the outer circle of debris, and I thought I could see a hole in the side of the derelict ship—either an open hatch or some other break.

It was, as far as I could guess, since my sight of it was limited by the mass of stuff about it, larger than the *Vestris*, perhaps closer to passenger liner. And its lines were not those of any ship I knew. Then—we were in the first wave of debris—

I waited for the crushing of those bits of jagged metal —until I saw that the floating stuff was parting before

65

the beam of the stone, as if that had the power to cut a clear path. Hardly daring to believe that such would be the case, I watched. But it was true, a great lump dipped and bobbed and moved reluctantly away.

So we came to that dark doorway. I was sure it was a hatch, though there remained no evidence of any door. But the opening was too regular to be a mere hole. Into and through that dark arch the ring continued to pull me, lighting up dim walls. And then my beacon hand struck painfully against a solid surface, and continued to beat through no desire of mine, hammering upon the inner hatch of this long-dead ship as if demanding entrance. Finally my gloved flesh came to rest on that resisting surface as if it were welded there, while I struggled until my magnetized boots struck the floor and I could stand, my right hand pinned to the door, my feet anchored once again.

SIX

There was such an overwhelming relief in being shut in, out of the void, that for a space that was all I felt—until the knowledge that I was now caught in another trap dispelled my only too short sensation of safety. My hand was still fast against the door and I could not pull it loose. Rather, it dragged me further and further forward, until my whole body was flat to that surface, almost as if the strength of the attraction could ooze me through the age-worn metal itself. And a second wave of fear arose in me at the thought that I would be held so for all time, trapped in this hatchway.

The glow from the stone was no longer so bright as it had been. In these confined quarters it would have been blinding had its brilliance shown as it had in space. But it was still flickering. I struggled wildly against the hold, until I wilted, exhausted, held upright by my hand against the door.

As I hung there, staring dully at the light, my hand, and the door, a fact broke through my bemusement. The flickering was now more deliberate. Almost it followed a pattern—on, off, on, off, with varying intervals between flashes. The suit was insulated, of course, but where the palm of my glove met the substance of the door, a reddish stain was spreading. Even through that insulation I could feel a tingle of concentrated energy.

Again I sensed I was only a thing to be used by the stone, that I was its tool and not it mine. The tingle became pain, and finally agony, with nothing I could do to ease it. The red stain brightened and at last I saw dark lines crack open. As the agony grew, the door began to give way. It fell in broken shards from the frame and I was pulled on.

I caught only glimpses of corridors, for it seemed that the stone now sped to make up for the time lost in defeating the barrier at the hatch. I was twice pulled past breaks in the hull.

My journey ended in a section where there were strange shapes of machines—or I believed them to be machines. And this part of the ship seemed intact, undamaged by whatever had struck to finish its life. The stone whisked me around and through a maze of rods, cylinders, latticework, piping, coming at last to a box wherein I could see a tray. And set on that were black lumps. With a last spurt the stone once more plastered my hand to the viewplate of the box. It flared in a burst of dazzling light. And behind the plate I saw a small answering flicker from one of those lumps. But it was only a flicker and quickly gone. Then the glow of the stone died, too, and my hand fell limply to swing by my side, a dead weight. I was alone in the dark bowels of a long-dead ship.

I collapsed, to float, and then felt the bump of the box in which my companion traveled. How much air I had left in my suit tank I did not know, but I doubted whether it was enough to keep me living long. The stone had clearly led me to my death, not in a void where I would have spun forever, but in this tomb of blasted metal.

There is the ancient fear of my species of the dark and what may creep therein. I raised my left hand and fumbled with the button on the fore of my harness until the sharp ray of a beamer glowed, picking out the case of lumps which might once have been stones to rival that in the ring. There was, of course, no hope that I could find any compartment with air remaining, or any form of escape. But neither would I stay supine where I was, just waiting for suffocation to finish me.

My right arm was still useless. I took that hand with

my left and wedged it into the front of my harness, keeping it across my chest. I would have cast off the box with the dead creature, only, when I looked down at that tightly curled body, to my vast amazement, I saw the head move, caught the gleam of eyes. So it had also survived our voyage to the derelict!

The magnetic plates on my boots allowed me to walk along the deck, though the slow spin of the ship made the deck become wall, or even ceiling. Finally I loosed the plates and pulled along by handholds.

All ships of my own time carried lifeboats, with directional finders which would locate the nearest planetary body and would then direct the boat there—though there was always a chance the survivors might be landed on a world inhospitable to human life. Perhaps this ship had a similar arrangement for the safety of passengers and crew. If so—and I could find one—though they might have all been used when the ship was first abandoned—I might still have a thin chance.

It is the nature of my species that we find it necessary to keep fighting for life until a last blow ends us. That inborn instinct drove me now.

The stone, I deduced, had brought me to the engine section of the ship. Whatever empowered it in space and acted as a homing device had drawn it straight to those burned-out bits in the box, once, perhaps, the motive power for the ship.

I pulled myself through the remains of the engine room. There might, I thought, be other energy sources in the lifeboats. They should be several decks higher, close to the crew and passenger quarters—always supposing this ship duplicated the general layout of those I knew.

I found no ladders, only wells which were cut through the levels. There were hints here and there that this vessel had never housed beings of my type. At the foot of the second well I hesitated. The ship rolled lazily; I might float through one of these—only my beamer showed no handholds to pull me along, and to be sucked in and then spin helplessly— At last I used my boot plates, walking up along walls which moved ever to make my head swim and induce a return of the vertigo which had been a symptom of my illness.

The next level had cabins, most of their doors open. I peered into one or two. There were shelves which might have been bunks, save that they were very short and narrow, and they were so uniform in the interior design I thought this must have been crew territory.

Once more I made a spin walk to the next level. There had been a carpet on the floor here and the cabins were larger. My beam illuminated a splash of color on the wall, focused on a picture or mural—queerly disjointed figures or objects, which my eyes could not follow, colors which hurt. Passenger territory. Now—along here I should find LB hatches.

There was something floating against the wall of the corridor. It seemed to lurch at me and I fended it off with aversion, refusing to look closely. Passenger or crewman, here was one who had not reached any LB. My touch sent it swirling back and away.

I had begun to think I was wrong in my hopes when I came to the first port and looked through its door into an empty socket. The LB had been launched, which meant live passengers had reached it. Some had escaped that long-ago wreck. And though the port was empty, it raised my flagging hopes.

The dial on my air tank had swung far toward red. I glanced at it once and then swiftly away. Better not to know how near I was to the end. Even were I able to find a usable LB and launch it, how long would it be before I reached a planet? If and if and if again—

Suddenly the numb arm across my breast twitched and pulled against the confining strap. I looked down. The stone shone. Was it answering once more a call from an installation similar to the one I had found in the engine room?

Though the pull tugged at my secured arm, it was not enough to jerk it free of the fastening. But it did provide a guide along this corridor. Past two more empty berths I traveled. Then my arm gave a hard jerk, which did tear it loose and bring its dead weight around to point to a surface now almost under me as the ship rolled. There was another hatch to an LB berth—but it was closed. Perhaps no one had reached it.

Again my glove went to that door, anchored me, and the light from the stone flared. But this time it did not burn through. The hatch cover rolled aside and I saw the projectile shape of an LB. Once more my arm dropped, but I pulled myself along with my left hand, pried at the hatch of the LB. It gave and I fell into its interior, bringing the box of the creature with me.

There was a flickering of light, not only from the stone, but on a panel at the nose end of the LB. There were hammock-like slings to take the bodies of passengers and one was close enough for me to clutch. I could feel a vibration through the small cabin. Whatever energized this LB was not dead—the thing had at least enough power to cruise out of its sling inside the skin of the parent ship. We shot forth with enough force to pin me down, and I blacked out.

"Air—"

I looked blearily about. The beamer still shown, now straight against a curving wall, to be reflected back dazzlingly into my eyes. Suddenly I realized that I was breathing in shuddering gasps, coughing a little. For the air I fought to draw into my lungs had a strange odor which irritated my nasal passages. On my shoulder was a furry burden, and a whiskered face was thrust close to mine, dark beads of eyes watching me intently.

"Air it is," I answered dreamily. More and more this had the cast of a weird nightmare. Logical, perhaps, after a fashion which nightmares seldom are, but certainly not believable. For now, however, I was content to lie half entangled in the hammock, rapidly breathing that disagreeable air.

When I turned my head a fraction I could see a board of controls. The numerous lights which had played so swiftly across it at my first entrance now were cut to three—one yellow-white, in the center and

71

a little above the other two, one red, and the other a ghostly blue. I looked down at my hand. There was still a glint of light in the stone, showing beneath the clouded surface, and a faint tingling prickled in my hand.

At least I was still alive, I was free of the dead ship in an LB, and I had air to breathe even if it was not the air my lungs craved. It would seem my entrance into the projectile had activated its ancient mechanism.

If we were on course for the nearest planet, how long a voyage did we face? And what kind of a landing might we have to endure? I could breathe, but I would need food and water. There might be supplies—E-rations —on board. But could they still be used after all these years—or could a human body be nourished by them?

With my teeth I twisted free the latch which fastened my left glove, scraped that off, and freed my hand. Then I felt along my harness. These suits were meant to be worn planetside as well as for space repairs; they must have a supply of E-rations. My fingers fumbled over some loops of tools and found a seam-sealed pouch. It took me a few moments to pick that open.

I had not felt hunger before; now it was a pain devouring me. I brought the tube I had found up to eye level. It was more than I could manage to sit up or even raise my head higher, but the familiar markings on the tube were heartening. One moment to insert the end between my teeth, bite through, and then the semiliquid contents flooded my mouth and I swallowed greedily. I was close to the end of that bounty when I felt movement against my bared throat and remembered I was not alone.

It took a great deal of resolution to pinch tight that tube and hold it to the muzzle of the furred one. Its pointed teeth seized upon the container with the same avidity I must have shown, and I squeezed the tube slowly while it sucked with a vigor I could feel through the touching of its small body to mine.

There were three more tubes in my belt pouch. Each one, I knew, was intended to provide a day's rations, perhaps two if a man were hard pushed. Four days—

maybe we could stretch that to eight. But the gamble was such as no sane man would have taken by choice.

I lay quietly until my strength began to return. The leaden weight of my right arm tingled a little, not from the action of the stone, but as if circulation returned. With that came a painful cramping. I forced myself to flex my fingers inside the glove, to raise and lower my forearm, setting my teeth against the hurt those exercises caused me.

In time my arm obeyed me as well as it had before the stone had taken over. I pulled myself up into a sitting position and gazed about the LB. There were six of the hammock slings, three on each wall, and I lay in the last to the right. None of them had been placed close enough to the control board for the occupant to reach it. This was true also of the regulation escape boats I knew. Their course tapes were set, so that if a badly injured man managed to reach one of them, it would serve without need for human manipulation.

Like the bunks I had seen in the ship, these hammocks, gauging by their size, were not intended for the human frame. And certainly the air still rasping my nose and lungs was not normal. I wondered briefly if it held some poisonous element which would in time finish me. But if that were true there was nothing I could do about it.

On the wall I traced outlines which I thought marked storage compartments. Whether E-rations lay behind those still— The dreamy state continued to hold me. Though my strength returned to my body; it was as if I watched all this from a distance and nothing really mattered. Once I raised my hand to look at it. Those dark patches which had been the purple, swollen blisters, and then scaling scabs, had rubbed off their rough surfaces inside the glove. The skin beneath was shiny pink and new.

Again the furred body moved and I felt the wiry hair rasp against my neck. Then my companion moved out, crawling down my body, reaching out a hand-paw to catch at the webbing of the next hammock. It was a long space to span, and at last the creature dug the claws of its hind legs into the stuff of my suit, lunged forward, and so was just able to grasp the edge of the web. With sinuous dexterity it took firm hold and swung over to its new position.

The hammock served it as a ladder and it climbed agilely to one of the outlined lockers. Holding with a left forepaw and both hind legs to its swaying anchorage, it ran the other set of small gray fingers over the surface. When it pressed or released, I could not tell, but a panel swung open with such speed that the creature had to duck to escape.

Behind were two tubes secured in a rack. Each had something vaguely resembling a laser grip, and I thought they might be weapons—or perhaps survival tools. Leaving that door aswing, the creature went methodically to the next. I was a little troubled as I watched it.

Even after our communication I had continued to think of my companion as an animal. It was clearly the offspring of Valcyr, strange though its begetting had been. I had heard of mutant animals able to communicate with man. But now it was brought home to me that whatever this creature was, it had intelligence above the level I had assigned it. And now I asked, my voice overloud in the small cabin:

"Who are you?"

Perhaps it would have been better to ask, "What are you?"

It paused, its forepaw still outstretched, its long neck twisting so that it could look straight at me. And for the first time I remembered I had awakened without my helmet, with the air reviving me. Surely I had not taken it off while unconscious—so—

"Eet."

A single word with a queer sound—if a word in one's mind may also register as a sound.

"Eet," I repeated aloud. "Do you mean you are Eet as I am Murdoc Jern, or Eet as I am a man?"

"I am Eet, myself, me—" If it understood my division of terms it was not interested. "I am Eet, returned—"

74

"Returned—how? From where?"

It settled back into the hammock, which swayed under its weight as light as it was, so that it must clutch at the webbing to keep its position.

"Returned to a body," it replied matter-of-factly. "The animal made me a body—different, but usable. Though perhaps it needs some altering. But that can come when there is time and the necessary nutriments."

"You mean you were a native, one of those we could not find? That because Valcyr ate that seed, you—" My thoughts jumped from one wild possibility to the next.

"I was not native to that world!" There was a snap to that, as if Eet resented the suggestion. "They did not have that in them which could make Eet a body. It was necessary to wait until the proper door was opened, the right covering prepared. The beast from the ship had what I needed—thus she was attracted to the seed and took inside her the core from which Eet could be born again—"

"Born again—from where?"

"From the time of hibernation." There was impatience now. "But that is past—it need not be considered. What is of importance in this hour is survival—mine—yours—"

"So I am important to you?" Why had it urged me out of the *Vestris*, saved me by removing my helmet in the LB? Did it need me in some way?

"It is true that we have need of one another. Life forms in partnership sometimes make a great one out of a lesser," Eet observed. "I have obtained a body which has some advantages, but it lacks bulk and strength, which you can supply. On the other hand, I have skills I am able to lend to your fight for life."

"And this partnership—it has some future goal?"

"That has yet to be revealed. Now we think of continuing to live, a matter of major importance."

"I agree to that. What are you hunting for?"

"What you have already imagined might be here, the food and drink intended to sustain those escaping in this small ship."

"If it is still here and has not dried to dust, or if it

will feed us and not be poison." But I pulled myself up yet farther in the hammock and watched Eet claw open another locker.

This contained two canisters set in shock-absorbing bands. And though Eet wrestled with them, he could not free either. At last I dragged my weak-legged self from my hammock to the next and managed to pry the nearest canister from its hooks.

It had a nozzled tip. I gripped it between my knees and used one of the small tools from my harness to open it. Then I shook the can gently. There was the slosh of liquid inside. I sniffed, my mouth dry again as I thought of the wonderful chance that it might actually hold water. The semiliquid E-ration contained moisture but not really enough to allay thirst.

Its smell was pungent, but not unpleasant. What I held could be drink, or fuel, or anything. Another chance among all those I—we—had taken since we had left the *Vestris*.

"Drink or fuel, or what have you?" I stated the guesses to Eet, holding out the canister so that he, she, or it could sniff in turn.

"Drink!" was the decided answer.

"How can you be so sure?"

"You think I say so just because I wish it? No. This much have I in this body: what is harmful to it, that I shall know. This is good—drink it and see."

So authoritative was the command that I forgot it came from a small furred creature of unknown species. I put the nozzle to my lips and sucked. Then I almost spilled the container, for though the stuff which filled my mouth *was* liquid, it had a sour bite. Not wine as I knew it, but certainly not water either. Yet after I had swallowed inadvertently, my throat was cool and my mouth felt fresh, as if I had drunk my fill of some cool stream. I took another drink and then passed it to Eet, holding the container while it sucked. Thus we had our necessary moisture. But for food we were not so lucky. We found in another locker blocks of a pinkish stuff, dried and hard. Eet pronounced them dangerous,

76

and if they were the E-rations of the LB, they were not for us.

He found some queerly shaped tools and another set of weapons, but that was all—except for a box, in the last compartment, that had various dials and two rods which could be pulled out from a place of safekeeping on its back. These extended, and between them there was a thin tissue which expanded to form a film. I judged it a com device—doubtless meant to beep a distress signal once the party aboard the LB made their landing. But those it might have summoned were long since vanished from this portion of the galaxy.

Since my species entered space we have known we were latecomers to the star lanes. There were other races who voyaged space, empires and confederations of many worlds which rose and fell, long before we knew the wheel and fire, and reached for metal to fashion sword and plow. We discover traces of them from time to time and there is a very brisk trade in antiques from such finds. The Zacathans, I believe, have archaeological records of at least three star empires, or alliances, all vanished before they pioneered space, and the Zacathans are the oldest people we have firsthand knowledge of, with a written history covering two million planet years! They are a long-lived race and prize knowledge above all else.

Even this LB, could we possibly by some fluke land on an inhabited planet, would bring me enough from its sale to set me up as a gem buyer. But the chance of that happening was so small as to be infinitesimal. I would settle gladly for any sort of a landing where the air was breathable and there was enough food and water to sustain life.

There was no reckoning time in the LB. I slept and so did Eet. We ate very sparingly, when we could no longer stand the demands of our bodies, and drank the liquid of the vanished voyagers. I tried to get more information out of Eet, but he stubbornly curled into a ball and would not answer. I say "he," for while he never stated his sex, if he had one, I came to think of him as male, and since he did not correct that assumption, I continued in it.

We had but half a tube of nourishment left when that white light on the board, so steady that it had ceased to interest us, flashed into yellow and there was a warning buzz along the walls. I hoped (or did I fear?) that this meant a landing. And I huddled back in the hammock, Eet sprawled flat against me, wondering how well we would set down in a craft ages old and powered by energy close to extinction.

SEVEN

We must have blacked out in shock following our entrance into the atmosphere, for when I was again conscious of my surroundings, we lay in a ship which no longer vibrated with life—though it swayed under my half-aware movements as if we were caught in a giant net and there was no stable earth under us. I screwed the helmet of the suit back into place and saw that Eet had been prudent enough to return to the box. Then I crawled, inch by inch, to the hatch, the LB slipping and shuddering under me in the most alarming way.

The inner catches on that were simple, devised for survivors who might have been injured and able to use only one hand. But when I tried to push it open there was resistance, and curls of white smoke trickled in. I had to fight the stubborn metal until I was able to wedge open a space wide enough to scramble through without tearing my precious suit.

There I was met by more puffs of thick smoke. I looked around for a stable foothold. The LB seemed to be sliding sideways and I had little time for choice. When it gave a convulsive tremble I jumped, into the smoke, and crashed through that veil into a mass of splintered and broken foliage, some of it afire.

A branch as thick as my wrist, with a broken end like a spear point, nearly impaled me. I caught it with both hands and hung for a moment, thrashing wildly with my feet for some hold. But it bent under my weight and I slid inexorably down it in spite of my struggles. I crashed on, down through more branches, bringing up at last on a wider one where my harness

79

caught on a stub of mossed wood and I found a precarious landing. There was a heavy tearing a little ways away. I thought that perhaps the LB had gone down. I clung to the stub which had hooked me and drew a deep breath as I looked around.

The masses of leaves screening me in were a sickly yellowish-green, which here and there shaded to a brighter yellow, or a dull purplish-red. The branch under me was rough-barked, wide enough for two men to walk, and splotched with purple moss, in which grew spikes of scarlet crowned with cups which might be flowers, but which opened and shut as I watched with the rhythm of breathing or of a beating heart.

There was a great ragged hole overhead which marked more than my own descent, probably the entrance of the LB. But elsewhere the canopy of growth was thick and unbroken.

I drew the box containing Eet up beside me and saw that he was sitting on his haunches, looking about him with reptilian twists of his long neck, so that sometimes he appeared to turn his head completely around on his shoulders. There was a crashing which I did not really hear, but rather felt as a vibration through the shaking tree, and then a final thud which set my perch rocking under me. I judged that the LB had at last met the ground. The fact that so heavy a craft had taken so long to fall suggested two things—that this net of vegetation grew well above the ground, and that it was tough enough to catch the entering ship, cushion it for a space, delay its final landing.

The smoke was thickening, coming from above. If there was a fire blazing there, then a withdrawal was certainly in order. To outrun a forest blaze in my unwieldy suit was nigh impossible.

I got to my feet and edged along the limb, heading, I hoped, for the parent trunk. At least it grew wider and thicker ahead of me. There were other aerial growths besides the moss with the breathing cups. One barred my way very soon. The leaves were yellow, broad and fleshy, curving up so that those in the center formed a cup. And in that, water, or some colorless fluid, gathered. Above this leaf-enclosed pondlet was the first animate life I had seen.

A flying thing perhaps as large as my hand unfolded gauzy wings to flutter away. It had been so much the color of the leaves that it was invisible until it moved. Another creature raised a dripping snout and bared teeth from where it crouched on the other side of the cup. Like the flying thing, it was camouflaged, for its wattled, warty covering was like the rough bark of the tree limbs, and of the same dark color. But the fangs it showed suggested that it was carnivorous, and it was about the size of Valcyr, with long legs which were clawed, clearly meant to grip and hold, perhaps not only the aerial trails it followed but also some prey.

Nor did it have any fear of me, but stood its ground, fangs bared, its ugly head down, its shoulders hunched, as if it was about to spring.

To advance I must cross the outer leaves of the pool plant. And while my challenger was small, I did not underrate it for that reason. There had been no laser with the suit—after ship custom all arms were locker-stored during the flight. Most Free Traders carried only the non-lethal stunners anyway. But I did not even have one of those.

"Let it be." Eet's command rang in my head. "It will go—"

And go it did, with a suddenness which left me believing it had vanished like some illusion wrought by a Hymandian sand wizard. I saw a flash across the bark beyond the pool plant, and that was all that marked its going.

Cautiously I stepped onto the broad leaves. Their surfaces broke under my weight, and yellow stuff oozed up and about my boot soles, the leaves themselves turning dark, seeming to rot away at once, flaking in great shreds from the holes. More of the gauzy things took to the air, to splash back, as my passing put an end to their world.

I slipped and slid, careful of every slime-coated step,

until I reached the other side. My face was wet with sweat inside the helmet, and I was breathing slowly and with an effort. I had come to the end of my air supply, and whether it would mean death or no, I must open my helmet.

Squatting down on the limb, I clicked open the latches and breathed, half expecting to have the lungs seared out of me by that experiment. But, though the air was laden with smells, and many of those noxious as far as I was concerned, I thought the air less bad than that I had encountered in the LB.

I could hear now, and there were sounds in plenty. The buzzing of insects, sharp calls, and now and then a distant heavy thud, as if someone beat a huge drum and listened to its echoes dying gradually away. There was a rustling and crackling, too. I could smell a stench which was certainly born of burning, though I did not see any movement of tree-dwelling things which would suggest that the inhabitants of these leafed heights were fleeing a fire.

Behind me the pool plant shriveled, its bruised leaves falling away in festering shreds. Now the inner petals or leaves which had cupped the water unclasped and a flood poured out, to cascade and then drip from the big limb into the mass of vegetation below, carrying with it wriggling, struggling things which had lived in it. The plant continued to die and rot until only a black blot remained on the limb, a most nauseating odor rising from it, making me move on.

The limb road grew wider and thicker. Now it was a running place for vines, which crossed it and looped around it, forming traps for the feet of the unwary. I continued to sweat as the muggy heat held me. And the suit became more and more of a burden. Too, I was hungry, and I remembered the drinker at the pool, wondering if I could turn hunter with any success.

"Out—!" Eet was economical with words now, but his meaning was plain. I put down his traveling box and opened it. He flashed out of its confines and stood poised on the limb, his head flicking from side to side.

"We must have food—" I remembered what he had said about being able to tell what was edible and what was not. The fact that on an alien planet practically all food might mean death to off-worlders was to the fore of my mind. We might have made a safe landing here only to starve in the midst of what was luxurious plenty for the natives.

"There—" He used his nose as a pointer, elongating his neck to emphasize his statement. What he had selected was an outgrowth on one of those serpentine vines. It rose like a stem, from which quivered some narrow pods, more flat than round. They shook and shivered as if they possessed some odd life of their own. And I could not see why Eet thought them possible food. They appeared less likely than the cluster of ovoid berries, bursting with ripe pulp and juice, which hung from another stem not too far away.

I watched my companion harvest the pods with his forepaws. He stripped off their outer shells to uncover some small, far too small, purple seeds, which he ate, not with any appearance of relishing that diet, but as one would do a duty.

He did not fall into convulsions, or drop in a fatal coma, but methodically finished all the buttons he could strip out of their pods. Then he turned to me.

"These can be safely eaten, and without food you cannot go on."

I was still dubious. What might be good for my admittedly half-alien companion might not nourish me. But it was the only chance I had. And there was another cluster of the trembling pods not too far beyond my hand.

Slowly I drew the space stone from my gloved finger, stowed it away in a pocket on my harness, and then unsealed the gloves, allowing them to dangle from my wrists as I reached for the harvest.

Once more I saw the healing scars of the blisters. My flesh was pink and new-looking in unseemly splotches against the general brown of my skin. Though I was not as space-tanned as a crewman might be, my roving life had darkened my skin more than was normal for a planet dweller. But I was now spotted in what I was sure must be a disfiguring manner, though I could not see my face to judge. Until the blotches faded, if they ever did, I would be marked as undesirable to any off-worlder. Perhaps it was just as well we had not made landing at a port; one look at me and I would have been sent into indefinite quarantine.

Carefully I husked the pellets. They were larger than grains of hoswheat, hard and smooth to the touch. I raised them to my nose, but if they had any odor, it was slight enough to be overlaid by the general blast of smells all about us. Gingerly I mouthed several of them and chewed.

They seemed to have no discernible taste, but became a floury meal between my teeth. I found them dry, hard to swallow, but swallow I did. Then, since I had taken the first step and might as well go all the way, I harvested all within reach, chewing and swallowing, giving Eet another two clusters when he signified they would be acceptable.

I allowed us some small sips from the canister of liquid out of the ship, which I had made fast to my harness. That cleared the dry-as-dust feeling from my mouth tissues.

Eet had been moving impatiently back and forth along the branch as I ate, progressing in darting runs, pausing to peer and listen, then returning. Although it had been but a short time since his birth, he had all the assurance of an adult, as if he had achieved that status.

"We are well above ground." He came back to settle down near me. "It would be well to get to a lower level."

Perhaps as I had depended upon his instincts to find us food, so I should harken to him now. But the suit was clumsy to climb in, and I feared a false step where the vines were so entwined.

I crawled on hands and knees, testing each small space in advance. Thus I came to the point from which those vines spread, the giant trunk of the tree. And that bôle was giant indeed. I believe that had it been hollow, it would have furnished room for an average dwelling on Angkor, while its height was beyond my reckoning. I wondered just how far it was to the surface of this vegetation-choked world—if the whole planet was covered by such trees.

Had it not been for the vines, I would have been marooned aloft, but their twists, slippery and unpromising as they looked, did afford a kind of looped stairway. I had two cords with hooked ends coiled in my harness—intended to anchor one during space repairs, though I had not discovered them in time to keep me on the *Vestris*. These I put to use now, hooking them to vines, lowering myself to the extent of the cord, loosing by tears to hook again. It was an exhausting form of progress, and I grew faint with the struggle. The muggy heat made it worse.

Finally I came to the jut of another wide branch, even larger than the one I had left. I dragged myself out on that, thankful to have reached such a small link with safety. The thick foliage made this a gloomy place, as if I were in a cave. And I thought that if I ever did reach the surface of the forest floor, it would be to discover that day was night under the sky-hiding canopy. Perhaps it was the tear made by the LB which allowed even this much light to filter through.

Those patches of moss with the breathing cups were not to be seen on this level. Instead there was a rough, spiky excrescence from which hung long drooping, thread-thin stems or tentacles. These exuded drops of sap or a similar substance. And the drops glowed faintly. They were, I believed, lures, attracting prey either by that phosphorescence, or by their scent. For I saw insects stuck to them, sometimes thrashing so hard to be free that the thread-stems whipped back and forth.

Eet halted beside me, but I could sense his impatience at the slowness of my descent. Unburdened by a suit, he could have already reached the ground. Now he kept urging me to go on. But if he had some special fear of this arboreal world, he did not share it with me. His attitude had grown more and more like that of an adult dealing with a child who must be cared for, and whose presence hinders and makes more difficult some demanding task.

Groaning, I began the descent again. Eet flashed by me and was gone with an ease I envied bitterly as I took up my crawl, hook, hold, free, hook, crawl. As the gloom increased I began to worry more about my handholds, about being able to see anchors for the hooks.

It was as if I had started at midday and were now well into evening. The only aid was that more and more of the vegetation appeared to have phosphorescent qualities and that the spike growths with lures became larger and larger, giving a wan light. This glow grew brighter as darkness advanced. Perhaps the dusk really was due to the passage of time, and planet night was nearly upon me.

The thought of that led me to greater efforts. I had no wish to be trapped in the dark, climbing down this endless vine staircase. So I passed without halting two other limbs which offered tempting resting places and kept doggedly on.

Since that creature which had drunk from the pool plant had vanished I had seen no life except insects. But there were those in plenty and they varied from crawlers on vine and bark to a myriad of flying things. Some of the largest of those were equipped with spectral light patches too. Their antennae, their wings, and other parts of their bodies glowed with color instead of the ghostly grayish illumination of the plants. I saw sparks of red, of blue, of a clear and brilliant green—almost as if small gems had taken wing and whirled about me.

I was sure it was night when I slipped over the last great loops of vine which arched out and away from the tree, and which carried me, as I clung to their now coarse-textured surfaces, down to the floor of the forest. I landed feet first on a soft sponge of decay, into which I sank almost knee-deep. And it was as dark as a moonless and starless night.

"Here!" Eet signaled. I was floundering, trying to get better footing in the muck. Now I faced around to the point from which that hail had come.

The roots of the vines stretched out about the monster bole of the tree, so that between them and the trunk was a space of utter dark, where none of the light plants grew. It seemed to me that my companion had taken refuge in there. Painfully I pulled loose from the sucking grip of the mold, using the vine stems as a lever, and then I edged between two of them into that hollow.

Save that we lacked light, and weapons, we had won to a half-safe refuge. I could not guess as to the types of creatures roaming the floor of the forest. But it is always better to assume the worst than to try for a safety which does not exist. And on most worlds the lesser life is tree borne, the greater to be found on the ground.

I half sat, half collapsed in that hollow, the spread of a tree root giving support to my back. I faced outward so that I could see anything moving beyond that screen of vine roots. And the longer I sat there, the more I was able to pick out, even in the dark.

In my harness was the beamer, yet I hesitated to flash it unless the need was great. For such a light might well attract attention we would desire most to avoid. I could sight some of the sparks of light marking flying creatures. And now there were others which did not wing through the air, but crawled the ground.

There were sounds in abundance. A dull intermittent piping began once I was settled. And later a snuffling drew near and then faded away again. I craved sleep, but fought it, my imagination only too ready to paint what might happen if I closed my eyes to a danger creeping or padding toward our flimsy refuge.

The beamer was in my hand, my finger on its button. Perhaps a sudden flash of light would dazzle a bold hunter and give us a chance of escape, were we cornered.

Eet climbed to what appeared to be his favorite resting place, my shoulders. His weight was more than I had remembered; he must be growing, and faster than I had known any animal cub or kitten to do so. I felt the rasp of his wire-harsh hair against my skin. Certainly Eet was no pet to be smoothed.

"Where do we go now?" I asked, not because I thought he could give me a good answer, but just for the comfort of communication with another who was not as alien as this place in which I crouched.

"At night—no place. This is as good as any to hide in." Again I read impatience in his reply.

"And with the morning?"

"In any direction. One is as good as another. This is, I think, a large forest."

"The LB crashed not too far away. Some of its survival tools—the weapons—if they still work—"

"Commendable. You are beginning to think again. Yes, the ship should be our first goal. But not our final one. I do not think any help will come seeking us here."

I found it harder and harder to fight sleep, and felt the tickle of Eet's fur as he settled himself more heavily across my shoulders and chest.

"Sleep if you wish," his thought snapped at me. "Treat your body ill and it will not obey you. We shall need obedient bodies and clear minds to face tomorrow—"

"And if some night prowler decides to scoop us out of this hole? I do not think it is any safer than a tark shell."

"That we shall face if it happens. I believe my warning senses are more acute than yours. There are some advantages, as I have said, to this particular body I now wear."

"Body you now wear— Tell me, Eeet, what kind of a body is really yours?"

I had no answer, unless the solid wall which I sensed snapping down between our minds could be considered an answer. It left me with the feeling of one who has inadvertently insulted a companion. Apparently the last thing Eet wanted to disclose was the life he might or might not have had before Valcyr swallowed the stone on the swamp world.

But his arguments made sense; I could not go without sleep forever. And if he had those warnings which animals possess and which have long been blunted in my species, then he would be alerted long before I could hear or sense trouble on the way.

So I surrendered to sleep, leaning back against the tree root with the night of the strange world dark and heavy about me. And I did not dream—or if I did, I did not remember. But I was startled out of that slumber by Eet.

"—to the right—" A half-thought as sharp as a spear point striking into my brain roused me. I blinked, trying to come fully awake.

Then I could see it, a glimmering. I thought that the dusk in which I had fallen asleep was not nearly as thick now.

It stood, not on four feet, but as a biped on two, though hunched forward, either as if that stance were not entirely natural, or as if it were listening and peering suspiciously. Perhaps it could scent our alien odor. Yet the head was not turned in our direction.

Like the colored insects and the plants, it had a phosphorescence of its own. And the effect was startling, for the grayish areas of light did not cover it as a whole but made a pattern along its body. There was a large round one on the top of the skull, and then below that, where the eyebrows of a human might be located, two oval ones. The rest of the face was dark, but ridges of light ran along the outsides of the upper and lower limbs, and three large circles such as that which crowned the head ran in a line down the center of the body. For the rest I could see that the four limbs were much thicker than those lines of light, and that the body was roughly ovoid, the wider portion forming the shoulders.

It moved a little away from the vines where it had stood and now I perceived that it carried a club weapon. This it swung up and down in one quick blow, and I heard an ugly hollow sound, which marked the striking of a victim. The attacker reached down a long arm and gathered up a limp body. With its kill in one hand and the club in the other it turned and was gone, bursting through the vines at a speed which almost matched that of the drinker from the pond plant.

It was certainly more than an animal, I decided. But how far up the ladder from primitive beginnings I could not guess. And it had been as big as a tall man, or even larger.

"We have company," I observed, and felt Eet move restlessly.

"It would be wisest to seek the LB," he returned. "If that is not too badly damaged— The day is coming now."

As I got to my knees to crawl out of our temporary shelter I wondered in which direction we should go. I certainly could not tell. And if Eet did no better we could pass within feet of the wrecked ship and perhaps never sight it. I had heard of men who wandered lost in circles in unfamiliar territory when they had no guides or compasses.

EIGHT

"Any suggestions as to how we *do* find the ship?" I asked Eet.

Without inquiring if I cared to be his mode of transportation, he had climbed to my shoulders. In this dank heat and with the weight of the suit pressing me down, his presence was a drag.

Eet's head waved back and forth, almost as if he could sniff out our path. There was a constant patter of drops from above. It might have been raining forever in the dusk of the forest—or rather, dripping from the condensation of moisture above.

No underbrush existed here, save for the parasitic plants, which apparently did not need sunlight and were rooted on tree or vine trunks. Most of these gleamed ghostlily.

But there was no clear vista in any direction. The trunks of the tree giants stood well separated one from the other because of their size, the large and strong forcing their way to the light and sun, the weaker dying. However, every one bore a lacy coating of vines, those twined and twirled from their own rootings to make a chocked maze.

Under the tree where we had seen the clubber make his kill we came upon a kind of path, maybe a game trail. It was tempting to turn into that easier way—tempting, but dangerous.

"Right!" Eet's head swung in that direction.

"How—?"

"Smell!" he rapped out. "Burning—hot metal— At least this body has some good points. Try right and walk softly."

91

"As I can," I snapped in return. Slogging through the soft muck of long-dead vegetation was not easy. The plated boots I wore sunk in at each step and I had to pull my way wearily through either sifting sand or glutinous mud. Yet I clung to the suit, unwieldy as it was for such travel, because it gave me a sense of security.

As usual Eet proved to be right. Light pierced the gloom ahead after we rounded two more of the giant tree boles and their attendant festoons of vine stems. In this dusk the brilliant, eye-dazzling shafts of sunlight made me stop short, blinking.

There was a mass of splintered limbs, torn and mangled vines. Smoke still arose in languid trails, the stench of burned vegetation as thick as gas. But so full of sap or moisture was that growth that the fire set by the crash of the LB had not spread, but been quickly smothered. The ship had rammed down on nose and side and was buried deep in the muck, the metal shell crumpled and rent in some places.

Across the forest hole its fall had torn, brilliantly hued insects darted or drifted, lighting to crawl over the still-oozing sap. I saw a scurry as some four-footed explorer crossed the burst hull. And, surveying that wreck, I was shaken by the closeness of our escape. What if we had not been able to scramble out before the LB had plunged from its first landing in the treetops?

Fighting my way over the mass of splintered, entangled, and half-burned debris about the ship was a slow and painful business. Eet had jumped from my shoulder and reached our goal with a couple of bounds, then raced along the sloping side.

"The hatch is buried," he reported. "But there is a break here—not large enough for you—"

"But all right for you." I snapped apart a nasty trap of spiky, splintered limbs, pulled it away, then stepped out on a charred crust, my tread raising smoke and a bad smell.

I was just in time to see Eet vanish into the rent. From here the wreck looked even worse, and I believed that the inside of the cabin must be folded and pleated until there could be room there for no explorer larger than the mutant.

"A line—" came my companion's thought command. "Drop me a line—"

I clumped through the smoldering debris and wriggled close to the break, dropping one of the hooked lines I had used in my tree descent. A weight swung upon it and I hauled in slowly, the line jerking as if Eet steadied whatever it raised.

One of those things I had thought might be a weapon appeared, butt first. I grasped it eagerly. To have some arm available gave one a feeling of security. It did not fit comfortably in my palm and I guessed it had not been wrought for use by a human hand. There was no firing button such as one saw on laser or stunner, only a small lever difficult to finger. I pointed it at a ragged stub of limb projecting not too far away and drew back on that lever.

There was a weak flash, hardly more than a blink of light, but nothing else. Whatever charge this weapon had once operated upon had been exhausted. It was of no more use to us now than an awkwardly shaped club. And I said so to Eet.

He expressed no disappointment, but dived once more into the ship, while I dropped the line. In the end we assembled a motley collection of survival equipment. There was another canister of liquid, a sharp-bladed, foot-long tool which at least was still effective, for my practice swings at spikes cut those neatly through. Lastly there was a roll of fabric which could be folded into a small packet, or shaken out into a wide square, and which appeared to be moisture-resistant.

I had found among the shredded debris some more of those pods, and had shelled their seeds into the canister we had already drained. We ate and drank before we decided in which direction to go.

There was no use in lingering by the wrecked ship. Had it been an LB of my own people, we could have set up a call signal and stayed hopefully nearby—though even then eventual rescue would have depended upon so many chance factors that we might never have been found. But we now had not even that slender tie with any predictable future.

"Where?" I asked as I made the fabric into a pack to lash to my harness. "Where—" And I added to myself, "Why?"

Eeet scrambled up on the elevated end of the wreckage once again. His head turned and his nostrils expanded, as if he cast about for some scent as a guide. But as for me I could see no goal in this wilderness. We could continue to wander through the dusk under the trees until we died, and find no way out.

"Water—" His thought reached me. "A river—lake— If we can find such—"

A river meant an open highway of sorts—but leading where? And how were we going to find a river?

I had a sudden inspiration. "The game trail!"

Surely any animals large enough to beat that slot in the forest muck would need water. And a well-marked trail could lead to it.

Eet ran back along the battered tail of the wreck. "An apt suggestion." He jumped to land heavily on my shoulder, nearly rocking me off balance. "To the left, no, more that way—" He used his forepaw to point. The path he indicated was not that which had been made by my blundering feet, but led off at a sharper angle to the left.

As we left the torn clearing, I glanced back. Eet's body somewhat masked it from view, but I saw that my dragging progress left very visible tracks. Anything with eyes could tail us. And what of the hunter with the club? Drawn to this break in the forest ceiling through curiosity, a native might well hunt us down.

"A contingency we cannot help. Therefore we can only be alert," Eet returned.

Alert he certainly was, and not to my comfort, he constantly changed his position. Too, since his weight was not inconsiderable, I was afraid of stumbling. The long knife from the LB allowed me to cut a path through the rim of debris beyond the burned space; then we were back in the dusky forest.

I would have been entirely lost as soon as the clearing was left behind, for we had to weave in and out to avoid the latticework of the vine roots. But Eet appeared to know just where we were going, sniffing at intervals and then directing me, until I almost fell into a sharp slot which marked the game trail. It had been so well used that it was cut more than a hand's breadth below the surrounding surface soil. On it were prints of what might have been hoofs and paws, and even odder marks, overlaid one upon another.

We came in time to another opening, where one of the giant trees had crashed to its death, perhaps seasons earlier, taking with it the lesser growth, giving living room to bushes and shrubs. So riotously had these grown that they made a vast matted plug in the opening. There were things which might be flowers, wide of petal, with deep throats. But I saw a green tentacle whip from one of those gaping throats, seize upon a small, winged thing which had lit on a petal, and carry the victim, still struggling, back into the cavity. The petals were brilliant yellow, striped with a strident green, and the whole thing gave off a sickly odor which made me turn away my head.

The trail did not cut across this space, but skirted around the perimeter, almost three quarters of the circle, so that we re-entered the forest not far from where we had come out. And it was just before we went back into that gloom that I paused in slashing at a looping vine to examine a sign beside the trail which proved to me that we were not alone in walking it.

There was a clump of tall stalks, lacking leaves to their very tips. On each of these tips was a cluster of tiny, feathery dark-red fronds. Two of the stalks had been so recently severed that a watery substance still oozed from the clean cuts across their hollow stems. I leaned to see them the closer and there was no doubt. They had not been broken, but cut. I sliced another to prove it. In my hand the smooth stalk was supple, whipping, but from the cut lower portion the liquid welled.

"Fishing—"

"What—?" I began.

"Silence!" Eet was at his most arrogant. "Fishing—yes. Now take care. I cannot read much of this creature's mind. It is on a very low band—very low. It thinks mainly of food, and its thought processes are very slow and primitive. But it is traveling toward a body of water where it hopes to fish."

"The one with the club?"

"Unless there are two native species of primitive forms," conceded Eet, "this one is like that. As to its being the same, who knows? I think this is a route often used by its kind. It walks the trail with the confidence of a thing going a familiar road on which it has nothing to fear."

I did not share his confidence. For there was a thunderous crash not too far away. I threw myself, and incidentally Eet, toward the nearest tree, planted my back to it, and stood with that sap-stained knife ready. My field of vision was too limited. I could see nothing beyond the vines and boles. But I tried to put my ears to service.

Nothing stirred. It had sounded as if one of those trees, which must have roots reaching to the very core of this world, had crashed. Crashed—? But the trees must eventually die. And having died and begun to rot, with the weight of the vines and parasites with which they were covered, would they not fall? As had the one which had made the second clearing? But what if the very one I had chosen as my backing would be the next? I moved away almost as fast as I had sought it.

I do not know how a thought can suggest laughter, but such a thought flowed from Eet. He was fast becoming, I decided, a less than perfect companion.

As if I were being punished for that, I caught one of my boots in a loop of root or vines and crashed as helplessly as the dead tree must have done. A thrust of irritation, sharp as any physical blow, struck me. Eet had leaped free in one of his flash reactions, and now sat a short distance away, his fangs bared, his whole stance expressing disgust.

"If you must clump about," he spat, "then at least lift your feet when you move them. But why do you continue to wear that burden of a useless overskin?"

Why indeed? I struggled to sit up. Inside the confines of the suit, my coverall was plastered to my body with sweat. I itched where I could not scratch, and I felt as if soaking in a bath for several days would not be enough to free me from the smelly burden of myself. Yet I clung to the suit as a shell animal might cling to its shell as a protection against the unknown.

I could never wear it into space again. When I examined if I could see tears which must have been inflicted during my descent of the tree. And the boots weighed my feet into a shuffle which could be dangerous in the muck. The harness which carried our very limited supplies could be adapted, but the suit itself— Eet was right. It had no further use. Yet when my fingers went to the various seals and buckles, they moved reluctantly, and I had to fight down the strong need to hold to my shell.

However, as I discarded that husk and felt the cool wreath about my damp body, I had a sense of relief. When we moved on, I had a small pack on my back, my hands were free to swing the cutting knife, and I found I was no longer slipping and sliding. For the tough web packs worn inside space boots not only protected my feet from close contact with the muck, but gave me purchase. Now I longed for a pool or stream in which I could dunk my steaming body and get really clean—though any such exercise on a strange world would be utter folly, unless I could be very sure that the water in question had no inhabitants who might resent intrusion.

"Water—" Eet announced. His head swung from right to left and back again. "Water—much of it—also alien life—"

Scents crowded my nose. I could put name to no one of them. But I accepted Eet's reading. I slowed my pace. Underfoot the game trail was no longer so hard of surface, and the slots of the tracks in it were deeper sunk, more sharply marked. I made out one, superimposed on earlier prints, which was a little larger than those I myself left. It was wedge-shaped, with indentations sharply printed in a fringe of points extending beyond the actual track.

I am certainly no tracker, nor have I hunted as a reader of trails. Though I had gone to frontier and primitive planets, it had been to visit villages, port trading posts. My acquaintance with any wilderness arts was close to zero.

But my guess was that whatever creature had so left his mark was large and heavy, as those indentations were deep and cleanly marked. And perhaps it was advancing at a deliberate pace.

"Water—" Eet repeated.

He need not have given that caution. The trail was mud now, holding no recognizable prints. There were here and there humps formed by harder portions of earth, and I jumped from one to the next where I could. In no time at all the mud was covered with a glaze of liquid out of which the trees and growth projected. And there were bits of refuse caught in tangles of vine roots, held there as high as my shoulder. It had the appearance of a land which had been flooded in the not too distant past, and which was now slowly drying off.

Puddles smelling of decay and bordered by patches of yellow slime showed between the trees, in hollows in the ground. And there were noisome odors in plenty. We passed a huddle of bones caught between exposed vine roots, and a narrow skull bared its teeth at us.

The puddles became pools and the pools linked into stagnant expanses of water. Here trees had been undermined, so that they leaned threateningly. And smaller ones that had been overthrown showed masses of upturned roots.

"Caution!"

Again I did not need Eet's warning. Perhaps his sense of smell was so assaulted by the stenches about that he had not sniffed that worker ahead until I had sighted him, her, or it.

On a tree trunk which was not yet horizontal, but leaned at an angle out over the largest pond we had yet seen, lurked a creature. In this light it was easy to see. It was humanoid, save that a bristly hair grew in a stiff upright thatch on its head, in two heavy brows, down the outer sides of its arms and legs to wrists and ankles, and in round, shaggy patches, three of them, down its chest and middle.

Around its loins was a skirt or kilt of fringe, and encircling its thick neck was a thong on which were strung lumps of dull green alternating with red cylinders. A heavy-headed club had been wedged for safekeeping beside a stub of branch, as its owner was busy with an occupation demanding full attention.

A withe, which I recognized as one of the slender canes cut from the patch we had passed, had been bent into a hoop, one end extending for a handle. This was held firmly between the back feet of the worker, gripped tightly in huge claws. In its hands the native held a forked stick in which was imprisoned a wriggling black thing that fought so furiously and was in such constant motion I could not be certain of its nature.

Its struggles did it no good as the worker passed it back and forth across the hoop, from one side to the other, then from top to bottom and back again. A thread trailed from the end of that whipping body, to be caught on the frame of the hoop and joined to its fellows, forming a mesh. With a last pass of the captive, the workman appeared satisfied with the result. Then, with a sharp flip of his wrist, he sent the forked stick and its prisoner out into the pond. As soon as the stick hit water there was a turmoil into which stick and captive vanished, not to appear again.

The hoop holder now got to his feet, the net in one hand. He was taller than I by a head. While his arms and legs were thin, his barrel body suggested strength.

His face was far from human, resembling more one of the demon masks of Tanth.

The eyes were deep-set under extravagantly bushy brows, so that while one believed them there, one did not see them. The nose was a fleshy tube, unattached save at its root, moving up and down and from side to side in perpetual quest. Below that appendage was a mouth, showing two protruding fangs and no real chin, the flesh, wattled in loose flaps, sweeping straight back from the lower set of teeth to join the throat.

Any traveler of the space lanes becomes inured to strange native races. There are the lizard-like Zacathans, the Trystians, who have avian ancestors, and others—batrachian, canine, and the like. But this weird face was repellent—at least to me—and I felt aversion.

When he reached the far end of the tree, which swayed under his weight, he moved with caution, trying each step before he put his full weight on it. Then he settled down, to lie full length, staring intently into the scummed water, the webbed hoop clasped in his left hand.

I did not dare yet to move. To skirt the edge of this lake meant coming into the sight of the fisherman, and I shrank from that. As I hesitated, Eet saying nothing though he watched the creature intently, the arm of the fisherman swept down and up again, scooping in his hoop a scaled thing about as long as my forearm.

He grabbed it out of the net, knocked it sharply against the tree trunk, and then knotted its limp length to a tie of his kilt.

"Go right—" Eet's thought came.

The fisherman was left-handed, his attention on that side. Right it was. I moved slowly, trying to put a screen of brush between us. But even when I was able to do so I felt no safer. It would be easy to become mired in a bog patch, and thus helpless prey for the club. My cutting knife was sharp but the native had the longer reach and knew this swamp. Also, to work any deeper into this flooded land and perhaps become lost in it was folly. And I said as much to Eet.

"I do not think this is a true swamp," he observed. "There are many signs of a great past flood. And a flood can be born of a river—"

"What is the advantage of a river—here?"

"Rivers are easier to follow than game trails. And there is this—civilizations are born on rivers. Do you presume to call yourself a trader and not know that? If this planet can boast any civilization, or if it is visited by traders from off world, you would find evidence of that along a major river. Especially where it meets a sea."

"Your knowledge is considerable," I observed. "And you certainly did not learn it all from Valcyr—"

Again I felt his irritation. "When it is necessary to learn, one learns. Knowledge is a never-emptied storehouse. And where else can one learn better of trade, traders, and their ways, then on such a ship as the *Vestris*? Her crew were born to that way of life and have a vast background of lore—"

"You must have spent some time reading their minds," I interrupted. "By the way, if you know so much—why *did* they take me off Tanth?" I did not really expect him to answer that, but he replied promptly.

"They were paid to do so. There was some plan there —I do not know its details, for they did not. But that went wrong and then they were approached and well paid to get you off planet and deliver you at Waystar—"

"Waystar! But—that's only a legend!"

If Eet could have snorted perhaps he would have produced such a sound.

"It must be a legend of substance. They were taking you there. Only they insisted upon following their regular schedule first. And when you took ril fever they decided prudence was in order. They would get rid of you lest you contaminate the rest. They would just not turn up at Waystar, but send a message to those who had arranged it all."

"You are a mine of information, Eet. And what was behind it—who wanted me so badly?"

"They knew only an agent. His name was Urdik and

101

he was not of Tanth. Why you were wanted they did not know."

"I wonder why—"

"The stone in the ring—"

"That!" My hand went to the pouch where I carried it. "They knew about that?"

"I do not think so. They wanted something you or Vondar Ustle carried. It is of great importance and they have been searching for it for some time. But can you not say now that the ring is your most important possession?"

I clutched the bag closer. "Yes!"

Then, startled, I looked down at the pouch. It was moving in my hand, and there was heat. We had come into the open and there was daylight around, but I thought I could also detect a glow.

"It is coming alive again!"

"Use it then for a guide!" urged Eet.

I fumbled with the seal on the pouch, slipped the ring on my finger. But the band was so large it would have fallen off if I had not closed my fist. My hand, through no volition of mine, moved out, away from my body, to the right and ahead. It would seem that once more the stone used my flesh and bone as an indicator. And I turned to follow its guidance.

NINE

"We are followed," Eet informed me.

"The fisherman?"

"Or one of his kind." My companion did nothing to relieve my mind with that report. "But he is cautious— he fears—"

"What?" I demanded bitterly. "This knife is no adequate defense, except at close quarters. And I have no desire to stand up to him as might a Korkosan gladiator. I am no fighter, only a peaceful gem trader."

Eet disregarded most of my sour protest. "He fears death-from-a-distance. He has witnessed such—or knows of it."

Death from a distance? That could mean anything from a thrown spear or slingshot propelled rock, to a laser beam, and all the grades of possible "civilization" in between.

"Just so." Eet had picked up my thought. "But—" I caught a suggestion of puzzlement. "I can read no more, only that he fears and so sniffs us prudently."

We holed up in a mass of drift thrust into a corner between two downed trees, eating from our supply of seeds, drinking from the ship's flask. The seeds might be nutritious, but they did not allay my need for something less monotonous. And I had seen none of them growing since we had come into the dripping country, so that I rationed carefully what we had. As I chewed my handful, I watched our back trail for any sign of a tracker.

I sighted him at last. He had gone down on one knee, his head almost touching the ground as that trunk-like, mobile nose of his quivered and twisted above my tracks. If it was not the fisherman, it was one enough like him to be his twin.

After a long sniffing, he squatted back on his heels, his head raised, that trunk standing almost straight out from its roots as he turned his head slowly. I fully expected him to point directly at us, and I readied my knife desperately.

But there was no halt in that swing. If he did know where we were, he was cunning enough to guess we might be alert, and did not betray his discovery. I waited tensely for him to arise and charge, or to disappear into the brush in an attempt to circle around for an ambush.

"He does not know, he still seeks—" Eet said.

"But—if he sniffed out our trail, how could he miss scenting us now?"

"I do not know. Only that he still seeks. Also he is afraid. He does not like—"

"What?" I demanded when Eet paused.

"It is too hard, I cannot read. This one feels more than he thinks. One can read thoughts, and the cruder emotions. But his breed is new to me; I cannot gain more than surface impressions."

At any rate, though my trail led directly from where the sniffer now squatted, he made no attempt to advance. Whether I could leave the cover we had taken refuge in without attracting attention, I did not know.

Two trees, not the huge giants of the forest, but ones of respectable girth, had fallen so that their branched crowns met, their trunks lying at right angles. We were in the corner formed by the branched part, a screen of drift piled not too thickly between us and the native.

I saw that the branches were bleached, leafless, but matted together. Yet the stone pulled me toward them, as if it would have me go through that mass. I hunched down and began to saw away at the obstructions. Eet was there, his forepaws at work, snapping off smaller pieces, while I dug with the point of the knife in the soft earth under the heavier branches. We moved very slowly, pausing many times to survey the open ground between us and the sniffer. To my surprise, for I knew we were far from noiseless (in spite of our best efforts), he did not appear and Eet reported he had not moved.

It suddenly occurred to me, with a chill, what his purpose might be—that he was not alone, and that when his reinforcements moved into place there would be a charge after all.

"You are right." Eet was no comforter. "There is one, perhaps two more, coming—"

"Why did you not tell me?"

"Had it been necessary I would have. But why add to apprehension when a clear mind is needful? They are yet some distance away. It is a pity, but the day is almost gone. To them, I believe, night is no problem."

I did not put my thoughts into words; Eet could read them well enough anyway. "Are there any in front of us?" I bit back and curbed my anger.

"None within my sensing range. They do not like that direction. This one waits for the others' coming, not because he fears us, but because he fears where we head. His fear grows stronger as he waits."

"Then—let us get farther ahead—" I no longer tried to be so careful, but slashed at branches, cutting our way through the springy wall in quick blows.

"Well spoken," Eet agreed. "Always supposing we do not run from one danger into a greater one."

I made no reply to that, but hoped that Eet was reading *my* emotions and that they would scorch him. Beyond the trees were more of the scum-rimmed pools, fallen trunks. But the latter provided us with a road of sorts. The fisherman had been armed with nothing more lethal than a club, which he could not use at a distance. He knew we fled, and it seemed to me that speed was now in order.

With Eet back on my shoulders, his paw-hands gripping the ties of my pack, I sprang onto the nearest trunk and ran, leaping from one to the next, not in a straight line, but always in the direction the stone pointed me. For I could not help but hope that it would guide me to some installation, or ship, perhaps even a settlement of those who had owned the ring, even as it had brought us across space to the derelict. The great age of that ship, however, suggested I would find no living community.

We were out of the gloom. Not only had the flood cut a swath among the trees, but the secondary growth had been undermined and was scanty. Now I could see the sky overhead.

But that was full of clouds, and while it was still warm enough to make one pant when exercising, there was no sun. Insects buzzed about, so that at times I had to swing my hand before my face to clear my vision. But none bit my flesh. Perhaps I was so alien to their usual source of nourishment that they could not.

There was no sign of any pursuit, and Eet, though he had ceased to communicate when we began this dash, would, I believed, raise the warning if it were needed. I appeared to possess some importance to him, though his evasiveness concerning that bothered me.

Again pools began to link together, forcing me to make more and more detours from the direct path the stone indicated. I had no wish to splash through even the shallows of those evil-looking, bescummed floods. Who knew what might hide below their foul surfaces? Perhaps the insects did not find me tasty, but that did not mean other native life would be so fastidious.

I had no idea of the length of the planetary day, but it seemed to me now that the cloud blanket overhead did not account for all the lack of light and that this might be late afternoon. Before night we must find some safe place in which to hole up. If the natives *were* nocturnal, the advantage of any encounter would rest with them.

The water pushed me back, farther and farther to the right, while the tug of the stone was now left, straight into the watery region. Its pull became so acute and constant that I finally had to slip the loop from my hand and put it back in the pouch, lest it overbalance me into one of the very sinks I fought to skirt.

There was much evidence that not only had this lake

been far larger in the not too far-distant past but it was still draining away in the very direction the ring pointed. It was hard going and from time to time I demanded of Eet reassurance that we were not being followed. But each time he reported all clear.

It was decidedly darker and I had yet found no possible place to lie up for the night. Too many tracks in the mud suggested that life, large life, crawled from pond to lake, came from the water and returned to it. And the size of some of those tracks was enough to make a man think twice, three, a dozen times, before settling down near their roadways.

I had passed the first of the outcrops before I really noticed them, so covered were they with dried mud which afforded anchorage to growing things. It was when I scrambled up on one to try for a better look at what might lie ahead that it dawned on me that they were not scattered without pattern but were set in a line which could not be that of nature alone.

My foot slipped on the surface and I slid forward, trying to stop my fall by digging the point of the knife well in. But the stone resisted my blade, which came away with an almost metallic sound, scraping off a huge patch of mud.

What I had uncovered was not rough stone, but a smooth surface which had been artificially finished. When I touched it I could not be sure it was stone at all. It had a sleekness, almost as if the rock had been fused into a glassy overcoat—though in places this was scaled and pitted.

In color it was dull green, veined with ocher strata. Yet it was not part of a wall, for the stones did not abut, but had several paces distance between them. Perhaps there had once been some link of another material now vanished.

The outcrops ran in the direction the stone urged upon me, marching down to the lake, partially submerged near the shore, water lapping their crowns farther out, then entirely covered.

As I continued along the lake, now alert to any other

evidence, I came across a second line of blocks, paralleling those swallowed by the water. These I took for a guide. They were certainly the remains of some large erection, ancient though they appeared. And as such they could well lead to a building, or even a ruin which would shelter us.

"Just so," Eet agreed. "But it would be well to hurry faster. Night will come soon under these clouds and I think a storm also. If more water feeds this lake—"

There was no need for him to underline his thought. I jumped from one of those blocks half buried in the muck to the next, listening for warning thunder (if storms on this planet were accompanied by such warnings) and fearing to feel the first drops of rain. The wind was growing stronger and it brought with it a low wailing which stopped me short until Eet's reassurance came:

"That is not the voice of a living thing—only sound—" He sniffed as thoroughly as the trunk-nosed native.

The blocks for the first time now were joined together, rising into a wall, and I dropped down to walk beside it. It soon topped my head. There were too many shadows in its overhang, so I edged into the open.

I would have climbed again after a while for a better look at the country ahead, but the tops of these blocks were not level. Instead they were crowned with projections, the original form of which could not be guessed, for they were eroded and worn to stubs which pricked from them at meaningless angles.

On this side of the wall the signs of flood ceased, except in some places where apparently waves had spilled over the top, in a few instances actually turning and twisting the mighty blocks of the coping over which they had beaten.

There were no trees here. We moved across an open space which gave footing only to brush that did not grow high. Where one of the waves had topped the wall, I saw that I walked on a coating of soil overlying pavement, some of which had the same fused look as the surface of the wall.

If I walked some road or courtyard, there was no other wall. The clouds were very thick and dark now, and the first pattering rain began. The wall was no protection, nor was there any other shelter in this sparsely grown land. I ran on, my tiring body having to be forced to that pace, both my pack and Eet weighing cruelly on me.

Then the wall beside which I jogged made a sharp turn left and ended in a three-sided enclosure. It had no roof, but those three sides were the best protection I had seen. We could stretch the shelter from the wreck over us to afford some cover. Also, I was not going to blunder on in the dark. So I darted into that enclosure, squatting down in the corner I judged easiest to defend. There we huddled, the covering draped over my head and shoulders, Eet in my lap, as the night and the storm closed down upon us.

But we were not quite in the dark. As I changed position I saw the faintest of glows from the pouch which held the stone, and when I pried open the top a fraction, there was a thin ray of light. Just as it had come alive before, so it was registering energy now. Was this ruin its goal? If so, had the LB led us directly to the home planet from which the derelict had lifted eons ago? Such a supposition could not be ruled out as fantastic. The LB could have been set on a homing device and the drifting ship might have met its fate soon after take-off. Unwittingly we might have made a full circle, returning the ring to the world on which it was fashioned. But the age of the stones at my back certainly argued that those who had dwelt here were long gone, that I had stumbled on traces of one of the Forerunner races, about whom we know so little and even the Zacathans can only speculate.

To spend a stormy night amid alien ruins of incalculable age was not my idea of a well-chosen pastime. My search for gems had taken me into many strange places, but then I had only been second to Vondar, leaning on his knowledge and experience. And earlier I had looked to my father, not only for physical protection, but for that teaching which would aid in survival.

As I crouched there with the rain drumming on the thin sheet which was my only roof, I was only partially aware of the night, the alien walls, the need for alertness. One part of my mind sought back down the years, to my father's first showing of the ring with the zero stone—for that was what he had once termed it, a challenge to his knowledge and curiosity.

It had been found on a suited body floating in space. Had that body been one of the crew of the derelict? And my father had died at the hands of someone who had then searched his office, the zero stone the prize the murderer sought.

Then Vondar Ustle and I had been entrapped at the inn on Tanth. And I could accept that that had not happened by a chance pointing of the selective arrow. It had been planned. Perhaps they had believed that, being off-worlders, we would resist the priests just as we had, and both be slain, as Vondar was. They could not have foreseen that I would break away and reach the sanctuary.

For the first time I resented my bargain with Ostrend. And the trader in me regretted the gems I had paid for a passage which had already been arranged by another. So—I was to have been transported to Waystar and turned over there to those paying for my rescue. For what purpose? Because I was my father's son, or his reputed son, and so might have possession of, or knowledge of, that very thing which now glowed faintly against my chest?

Again by chance I had escaped—the fever—a contagion picked up on Tanth, or on that unnamed world where the people had so mysteriously disappeared? That sickness which had so oddly struck just at the proper time— Oddly struck!

"Just so," Eet answered with his favorite words of agreement. "Just so. You alone of the crew sickening so—why did it take you so long to wonder about that?"

110

"But why? I know Valcyr picked my cabin to give birth—that must have been chance—"

"Was it?"

"But you could not have—" What if he could? As helpless as Eet's body had looked when I found Valcyr with him on the bunk, did that necessarily mean that his mind—?

"You are beginning to think," Eet replied approvingly. "There was a natural affinity operating between us even then. The crew of the ship were a close-knit clan. It was necessary for me to find one detached from that organization, one who could furnish me with what I needed most at that time, protection and transportation away from danger while I was in a weak state. Had I encountered them at a later period I would not have been so endangered. But I needed a partner—"

"So you made me ill!"

"A slight alteration of certain body fluids. No danger, though it appeared so." There was a complacency in his answer which for a moment made me want to hurl Eet out into the dark and whatever danger might lurk there.

"But you will not," he answered my not completely formulated thought. "It was not only a matter of expediency which made me choose to reveal myself to you. I spoke of natural affinities. There is a tie between us based on far more than temporary needs. As I have said, this body I now wear is not, perhaps, what I might have chosen for this particular phase of my existence. I have modified it as much as I can for now. Perhaps there will be other possible alterations in the future, given time and means. But I do have senses which aid you. Just as your bulk and strength do me. I believe you have already discovered some of the advantages of such a partnership.

"We are still far from any situation you may term safe. And our alliance is very necessary to both of us. Afterward we can choose whether to extend it."

That made sense—though I disliked admitting that this small furred body I could crush in my two hands contained a personality forceful enough to bring me easily to terms. I had had few close contacts with anyone in the past. My relationship with Hywel Jern had been that of pupil to teacher, junior officer to commander. And while Vondar Ustle was a man of easier temperament, far more outgoing than my father, the relationship had remained practically the same for me when I entered his service. Beyond that I had had no deep ties with any man or creature. But now I had been summarily adopted by Eet, and it appeared that *my* will did not enter into the agreement any more than it had with Hywel or Vondar—for it had been of their desire in both cases. But—my anger arose—I was not going to stand in the same relationship to *Eet!*

"They come!" Eet's warning shocked me out of my thoughts.

We had been so long without any contact with the natives that I had believed they had given up. If they moved in now, we might find our shelter a trap.

"How many and where?" Eet was right; in such a situation I must depend upon his senses.

"Three—" Eet took his time to answer. "And they are very hesitant. I think that this place represents danger to them. On the other hand—they are hungry."

For a second or so, that had no meaning for me. Then I stiffened. "You mean—?"

"We—or rather you—represent meat. Contact with such primitive minds is difficult. But I read hunger, kept in check mainly by fear. They have memory of danger here."

"But—by the signs we have seen, there is plenty of game here." I remembered the fresh tracks, the evidences of life we had seen in profusion, and how easy it had been for the fisherman to scoop out his prey.

"Just so. A puzzle as to why our trail would draw them past easier hunting." Eet did seem puzzled. "The reason, I cannot probe. Their minds are too alien, too primitive to read with any clarity. But they are aroused now past the limit of prudence. And they are most dangerous in the dark."

I fingered the beamer on my harness. If the creatures

112

were mainly night hunters, a flash in their eyes would dazzle them for a moment. But my own folly in picking this hole with its towering walls about us might be the deciding factor—against us.

"It is not as bad as all that," Eet broke in. "There is a top to the wall—"

"Well above my reaching. But if you can climb it—climb!" I ordered.

I felt a sharp tug at one corner of the covering I had drawn over us.

"Let this free," Eet countered. "Climb I can, but prehaps we shall both be safe because of the fact that my claws are useful." He was out of my lap, dragging the cover behind him, though it was a burden which pulled his head to one side.

"Hold me up," he commanded then, "as high as you can reach, and take some of the weight of this thing!"

I obeyed, because I had no counterplan, and I had come, during our association, to give credit to Eet. I lifted his body, held it above my own head, and felt him catch hold, and draw himself up. Then I fed along the length of the shelter cloth, keeping its weight from pulling him back as he went. Suddenly it was still, no longer tugged.

"Tie the knife to it and let go—" Eet ordered.

Let my only weapon out of my hands? He was crazy! Yet even as my thoughts protested, another part of me set my hands busy knotting that tool-weapon to the end of the dangling cloth. I heard it, even through the storm, clang and rap against the stone as it was drawn aloft by Eet.

I faced around, to the open side of the enclosure. Though I did not have Eet's warning alert, I was sure that the aliens no longer hesitated, that they moved through the darkness. I pressed the button on the beamer, looking down the ray path.

They did indeed gather there, half crouched, their clubs ready in their fists. But as the light struck them full on, they blinked, blinded, their small mouths opening on thin, piping cries. The middle one dropped to his knees, his arm flung up to shield his hideous face from the light.

"Behind you—up!" Eet's mental cry was as loud as a shout might have been in my ear. I felt the brush of something at my shoulder, flung out my hand to ward it off, and touched the fabric of the shelter. My fingers closed about it and I tugged. But it did not fall; somewhere aloft it was anchored, to give me a possible ladder to safety.

Dared I turn my back upon the three the light still held prisoners? Yet how long could I continue to hold them so? I must chance it—

If only that improvised rope and whatever Eet had found aloft to anchor it would hold under my weight! But that was another chance I must take. I gave a short leap and caught the dangling folds with both hands, swung out a little to plant my feet against the wall, and climbed, or rather walked up that surface, the shelter my support.

TEN

I was not to escape so easily. There arose behind me a shrilling that topped the sound of the storm. Something thudded against the wall only inches from me, rebounding to the ground. I had kept the beamer switched on and the light jerked back and forth as I struggled to put distance between myself and the natives below. Perhaps that moving light misled them, or perhaps they were less adept with their clubs than we credited them with being. However, one hurled weapon grazed my leg and almost broke my hold on the fabric rope.

Fear alone gave me the strength to pull up on the rough crest of the wall. My leg was numb and I was afraid to trust my weight to it, so I dragged along like a broken-legged creature. The claws of the natives stuck in my mind. Those should aid them in gaining our perch.

Up here the wind and the rain buffeted us. I had not realized how much protection the walls had afforded below. I clung to the knobs and broken projections and pulled myself along, though I took time to switch off the beamer that I might not so brightly advertise our going.

"On, to your right now, and ahead—" Eet ordered.

I followed the line of the fabric to its end, found where the knife pinned it firmly into a crack between an eroded knob and the wall, paused long enough to worry it loose, and thrust that weapon into my harness.

To the right and ahead? The blasting of the storm was such that for some long moments I was not sure of the difference between right and left, having to think of my hands as guides. Eet's direction would apparently take me over the wall. Yet I was certain he did not mean us to descend again.

I discovered as I crawled on, dragging my aching leg, that here the wall was joined by another, leading off at a sharp angle in the direction Eet had indicated. It was slow and rough going, for the crest was as encumbered with humps, hollows, and stubs as the other had been. But at least they now served as anchorages against the wind and drive of rain.

The visibility was nil as far as I was concerned. I had to depend upon my sense of touch and Eet's guidance. Every moment I feared to hear the shrilling which would announce that the club holders were hard behind us.

The numbness in my leg was wearing off, leaving behind an ache which, when I barked that limb against one of the projections, made me yowl with pain. But I did not try to get to my feet. Crawling this uneven way seemed the safest.

We were heading out from the place where we had sheltered, directly into a dark unknown. Now I could hear, above the storm, not the shrilling of pursuers, but a roaring. And it was toward that that we headed.

At last I became so uneasy I paused in the lee of a large lump to use the beamer, sweeping the way before me. For a space the ray showed wall—then— nothing!

I swept the beam down, along the right-hand side of the wall. Water—raging water, beating its way around a vast tumble of rocks. As I sent the ray left, it caught the edge of something else, and I swiftly centered on that.

A rounded swell of mound? No, though it was patched with plants and moss which caught the light and held it, continuing to glow after the beam had passed. A curved object, taller than the wall at the highest point, stretching back and out into darkness where my beam could not reach.

The water which battered at the outer end of the wall washed it on one side, but apparently it was too securely rooted to be moved by that flood. I kept the ray playing on the portion nearest the wall, trying to calculate if I could cross to it. But that other surface, in spite of the growth of plants, suggested too smooth a landing, especially since my take-off room would be limited on this side.

"Well," I shot at Eet, "where do we go? On into the water? Or do we grow wings and head straight up?"

When he did not reply, I was suddenly afraid I had been left alone. Perhaps Eet, aware of his own ability to travel where I was a handicapped drag, had struck out for himself. Then his answer came, though I could not tell from what direction.

"To the ground, on the left. The water does not come this far. And the ship will give us shelter—"

"Ship?" Once more I swept the beamer ray, studied the mound. It could be a ship—yet it was not shaped like—

"Do you think there is only one pattern of ship? Even among your own people there are several."

He was right, of course. There is little resemblance between a slender Free Trader, meant to cut into planetary atmospheres, and a colonizer—so large it does not enter atmospheres at all, but uses ferry ships to load and unload passengers and supplies.

I edged to the left side of the wall. The nose of the vast object on the ground projected not far below. On that stood Eet, his wiry fur not in the least plastered down by the rain, his eyes pin points of light as the beam touched them. I swung over and allowed myself to drop, hoping I would be able to find secure footing.

Had I worn the magnetic boots, my feet might have clung. As it was, my fears were realized. I landed squarely enough, but skidded on, my hands and feet unable to find anchorage in the frail plants, tearing those out by their roots in thick wet pads as I went. I met the ground with a bump which drove most of the breath out of me. From my bruised leg there was such a stab of pain that I blacked out for a space.

117

But the drip of water falling on and running down my face restored me.

Half of my body lay under the curve of the ship, if ship it was. But the rest of me was exposed to the storm. I scrabbled feebly with my fingers in the mud and somehow pulled back under the shelter.

There I huddled stupidly, not more than three-quarters conscious, without the energy or will to move again. The beamer had gone out and the dark closed in as completely as any of those monolithic walls I had been climbing.

"There is an opening—" Eet's words in my mind were only an irritation. I put my hands over my eyes and shook my head from side to side slowly, as if by that effort I could refuse communication. It was a call to action and I had no intention of obeying.

"Around here—there is an opening!" Eet was peremptory.

Stubbornly I looked to see where I was. My leg ached abominably and my exertions since we had landed on this inhospitable world had caught up with me. I was content to have it so. In fact, I thought dully, since that long period of boredom on the *Vestris*, I had not had a moment of rest.

Hunger gnawed at me with an ever-growing pain. There might be a few of the seeds rattling around in the container swinging from my pack, but I had no desire to mouth them. They were not food— Food was a platter of sizzling vorst steak, a mound of well-cooked lattress, beaten, creamed with otan oil and herbs; it was an omelet of trurax eggs sweetened just enough with a syrup of bargee buds; it was—

"An empty belly about to be gutted by the sniffers!" Eet rapped out. "They no longer sniff along the wall— they have found a way around it!"

A moment earlier I could not have moved, but Eet's words, whether by his will or not, projected a mental picture which acted on me as a whiplash might on a reluctant burden bearer. I moved, on my hands and knees still, but at what speed I could muster, under

118

the overhang of the ship, around to where Eet waited.

When I tried to use the beamer there was no response. I supposed my fall had finished it. But somewhere above, Eet waited and gave directions. He had not found an open hatch, but rather a break in the fabric of the ship, and I climbed, using the edge of the rent to pull myself in. At last I lay on a slanting surface in a wan light.

That gleam came from a crowding of the plants which I had first seen in the forest. The shell of the ship might have been of an alloy which resisted the tearing claws of time. But here there must have been inner fittings which afforded rooting to the parasites as they rotted. The plants had grown and flourished, first on that, and then on the debris of their own ancestors, until the accumulated products of that cycle of life, death, decay, and life again had filled most of the open space. These broke off in huge, ill-smelling chunks which sifted to powder and arose in dust around me as I moved slowly and clumsily about.

The surface on which I half lay might be a floor, or the wall of the corridor. It was choked by plants, but those thinned out as one penetrated farther. I braced myself against the wall and looked back. I was certainly not as heavy of body as the sniffers and it had taken determined wriggling to enter. The opening my exertions had left would admit no more than one at a time, and that one only after a struggle. With the knife I could defend my new lair. We were out of the storm, and the wind was now but a muffled sighing.

Was this, I wondered suddenly, the goal to which the stone had been guiding us? If I explored farther into this disintegrating hulk would I come upon another long-deserted engine room with a box of dead stones?

I looked down at the pouch which held my strange guide. But that slight glow I had seen in the bog land was gone. When I brought out the ring it was as dull and lifeless as it had been before our venture in space.

"They sniff around—"

One of the glimmering plants guarding the rent

shook and I made out the shadow of Eet crouched there, his neck outthrust at what seemed to me an impossible angle as he nosed into the night. "They sniff but also they fear. This is a place filled with fears for them."

"Maybe they will go then," I answered. The lassitude of moments earlier had again closed upon me. I was not sure that even if one of the natives tried to force his way in I could raise knife in defense.

"Two do—" Eet replied. "One remains. He waits underneath, but where he can watch this door. I think he is settling in for a siege."

"Let him—" I could not keep my eyes open. Such crushing fatigue was new to me. It was like being drugged. If I lay ready for the slayer's club, I could not help it. I was done.

If Eet tried to rouse me, it was in vain. Nor did I dream. Perhaps the dust of the plants, the crushing of their leaves, produced a narcotic which overcame me. When I finally did awake, light lay across my eyes and I blinked, dazzled. At least, I thought sluggishly, I was not killed in my sleep.

The refuse caused by my entrance into this lair was all about me. Plants torn from their roots were already decaying with strong smells. It was not their phosphorescence which gave the light, but day beyond. I began to crawl toward that more wholesome gleam as an escape from the evil-smelling mass holding me. But there was agitation at the jagged opening and Eet's body humped up, as if, small as he was, he would interpose that insignificant bulk between me and some danger.

"There are many now—waiting—" he warned.

"The sniffers?"

"Just so. Many—and they are always on watch."

I retreated crabwise from the light. The plants thinned and finally I reached a place relatively clean from their rooting.

"Another door—hole?"

"There are two," Eet replied promptly. "One is on the underside and too small for you. There can be no digging to enlarge it, for it is pressed against stone paving. I think it was once a hatch. The other is on the other side of the ship and they watch there also. They are showing more intelligence than I thought they possessed."

"Never underestimate your opponent." Those were not my words but ones I had heard often from Hywel Jern in the old days. I had not, I thought now, done much credit to his teaching.

"I do not understand what moves them." Eet sounded fretful, lacking in that assurance which could irritate one. "They have a fear of this place. That emotion is strong in them. Yet they stay here with great patience —waiting for us to come forth."

"Perhaps they did this once before—ran a quarry to earth, had it come out. You said they look upon me as meat. Yet the land abounds in other game—"

"Among some primitive races there is another belief." Eet had returned to his instructor role. "To eat of the body of a creature looked upon with superstitious awe or fear, is to imbibe the unusual quality of that prey. This may be such a case."

"Which could mean that they have seen men, or humanoids, before." I seized upon that as a small hope. "But they surely could not hold memories of the people who built those walls, this ship—the remains are too old. And those are primitives, who normally do not remember events, save as vague legends, from one season to the next."

"Take your own advice," Eet made answer. "Do not judge all primitives alike. These may possess a form of memory more acute than any you have encountered before. Knowledge of events may even be handed down through a special body of trained 'rememberers.' "

He could be very right. Did those sniffers with their clubs, their near-to-animal look, treasure some tribal legend of a race which had once built here, had perhaps enslaved or mistreated their far-off ancestors—who had come to death in some fashion (perhaps at the hands of those same ancestors)? And now did they believe they had cornered one of the old masters and intend to have him out for the purpose of refreshing some inner strength?

"On the other hand," Eet continued, "there may have been landings of off-world ships, and you could be right in your first guess that men of your type have been hunted, killed, and their 'spirits' so absorbed by their slayers."

"All very interesting, but it does not get us out of here. Nor provide us with food, water, and the means of keeping alive while they cork us in here."

While I talked I brought out the two containers. The one with the seeds rattled faintly. But to my surprise the other was heavy and gurgled encouragingly.

Eet was amused. "Rain is water," he observed. "We had enough of that last night to fill a well-placed bottle."

Again he had put me to shame. I tested the contents for taste. The sharpness of the ship's liquid was still present, but much diluted. I sipped when I wanted to gulp, and then held it for him to do likewise, but he refused.

"There was much to drink last night. And this body does not need much moisture. That is one advantage in being small. But for food we do not fare so well—unless —" His neck went up to its full length. He was intently watching something which moved at the door rent. I could not make out the nature of the thing crawling in, nor did I have time to see it plainly before Eet sprang.

His feline ancestry went into that sharp attack. He bent his head and used his teeth, then came back to me dragging a body which dangled from his mouth, weighing down his head.

It was long and thin, with three legs on either side. The body was covered with plates of a horny substance, the head a round bead with four feathery antennae. Eet flipped it over to expose a segmented underside of a paler hue.

"Meat," he commented.

My stomach turned. I could not share his taste and I shook my head.

"Meat is meat." Eet was scornful of my squeamishness. "This is a feeder on plants. Its shape may not be that of a creature you know, but its flesh is of a type you and I can assimilate and live upon."

"You live upon it," I said hurriedly. The longer I studied that segmented insectile body, the less I wanted to discuss the matter. "I will stick to the seeds."

"Which are few and will not last long," Eet pointed out in deadly logic.

"Which may not last long, but while they do, I stick to them."

I averted my eyes and crawled a little away. Eet was a dainty eater. That, too, he took from his dam. But even though he was fastidious about the business, I had no desire to watch him.

My crawl brought me into a portion of the ancient corridor where I felt inequalities under me. I ran my hands over the surface and decided I had found a door and that the ship must lie on its side. I worked at the latch, if latch it was, trying to open it. There was always a chance that a small discovery might lead to a larger—even a way out past the sentries.

At last I could feel a slight give—then, with a suddenness which almost carried me with it, a plate gave way and fell with a clang, leaving my hands braced on the edge of a square space. I felt around carefully. It must be a door. But I could not explore below without light. Once more I clicked the beamer, but to no purpose. I glanced at the daylight coming from the rent. There was no way to introduce that to this point. But my eyes fastened on some of the plants which still grew unbroken above the level where I had crawled the night before. They were certainly very feeble torches, but they were better than nothing at all.

I crept past the busy Eet. The passageway was so full of debris at this point that I could not stand upright. And my badly bruised leg was a further hindrance. But I was able to jerk from their rooting two good-sized plants. With one in each hand I came back to the hole.

The phosphorescence was indeed very pale, but the longer I crouched with my back to the daylight, and held them over that dark drop, the more my eyes adjusted. And I was able to make out a few details.

At last I twined the dangling roots of the two together, and using those for a cord, I lowered the ball of plants into the dark. What I had uncovered was a cabin right enough. And as I examined it, allowing for the greater ruin and decay, I thought it twin to those I had seen in the derelict. There was nothing below to aid us, either as weapon or tool. But when I drew up my luminous plant ball, I had learned this much—with such a lamp I dared go deeper into the ship. For the darker the space into which it was thrust, the brighter by contrast became its glow.

With it again in hand I set about surveying the passageway. Eet had said he had found only two other exits. But had he fully explored the ship? Suppose there was another hatch not jammed against the ground which we could force open to escape?

Leaving my improvised torch ball at the open cabin door, I climbed back to the rent to examine the rest of the plants. They were, judging by their stalks and leaf structure, of several different varieties. One, with long slender leaves parting into hair-fine sections, possessed a bulbous center which was particularly effective as a light-giver. I snapped off four of these. They were brittle and yielded easily to pressure. I knotted them together, using their fine leaves, and carried the mass in my hand as one might carry a bouquet of more fragrant and entrancing growths.

Eet had finished his meal and I found him sitting by my first torch, using a hand-paw to clean his face and whiskers, licking his fur in another entirely feline gesture.

"There is a division of corridor beyond. Which direction?" he asked, apparently willing to join in an expedition.

"There might be another hatch—"

"There is surely more than one for any ship," was his withering reply. "Right, or straight ahead?"

"Straight ahead," I said, choosing instantly. I did not have any idea how long my torch would last, and I had no desire to be caught by the dark in some inner maze.

But when we reached the crossway Eet had mentioned, he suddenly hissed and spat, his whip tail shooting up, his back arching, until he was a weird caricature of a cat.

What he had sighted was a shining trace along the wall. It was a little higher than my ankle at first, but ascended until it striped that surface at about shoulder height. I did not touch it. There was that about it which was so disgusting that I wanted no close contact. It was as if the slime which had ringed the dying lakes and ponds had here been used to draw a marker, fresh, as a warning.

"What is it?" So much had I come to depend upon Eet that I now asked that almost automatically.

"I do not know—except that it is nothing to be meddled with. And darkness is its choice of abode." I thought he seemed shaken as I had never seen him before.

"You must have been along here before, for you knew about this side passage. Was it here then?"

"No!" His denial was sharp. "I do not like it."

Nor did I. And the more I surveyed that sticky trail with its suggestion of utter foulness, the way it climbed the wall so that whatever made it might hang overhead—waiting— My imagination began to work. And in that moment I knew that only desperation worse than any I had faced so far would ever drive me to take that road deeper into a dark where such horrors might lurk.

I turned back, nor did it matter to me that Eet could read my mind and knew just what fears rode me. But I wondered if he cared, for he was streaking back along the passage as if some terror lashed also at his flanks.

ELEVEN

Our precipitous retreat was in itself so unnatural as to startle me when, back at the door rent, I paused to think. That the sight of a mere trail could so unnerve one was a disturbing thing. Eet caught my thought and answered:

"Perhaps that leaver of trails uses fear for a weapon. Or else it is so utterly alien to us that we are repelled. There are things on many worlds which cannot be contacted by another species, no matter how willing one is. However, I do not want to walk ways in which that prowls."

I edged forward on my belly, pushing before me, though my nose revolted, a small screen of debris. The air outside was bright with sunlight. I stared out longingly. For my kind were meant for the open day and not dark burrows and night's dusk. We were, a quick glance from side to side told me, close to the ground, and that was covered with patches of shaggy, yellowish grass. Between those were expanses of glassy surface which might mark ancient rocket blasts, as if this had been a port site.

For one or two heart-lifting moments I could believe that we were free, that no sentries lingered. Then I heard a shrilling, such as had been voiced the night before. But this was infinitely louder, since there was no storm. It hurt my ears with the pitch of its note. And it came from almost directly below me, so that I jerked back from the rent.

Eet's report reached me. "They are beneath, along the side. They wait for hunger, or perhaps what lurks in the depths of this wreck to drive us out to them."

"Perhaps they will lose patience." My hope was a forlorn one but I knew that the powers of concentration varied to a great degree, and intelligence had something to do with it. Intelligent purpose could teach patience which was unknown to those of lesser brain capacity.

"I think they have played this game, or heard of it played, before, with success." Eet refused to feed my hope. "There are too many factors of which we are not aware. For example—"

"For example—what?" I demanded when he hesitated.

"The stone led you here, did it not? But is it alive now?"

I freed the zero stone and held it out into the daylight. The gem was dead and murky. I turned it this way and that, hoping to awaken some response. Certainly it did not beckon us any deeper into the wreck. But as I inclined it outward, in the general direction of the rush of water along the other side of the ship, its condition suddenly altered. There was no bright flash, not even a glow to outshine the corridor plants, but there had been a small spark. Only now the width of the ship lay between us and the direction in which it pointed.

"There is one way." Eet set his hand-paws on my knee and stood with his nose almost touching the stone, as if it gave forth some scent he could trace. "I can get out of this hole, cross the ship above with that. I could perhaps trace it to its source."

I thought that he spoke the truth. Being small and wary, using the growths on the hull for cover, he could well do it. Though of what benefit such knowledge would be to us—

"All knowledge is of benefit," he countered.

I laughed without humor. "I sit waiting to be gathered up and put in some native's cooking pot and you speak of gaining knowledge! What good will it do a dead man?"

My thoughts probably did me no credit. It was true

that a trap holding me was not one for Eet. He could leave at any moment he chose, with a good chance for freedom. In fact I did not know why he had remained as long as he had. But the zero stone—there was that in me which could not lightly surrender it, even for a space. I did not covet it, as one might covet some gem of beauty. It was rather that I was, in a manner I could not describe, tied to it, and had been ever since my father had first shown it to us. The more so since I had taken it from the hiding place he had devised for it.

To give it to Eet would be a breaking of ties I could not quite face. I turned the ring around and around, slipping its large circlet on and off my fingers, my thoughts disjointed, but mainly occupied with the fact that more than all else I did not want to remain here alone.

Eet said nothing more. I did not even sense that faint mind touch he maintained most of the time. It was as if he had deliberately withdrawn now to allow me some decision which I alone could make, and which was of great importance.

"There is also the matter of food—" Eet finally broke that utter silence.

I still turned the ring around and stared almost unseeingly at the stone. "Do you think this will gain that?" I half sneered.

"No more than you do," he replied. "But neither do I propose to sit here and starve."

Which I thought was the truth, since he seemed well able to provide for himself. And there was something in that realization which held a sour taste for me.

"Take it!" I pulled from the rotting vegetable stuff a long string of fiber, made it into a necklet supporting the ring, and slipped it over Eet's head. He sat up on his haunches when I dropped it around his neck, folding his hand-paws over it for an instant, his eyes closing. I had the feeling he was seeking—though how and where, and for what, I did not know.

"You have chosen well." He fell to four feet and crept to the doorway. "Better than you know—"

With no more than that he was gone, climbing to the top of the rent where plants still stirred in a ragged curtain, pushing through them.

"They are still here," he reported. "Not only under the ship, but along the wall. I think they do not like the sunlight, for they keep to the shadow. Ah—on this side—there is the river! And—another wall—it once fell to make a dam. But now it is broken in two places. Across the water—there lies what the stone seeks!"

He had gone successfully up over the top of the ship. Could I make the same climb? I touched my bruised leg, winced from the pain that followed. I tried to flex it, but it was too stiff. Eet might run easily along that path, but I would have to move slowly. I would have no hope of eluding the watchers, or even of climbing well enough to transverse that slippery surface.

"What lies across the river?"

"Cliffs with holes in them, more tumbled walls," Eet told me. "Now—"

He ceased to communicate. Instead I had from mind to mind as one might pick up a scent, a sharp emanation of violence.

"Eet!" I tried to get to my feet, bringing down upon my head and shoulders more of the plant life, so that I choked and coughed, and I beat the air, trying to brush aside the foul stuff and get a clean breath again.

"Eet!" Again I sent out that mind call in alarm. There was no answer.

I scrambled to the rent. Had some thrown club knocked him down?

"Eet!" The silence seemed greater than a silence which was only for the ears. For I could hear well enough wind, water, and other sounds of life outside.

And—something else!

No one who has ever heard the sound of a ship cutting atmosphere, coming in on deter rockets for a landing, can mistake it. The rumbling—the roar. About me the wreck quivered and vibrated in answer to it. A ship under control was about to set down, and not too far away. I slipped back from the rent. The roar was too loud; it sounded as if the ancient ship might be caught in the wash of rocket fire. As the corridor shook about me, I slid down it, striving to break my descent with my hands, around me the foul mess from the rent cascading to blind and choke me. There was a blast and even through the walls I could feel a wave of heat. Whatever had been exposed to that must have been instantly crisped. I wondered about the sniffers. Now would be my chance to escape.

But—who had landed? Some First-in Scout of Survey on a preliminary check of a newly discovered world? Or had there been landings here before for some mysterious reason? At any rate there was a ship down, and from the sound, a small one of a design made for such touchdowns, nothing larger than a Free Trader.

I clawed the debris away and crawled on hands and knees back to the rent. There was a stiffling smell of burning. Eet—if he had still been alive on the outer shell when that ship—

"Eet!" My mental call this time must have held the force of a scream. No answer.

A thick steam rose outside, enough to veil most of the landscape. The heat made me cower back for the second time. No one would be going out there until it had had a chance to cool a little. Perhaps some of the rockets' fire had struck into the river, boiling its flow. I shifted impatiently, eager to be out, to see the ship. A very faint chance had come true, as I had never really thought it would. We would not be marooned here for the rest of our lives— We? It seemed I was alone now. If Eet had not died in that burst of violence, then certainly he had at the landing of the ship.

The time which passed while the ground cooled and the steam mist cleared was as long to me as those dragging hours when I had been pent in the sanctuary of Tanth. Every impulse pushed me to the rent, to go to claim aid from my own kind. For by one of the most ancient laws of the star lanes any wayfarer marooned as I had been could claim passage on the first ship finding him and be taken off without question.

At last, though the heat was still that of the Arzorian dry lands in midsummer, I pulled myself through the rent and dropped to the charred ground, favoring my bruised leg as best I could. There was a huddled form some distance away, one of the sniffers who had been caught in the backwash of rocket fire. I limped in the opposite direction.

The sound and the heat had made me believe the newcomers had finned down very close to the wreck, but that was not so. However, the rocket wash had cleared that ancient ship of the growth on it. It was not, I saw now, as large as the space derelict, but more the general bulk of a Free Trader. Perhaps it had been left upright on its fins, just as the recently arrived ship was standing a goodly distance away, and the passing of time or some disaster had thrown it over.

I came slowly around to the erose, pitted fins, to look across a fire-bared space at the new ship. It was about the size of the *Vestris*. But no Free Trader's insignia was etched on its side. Nor did it have the blaze of Survey, nor of the Patrol. Yet why would any private vessel land on such a planet as this? There are wealthy Veeps, with a taste for hunting, who crack laws by searching out uncharted worlds where they may indulge their bloodthirsty tastes without falling afoul of the Patrol. If such a hunter had landed here before, that would explain the hostility of the sniffers. But—I drew back into the fin shadow—it would also mean trouble for me. Witnesses to illegal actions are accident prone, and there would be none to ask questions about me.

Only—a Veep's star yacht would have a set of code numbers. There was only one type of ship which would deliberately remain anonymous. I had never seen one, but there were tales in plenty heard in ports. And Vondar's connections had reason to gossip about such matters. The Thieves' Guild maintained ships. Some, under the cover of false papers, made legitimate trading voyages, with only now and then a reason to touch the other side of the law. I suspected the *Vestris* might have been such a ship. But there were other swift cruisers, often fitted with equipment which was experimental, stolen, or bought up before it was generally known.

These were raiders. They did not prey as pirates in space, because that was a very chancy business, to be tried only if a cargo was of such value that one dared a costly gamble. Instead, they looted on planets. Waystar was their legendary base, a satellite or small planet, fortified, hidden, save from those who satisfied its rulers they had no connection with the Patrol or any other law. There had been so many stories, wild tales of Waystar and the shark fleet which operated out of it, that one did not believe in them much. Yet Eet had insisted that I had been unwittingly bound for that place before he had taken steps to separate me from the *Vestris*.

A raiding ship would carry no markings, or else ones which could be changed at will. But a Guild raider here? It was entirely past the bounds of credibility that it was seeking me. My back trail was now so tangled they could not believe me alive, let alone that chance would land me here.

Therefore they had some other mission. And the last thing I must do—until I was sure of that ship— was to contact its crew or passengers. Though it was closed now, I could not be sure that I had not already been sighted on some visa screen. I began to edge back, keeping under the curving side of the wreck, retreating as eagerly as I had earlier advanced.

There was a sharp clang and the hatch opened, the landing ramp protruding like a tongue out over the smoking ground, hunting anchorage on the untouched land. It angled away from the wreck, so those using it could not clearly see it or me—I hoped.

I retreated further; I longed to dart back, away now from the wreckage, which could only draw curious explorers. There was a brush screen still standing, but I could not be sure that some of the sniffers were not lurking there.

The men who came out on the ramp had no protective suiting, proving that they were aware of the nature of this world, ready to be about their purpose here. They wore side arms, and even from this distance, I saw the short barrels of the lasers, not the long ones of the more ordinary stunners. So they were prepared to kill.

Though they wore the conventional planetside dress of any crewmen, coveralls and boots, those had no insignia on breast or collar. Nor was there any choice of color to suggest a uniform. The first two were human or humanoid, but behind them came a shorter figure with four upper limbs which hung at his sides in a way to suggest an unusual flaccidity. His head, which was round, lacked hair and appeared to rest directly on his shoulders, with no support of neck. Where a human skull would show ears, he wore tall feathery appendages which moved constantly back and forth, as Eet's head had moved when he tested for signs of life around him. And of the three I saw, I feared him the most. For as Eet had said, who knows what extra talents an X-Tee might possess. And any among a human crew would be there for no other reason than that he had attributes they found highly useful.

To re-enter the wreck was to be trapped. I must make up my mind to leave the dubious protection of its overhang and try to reach the bush or the river. And it seemed to me that the river offered the lesser menace.

For as long as I could I watched the three from the ship. They reached the end of the ramp, fanned out. The two humans on either side flanked the X-Tee in the middle. His feathery appendages were no longer whirling about; instead they now pointed their tips straight before him, and I could see more of his face. His features were not as far removed from the human norm as were the sniffers'. He had a short nose, two eyes, and if they were set far to the sides of his head and lacked brows, and if his mouth was wider than seemed symmetrical, he was still not too unlike his crewmates.

Suddenly he halted and in lightning draws two of his upper arms caught at the double set of weapons he wore. The brilliant splash of laser fire pencil-beamed from their tips, blackening the brush. His attack was followed by a scream and a thrashing, which marked the passing of either a sniffer or something of similar bulk. The two humans went into a half crouch, their weapons out and ready. But they had not fired, and it would seem they depended upon the X-Tee for leadership in attack.

I crawled back. Now the ship was between me and those killers. When I came to the river, I saw that blocks had been uprooted from the ruined wall and tumbled by the force of the water. At one time some structure on the other side of the stream had fallen, its masonry joining to the walls on this side to provide a dam. Perhaps that had caused, until the water had broken through again, the flooding of the country.

Now there was a crazy jumble of rocks and stones washed and ringed by the water, forming a broken bridge across that ribbon of river. On the other side was the cliff, some distance away, and as Eet had reported, that was holed with dark openings. Between the water and its face were the remains of buildings.

On this side of the ship the clinging vegetation had not been burned away so thoroughly. Perhaps the river spray gave more moisture, for in some places it grew into long trailing vines.

"Eet?" I tried that call, the life here leading me to hope that he might have survived after all. Or had he fallen to a club? I looked along the rocks, down to the water-washed stones, half expecting to see there a small body lying twisted and broken.

"Eet—?"

The answer I hoped against hope to hear did not come. But what did was an awareness of another kind, a strange groping which could not touch minds as

Eet did, but which noted my call. Not that it could trace it back to its source. Only it was alerted.

The X-Tee—could he have "heard" me somehow? My folly struck home as I teetered on the edge of a block, looking down for a possible bridge over the river. To attempt the drop with my dragging leg was more than I dared. I could be caught out there, helpless, vulnerable to any laser beam.

And so I betrayed myself. For as I hesitated I heard from behind:

"Hold it—right there!"

Basic, spoken with a human intonation. I turned slowly, holding on to a block for support, to face one of the humans from the ship. He was like any other crewman, save that in his hand was a laser pointing directly at me.

I knew then that I had thrown away one small advantage. Had I come out to greet the ship's people in wild joy, as they would expect from one marooned, made up a plausible story, they might not have been suspicious. Of course, it would have been dangerous for me if they wanted to cover up their presence on this world. But I would have gained time. Now my own actions made me suspect. I still had a small trick I could play—I could accentuate my lameness, allow my captors to believe that I was far more handicapped than I really was.

So I waited for the other to approach, making a display of holding to my support as if to loose it for a moment would allow me to collapse. And I hoped my general disreputable appearance would add to my claim of injury. Perhaps I could even build upon those patches of new skin so apparent on my body, using a story of being set adrift in an LB when plague was feared. It would not be the first time such an incident had happened.

My captor did not come too close, though he could see both of my hands in plain sight on the stone and that I had no weapons. And his laser never wavered from its sighting on my chest.

135

"Who are you?" he demanded in Basic.

In those few moments I had determined on the role which might save me. I cowered away from him and shrieked, in the wildest and lest sane voice I could counterfeit.

"No—no! Do not kill me! I am well, I tell you! The fever is gone—I am well—"

He halted and I thought I saw his eyes narrow as he studied my face intently. I trusted those pink patches were very visible.

"Where did you come from?" Was there a subtle alteration in his tone? Could I make him believe that I was a deportee from a plague ship, and that I expected to be burned down on sight for no other reason than that I had been cast adrift?

"A ship— Do not kill me! I tell you I am clean now—the fever is gone! Let me go—I will not come near you—your ship—just let me go!"

"Stand where you are!" His order was sharp. Now he cupped his free hand before his mouth and spoke into a com mike. The words he used were not Basic and I could not understand, save that he must be reporting to a superior. This was a dangerous game I played; a hair's difference could mean life or death.

"You—" He motioned with the laser. "Walk ahead—"

"No—I will go—I will not infect—"

"Walk!" A beam, cut to a finger's breadth in diameter, clipped the stone not far from my left hand. Its heat was searing. I cried out as he expected me to do.

I saw him grin. "Touched you? Want another—closer this time? I said—walk! The Captain's interested in you."

Walk I did, making a clumsy business of pulling myself along as if my bruised leg were hardly more than a dead weight.

"Got hurt?" my captor asked, viewing my very slow progress with impatience.

"There are natives—with clubs—they hunted me—" I mumbled.

"So? They have a liking for meat, and you would be

that, as far as they are concerned. Not good—meeting with them." He might have been remembering some earlier experience of his own.

I lurched along as slowly as I could, magnifying my limp. Once more I rounded the end of the wreck and now both the other human and the X-Tee came toward us. The X-Tee had holstered his lasers, but both those feather fronds inclined in my direction.

Whether my communication with Eet had sharpened any esper talent I might have had, though I was sure I was not talented at all, I could not tell. But I was aware of an impact from the alien which was not physical, but mental. Only, if he was trying to batter his way into my mind, he was not successful. There was no smooth meeting as I had known with Eet. And I hoped I could completely bar his probe. It was necessary that I remain what I seemed to be—

"So you flushed him," the other human observed. "What was he trying to do—scramble?"

"Not with that leg. And he may have more wrong with him—take a good look at that face."

So bidden, he did, with a searching stare. And his expression suggested he was not in favor of what he saw. I wondered just how bad my sloughing skin and the shiny new patching looked. It was no longer so noticeable on my hands, or so I thought. But then I was used to seeing it and any fading from those violent purple splotches was an improvement as far as I was concerned.

"Perhaps you had better keep him well away," was the newcomer's verdict. "Tell the Captain about him."

"Captain's waiting—up there. March, you!"

There was someone standing on the ramp. A jerk of the laser sent me on. I stumbled along, hoping I was indeed a miserable object for anyone's eyes to rest upon.

TWELVE

We came to the foot of the ramp and there they bid me stand, ringing me in, their weapons ready. The man awaiting us came several paces farther down to study me in slow appraisal.

He was from one of the old worlds, those first colonized Generations living under alien conditions had given him differences of physique which were noticeable at more than the first glance. His body, under the coverall with the Captain's shooting star on its standing collar, was thin and lank, his skin dark even beneath the space tan; but his eyes and hair were even more indicative of mutation from the parent stock. The hair, of necessity worn very short to accommodate a helmet, was more blue than gray, thick, and it grew in straight, short spikes. His eyes were a brilliant blue-green, larger than ordinary, and with double eyelids, one almost transparent against the ball, the other, heavier, fitting over it. He visibly lifted both to view me, but I think that the sunlight bothered him, as he quickly dropped the inner ones.

But—I knew him! Not by name, but from the past. Whether the recognition would be mutual, I did not know. I hoped not. This man had visited my father's shop, had been one of those escorted into the inner room, exiting through the private door. He had not worn a Captain's tunic then, nor aught to suggest he was a ship's officer. In fact his hair had then been long enough to brush the outsized, wing-padded shoulders of his foppish tunic—the elegance of an inner-planet dandy. That he was of the Guild I did not now doubt. But would he know me for Jern's son? And if I were recognized, could such a relationship be useful to me?

I was not to be left long in doubt on either point. He advanced another step and then laughed, raised his hand to his mouth, and made a vee with his two fingers, through which he spat deliberately right and left.

"By the Lips and Limbs of Sorelle Herself! After this day will I burn farn leaves to Her in any shrine I see! That which was lost is found. And see, boys, that it be not lost again. Murdoc Jern—how did you get here? I will believe any tale you spin me after this."

The three guarding me stirred and moved in, making very sure that I was not going to disappear— or even have a chance to attempt escape. I had only my role of late plague victim left. Aside from that, I would use as much of the truth as could be checked if later they set a scanner on me.

I allowed my mouth to hang open a little, and wavered as if I kept my feet only through an exhausting effort.

"Do—do not kill me! The fever—it is gone—I am whole now—"

"Fever?"

"Look at him, Captain," my captor urged. "He is two colors—best take care—"

"You, Jern, hold your head up! Let us see—"

I swayed back and forth. They were still afraid of coming too close. The terror of plague deflated the toughest starman when he faced it.

"I am—am clean—" I repeated. "They put me off in an LB—but now I am well—I swear it."

The Captain palmed his com and spoke into it with a snap in that tongue that was not Basic. We waited in silence until a second man came running lightly out on the ramp. He held before him a small box, from which extended a length of slender cable, ending in a disc not unlike a hand com. I knew it for a portable diagnostic. The ship was apparently very well equipped.

Advancing within touching distance of me, the medico swung his search disc in careful examination, his eyes ever on the indicators of the box.

"Well?" It was plain the Captain found this interruption irritating.

"He is clean, by what we can judge. There is always the possibility though—"

"To what point?" pressed his commander.

"The hundreth perhaps. Who can say definitely?" The medico expressed the caution normal to his calling.

"We shall settle for that." The Captain waved him back. "So," he said to me, "it seems you are right. Your fever or whatever it was is gone and you are no plague risk. But you were on board ship when it struck?"

"On a Free Trader—out of Tanth—" I raised my hands to my head, rubbed them across my forehead as if I were dazed or in pain. "I—it is hard to remember. I was on Tanth—I had to escape. There was trouble. So I paid gems and Ostrend gave me passage. There was another world—the natives were all gone. And after that I was sick. They said it was plague—put me out in the LB. It made landing here—but there were natives—they hunted me—"

"To this place?" The Captain was smiling. "But how fortunate for you. The hunt ended in the one spot you might meet an off-world ship."

"There was a wall—I followed it—and the wood people—they seemed afraid. I got in a wrecked ship, they did not come after me—"

"What fortune favored you, Jern, and us too! We might have met you elsewhere, but time is saved because we meet here. You see, you have been a focus of interest to others. We have long wanted to meet you."

"I—I do not understand—"

"What is the matter with him?" The Captain rounded on the medico. "He is not rated as stupid in our reports."

The medico shrugged. "Who knows what happens to

140

a man when a plague strikes? He is clean of infection as far as I can tell, but I cannot vouch for any changes a strange virus may have caused in mind or body."

"We shall turn him over to you." The Captain had lost his smile. "Suppose you make all the tests you need, and then let us know whether we have an imbecile or a source of reliable information."

"Take him on board?" The medico hesitated.

"Where else? I thought you said he was clean—"

"There is always the chance it is something new."

I felt rather than saw the Captain's indecision. But that did not last long.

"What equipment will you need? Can it be brought out of the ship?" he asked.

"Most of it—yes. Where will you put him?"

"In the workings, where else? Segal, Onund, get what the medico needs. And you, Tusratti, take him over to the west tunnel."

It was as if I had ceased to exist as a person, but had become an object to be moved around at their desire. In my role of dazed plague survivor I was willing to have it so. The X-Tee crewman urged me down to the riverbank, I moving as slowly and with as much of a limp as I could manage. There were others already at work there. Across the rocks and foaming water a section bridge had been anchored into place. It would appear they knew this place very well and had visited it before, making their preparations for setting up a base, if even a temporary one.

At the urging of my guard I wavered across the bridge, and through the ruins beyond. Our goal was one of those holes in the cliff face. But not the one to which the other crewmen were heading. What they carried were mining tools of the kind such as were used to pick riches from dead moons and asteroids.

"In—" commanded the X-Tee. The hole to which he pointed was the farthest to the left. Then was debris from recent digging dumped on either side of the opening. But whatever they had been hunting they had not

141

found here. They must be taking the holes in turn and were now working that two away from the one into which I was being ushered.

"I am—am hungry—" I halted as if to get my breath, being careful to steady myself against a rock. "I am hungry—I need food—"

There was no readable expression on the X-Tee's face. The hands of his upper pair of arms rested warningly on the butts of his double supply of lasers. For a long moment he stared at me and then he turned and called to one of the men on his way to the other tunnel.

In answer the other detached a packet from his belt and tossed it in our general direction. He had trusted to the unusual talents of my guard, and it did not fall short. Instead one of the X-Tee's upper limbs snapped out to twice the length I would have believed possible, caught the flying object, and pulled back to hand it to me.

My fingers closed about a tube of E-ration and I did not have to fake the avidity with which I gripped its tip between my teeth, bit through the stopper, and spit it out, before sucking the semiliquid contents. No meal of my imagination could have topped the flavor of what now filled my mouth, or the satisfaction afforded me as it flowed in gulps down into me. The mixture was meant to sustain a man under working conditions; and it would renew my strength even more than usual food.

"On!" My guard thumped me on the shoulder with a stick which one of the extraordinarily agile limbs had picked up from the ground. He was careful, I noted, not to touch me. Apparently X-Tees also shared the fear of plague.

Sucking at the tube, I lurched on. And it seemed that the promised strength of the food was already working in me.

The tunnel was a dark mouth opening to engulf us. But the X-Tee produced a beamer. That this was an artificial way was most apparent. And for some distance inside, the stone showed only the marks of its first working. Then recent scars were displayed in great slashes, both horizontal and vertical, until in places they formed a grid.

I saw the glisten of crystals still embedded in the slashes or lying in broken lumps on the ground. And my interest almost made me betray myself. But I remembered just in time that I was playing stupid. Apparently these were not what the crewmen had been searching for. Though they now caught and reflected the light as if a wealth of gems were spilled, yet they had been discarded. This struck me as odd, since ordinarily no Guild ship would pass up anything remotely suggesting profit.

We came to a hollowed-out space where the tunnel ended. Here the walls had been quarried in great rough arches and niches, as if those who had worked here had been so sure they were about to find what they sought that they had used their tools in a frenzy. The X-Tee motioned to a pile of rock. "Sit!"

I lowered myself stiffly to obey his order, still sucking at the tube of E-ration. He planted the beamer on another pile across the open space and turned it to high-diffuse, to light all but the innermost portions of the hollows in the walls. Then he took his place between me and the tunnel entrance.

During the silence which followed I could hear the drip-drip of water somewhere, though there was no evidence of moisture in the tunnel. And a little later I could both hear and feel through the rock the activities of those working farther along in the cliff.

Was this the place to which the zero stone had been pointing us? The discarded crystals here had no resemblance to that murky stone. But that had been exposed to centuries in space, and to whatever use as a source of energy its discoverers had put it to.

I leaned over to pick up one of the broken prisms. My guard placed a hand on the butt of a laser, but he made no move to stop me. This was a piece of quartz, I thought. But of that I could not be sure. One must never make snap judgments about finds on unknown planets. Vondar would have put any such material through exhaustive tests before he might venture an opinion, and even then I had known him to reserve final classification. He carried with him certain finds he was not sure of, even after years of study, since they possessed qualities which were beyond any code. All dealers accumulated a few such, and one of their principal activities when meeting a fellow gemologist was producing these mystery stones for comparison.

So what I held could be worthless quartz, or something quite different.

There was a sound from the tunnel and the medico entered, pushing before him a box which ran on rollers. Behind him came the two crewmen with other equipment. Then I became the object of tests.

I think first they still tried to find in me some seeds of the disease which had left such visible marks on my body. And the medico also applied a renewing ray to my bruised leg, so that I could no longer use lameness as a cover. But I could not, dared not resist—even when they at last locked me into a reader-helm. The very fact that they carried such a thing with them suggested they found its use necessary, illegal as that was.

With its pads locked to my forehead and the nape of my neck I could only answer with the strict truth, or what I thought was the truth. After they had reached that stage of the proceedings they summoned the Captain and it was he who fed me the questions.

"You are one Murdoc Jern, son to Hywel Jern—"

"No."

He was startled by that and looked to the medico, who leaned quickly to read the dial and then nodded to his commander.

"You are not Murdoc Jern?" the Captain began again.

"I am Murdoc Jern."

"Then your father was Hywel Jern—"

"No."

The Captain looked once more to the medico and received a second nod of assurance that the machine was functioning properly.

"Who was your father then?"

"I do not know."

"Were you a member of Hywel Jern's household?"

"Yes."

"Did you consider yourself his son?"

"Yes."

"What do you know of your real parents?"

"Nothing. I was told I was a duty child."

An expression of relief flickered momentarily on the Captain's face.

"But you were in Jern's confidence?"

"He taught me."

"About gems?"

"Yes."

"And he apprenticed you to Ustle?"

"Yes."

"Why?"

"Because, I believe, he wanted a future for me. Since his true son would have the shop upon his death."

I could not stop the flow of words. It was as if I stood slightly apart and listened, as if it was I who answered. Now I sensed that once again the answer I had given was baffled.

"Did he ever show you a certain ring, one made to fit over the glove of a space suit?"

"Yes."

"Did he tell you where it came from?"

"That it had been brought to him for hock-sale. That it had been found on the body of an alien floating in space."

"What else did he tell you?"

"Nothing except that he believed there was something to be learned about it."

"And he wanted you, during your travels with Ustle, to discover what you could?"

"Yes."

"And what did you discover?"

"Nothing."

The Captain seated himself on a folding stool one of his men had provided. He took from a seal pocket of his tunic a pale-green stick, put it between his teeth,

145

and chewed upon it reflectively, as if studying on some new and vital question. At last he asked:

"Did you ever see the ring in later years?"

"Yes."

"When and where?"

"On Angkor after my father's death."

"What did you do with it?"

"I took it with me."

"You have it now?" He leaned forward, his eyes fully open, both pairs of lids raised.

"No."

"Where is it?"

"I do not know."

Again exasperation, this time strong enough to bring a sharp exclamation from him.

"State the last time you saw it and under what circumstances."

"I gave it to Eet. He took it away."

"*Eet!* And who is Eet?"

"The mutant born of the ship's cat on the *Vestris*."

I think that had he not been so sure of the infallibility of the reader-helm, he would not have taken that for the truth. For it must have been the last answer he expected.

"Was that"—he spoke slowly now—"here on this planet, or on the *Vestris?*"

"Here."

"And when?"

"Just before your ship planeted."

"Where is this Eet now?" Again he leaned forward eagerly.

"Dead, I believe. He was crossing the top of the wreck when you flamed down. He must have been burned off by your deter rockets."

"You—" The Captain turned his head. "Thangsfeld, jump to it! I want every palm's width of that ship's surface searched and all the ground around it! Now!"

One of the crewman left at a run. Once more the Captain turned to me.

"Why did you give the ring to Eet?"

146

"The ring pulled us toward this place rather than to the wrecked ship. Eet wanted to know why."

"*Eet* wanted to know," he repeated. "What do you mean? You have stated that this creature was a mutant born of a ship's cat—not an intelligent being." Once more he looked to the medico for confirmation of my truthfulness.

"I do not know what Eet is," I replied. "But he is not an animal, save perhaps outwardly."

"Why did he and not you take this ring to the source of attraction?"

"We were beseiged by the natives. Eet had a chance of getting out, I did not."

"But why was it so important that the ring get out, via this Eet?"

"I do not know. Eet wanted to take it."

"In what direction?"

"Farther on—over the river."

"So!" He was on his feet in one lithe movement. "We are on the right track after all." Once more he looked down at me. "Do you know what the ring stone is?"

"A source of energy—I think."

"A good enough answer." Still he looked at me, his inner eyelids almost closed, giving his eyes a disquieting opacity.

"What do we do Captain, with him—?" one of the human crewman asked.

"For the present, nothing. Keep him here. But then, even if he runs loose, I do not think he is going anywhere." He laughed. "After all we owe him some small thanks. More if we find the ring at the wreck."

They unstrapped me. I was very tired and willing to yield to my fatigue. But I remembered they had not asked me the why and how of my leaving the *Vestris*. Had they swallowed my plague story and so would not question me about that? The indications were that they had not been in touch with the Free Trader, at least not since my escape. If these represented those who had bought me free from Tanth for their own purposes, they

147

had not been in direct contact with other members of their team lately.

But this time I did not have Eet to depend upon, and thinking of Eet hurt more than I would have earlier believed possible. I hoped that he had not suffered, that that flash of violence had marked an instantaneous ending for him.

Would they find his body with the ring still tied about his neck? And what did they want it for—to lead them to others of its kind as it had guided me across space to the dead stones in the derelict? That such gems might be a revolutionary source of power was an easy guess. And such power, in the hands of the Guild, was worth far more to them than the ransom of a whole system of planets.

The medico and the other human crewman gathered their apparatus and left. But the X-Tee continued to sit by the door of the tunnel, on the stool left by the Captain. He, too, had pulled a green stick out and was chewing on it, but, while his eyes were half closed in enjoyment, his fronds pointed in my direction.

I slept then, and awoke to a shaking of the rock around me, a roar in my ears. There was another ship coming in. Perhaps the *Vestris*. If so, the Captain might be back with more questions. I lay listening, watching my guard.

He stood looking down the tunnel. However, the fronds still pointed at me, and his upper hands hovered over laser butts.

It was clear from the attitude of the X-Tee that this second ship was not expected. Therefore—who? The Patrol? Or some innocent scout or trader arriving just at the wrong time? That the new arrival was about to walk into a trap, I did not doubt.

The thunder of the planeting died away. Now I could not feel or hear the vibration caused by the workers in the other tunnel.

"What is it?" I dared to ask my guard.

His attentive fronds twitched, but he did not turn his

head. Only now the lasers were drawn as if he were prepared to repel an invasion.

We continued to wait. I tried other questions until the wave of a weapon in my direction silenced me. Then there was a tramp of feet in the passage and a voice raised in a hail. My guard restored one laser to its holster, held the other ready.

Three of them came in, human crewmen. They carried a struggling bundle which they dumped without ceremony and with extra roughness on the floor. Once in port I had seen a crewman, drunk on the maddening lorthdrip, subdued by a police tangle gun. And now I looked upon a captive completely enmeshed in the same fashion. Among the coils of gummy rope I caught sight of the black tunic known across space. They had bagged a Patrolman, and securely.

THIRTEEN

He had sense enough to cease struggling as he was dropped, so that his bonds did not tighten. Luckily none had crossed his face or throat. But his captors were so sure of him they walked away, leaving the two of us to the X-Tee. He surveyed the Patrolman, no expression on his face. Then he returned to his stool.

The Patrolman's eyes were open and, I judged, he was busy examining his prison and its occupants. He stared a long time at me. The ordeal of questioning under the probe, though sleep had followed, had left me weak. And not only weak, but caught in a curious lethargy, disinclined to action. I could foresee that at any moment the X-Tee might turn a laser on me. But I was no longer afraid.

After a while one of the human crewmen came in, pitched in my general direction another tube of E-ration. Though I felt hunger stir in me when I saw it, a strong effort of will was required to put out my hand, shift my body to reach it. And I held it in my shaking fingers for some time before I could summon the energy to suck at its contents.

With the flow of food into my mouth, that dreamy, half-awake state broke, and I aroused enough to know that this was no nightmare but grim and threatening reality. The entangled Patrolman lay where they had dropped him, watching me. I had sucked about half the tube before I realized they had left nothing for him. Nor could he feed himself. I started to crawl to where he lay.

"Naw—" It was not good Basic, no more than a guttural bark. A laser appeared in our guard's hand, his intent of using it plain. I halted. He waved me back.

"Staaay—tharrr—"

I stayed. But I did not finish the tube. It would appear that our guard was determined to keep his two charges well apart.

Now I returned the Patrolman's stare. He was immobile in the net casing. Had he landed here alone, as a scout? Or did he have companions who would come seeking him? I would have given a great deal at that moment to be able to communicate with him as I had with Eet.

It could well be that I *was* a latent esper, and my talent—though limited—had been so aroused by Eet that I could at least make my fellow prisoner aware I was striving to contact him. So I put most of my energy into a beamed call.

What followed was so great a surprise that I betrayed my astonishment and had to dissemble quickly by throwing both hands to my head as if struck by a sudden pain—though how good a cover that could be I did not know. The X-Tee was on his feet, his feather fronds sweeping swiftly back and forth.

I had been answered. Not by the man who lay across the cavern—but by *Eet!* And as quickly as that touch of recognition had come, it was gone—a single flash of light across the dark of a moonless night.

The X-Tee advanced to the center of the working, his fronds still swinging, as if those antennae could pick up our communication. And the Patrolman looked from one of us to the other, inquiry plain on his face.

There was nothing more, and I could guess the reason for Eet's caution. If the X-Tee had been able to sense that touch, then mind speech was to be avoided. But the very fact the mutant was alive was almost as good as if someone had dropped a laser into my reach.

I continued to play a part, huddling together, my hands to my head. The guard halted by me and kicked out, the metal-enforced tip of his boot landing painfully against my shin.

"Whaaat—do—you—?" His guttural mouthing of Basic was hard to understand.

"Pain—in my head—hurts—"

"Mind—talk—you—" He did not make that a question.

I felt then a kind of clumsy, fumbling thought approach which was only a feeble pushing, bearing no relation to Eet's. It was easy to withstand such a probe. The X-Tee must have esper powers to a degree, but perhaps they worked better among his own kind. At any rate he got nothing from me.

Now he began a crisscross search of the cavern, his fronds ever in motion. That they were highly astute sense organs, I did not doubt. But whether they could nose out Eet I did not know.

My confidence arose as I saw that the uneasiness of the X-Tee did not abate, but rather grew. Had he been able to get a quick line on Eet, he would not have continued to prowl but would have gone into action.

Where *was* Eet? I had no idea from which direction that flash of recognition had come. But that he was alive—! Now I hoped furiously that they would not question me again. But if the guard continued to be suspicious perhaps they would.

He stood close to the Patrolman now, his fronds still seeking. Slowly he turned, then put his head back and looked up at the dim expanse overhead. Eet—was Eet up there somewhere?

Clearly the X-Tee's attention was now riveted and I could only believe that he had a line on the esper tie. But how could he? Eet had been quiet.

The laser swung up, pointed at a spot almost directly above the guard. There were hollows in plenty there, and they might hide anything. A mass of crystals larger than my head was visible. He fired—

A flash of light blinded me. I had reason enough to cry out and cover my eyes now. I heard a gasping which could have come from either the Patrolman or the guard. A thud—and a rattling—

To be blind was horror at that moment. I feared to move, sure that ray was bringing down the rocks over us, to bury us alive. When that did not follow, I tried vainly to see through a blood-red fog.

"Are you dead?" That demand which penetrated my dark was no call from Eet, nor was it the bark of our guard. Basic in human voice—it could only come from the Patrolman.

"Where are you?" I asked, groping out with one hand.

"Ahead, a little to your right!" he answered swiftly. "You must have been looking up as he fired—"

"What happened?" I did not try to get to my feet, but crawled forward on hands and knees, sweeping now and then a hand before me.

"He beamed straight up. Brought down a hunk of crystal on his head. Look out, he is right before you now—"

But my hands had already encountered the body. I made myself examine it by touch, locate one of the lasers. And all the time I feared I was blind.

I edged around the body and crawled on until one of my hands touched the Patrolman. To burn off his bonds was a job demanding good sight, and I could not do it blind.

"Wait!"

I settled back on my heels, a surge of relief breaking like a high tide in me. "Eet!"

He came out of nowhere as far as I was concerned. I felt the pat of his hand-paws on mine and I released the laser into his hold. I guessed that he was quick and efficient about freeing the Patrolman. For it was only moments later that a human hand fell on my shoulder, drawing me up to my feet. I wavered there, almost as I had when I had played the role of plague wanderer for the Captain. Eet climbed me as if I were a tree and his weight once again ringed my shoulders. I felt the tickle of his whiskers against my cheek.

"Hold still! Let me see your eyes—" That was the Patrolman. I flinched involuntarily from his touch and then obeyed. I could feel him spread the lids, the sting of moisture against the balls.

153

"Close and hold!" he ordered. "From my aid kit—that ought to help."

"They will have heard—" I put up my hand to touch Eet's wiry fur. "They will come—"

"Not for a while," Eet answered quickly. "It is night and they have posted an outer guard, but there are none in any of the tunnels. We have a good chance of getting free. This guard was the only sensitive among them."

My hand was caught in a firm grip which pulled me on. Eet meanwhile directed my steps around piles of debris. We must have re-entered the tunnel, heading for the outside.

"Who are you?" the Patrolman asked. "A hostage?"

I gave him the version I had edited for the Guild men. "I caught an unknown disease, was spaced from a ship in an LB. It made tape landing here and I was hunted by natives. I took refuge in a wrecked ship. Then these landed. They made me prisoner after their medico pronounced me clean."

"You are lucky they did not just beam you down," he returned. "I wonder why they did not."

I had to supply him with a plausible answer. "They thought I knew about what they hunt here. I am an apprentice gemologist."

"Gems!" He paused and then added, "They are conducting mining operations—that is true."

"Were you tailing them? And where is your ship?" I counterquestioned.

"I am a scout." He gave me the most disheartening answer for one hoping for a quick way out of trouble. "They took me when I came out after landing. But my ship is on time lock—they cannot break into her. If we can reach her— But what—or who—is your friend?"

"I am Eet," Eet answered for himself. "This human and I are in defensive alliance—which was good for you, Patrolman. To get him free I had also to extend aid to you."

"Then you did engineer that fall of rock," I observed.

Eet corrected me. "No, the creature brought it on himself. I only gave him mind direction, confused him to

154

make him think he saw something threatening above. He was esper, but to a limited degree save with his own kind. He lost his head and shot at a shadow which was not there, bringing down the rock."

My hand slipped along Eet's body and he suffered that examination by touch. I did not feel the twined roots about his long neck, or any indication that he still carried the ring. Nor in that company could I ask questions. For the less the Patrolman knew the better. The Patrol ever takes the view that the good of many is superior to the good of the individual.

I sensed that Eet was in complete agreement with me on that point, and that the ring was in a safe place. But I fretted a little—no place save my own custody really satisfied me.

"Try to use your eyes," said the Patrolman.

The sensation of being closed in was gone, and a cool wind laden with outdoor scents blew about us. I lifted my lids and blinked rapidly. That sweep of violent red had faded, and though there were some shadowy blotches, I could see blearily.

Not too far away a rude sentry post had been erected from debris of the mine tunnels and blocks of the ruins. There was a beamer mounted on its uneven wall, and at intervals that swept, not toward the tunnel mouths, but across the jumble of ruins, touching the broken walls which had once dammed the river.

"They fear an attack from the natives," Eet explained.

"Clubs against lasers?" I scoffed.

"Clubs in the night, when one cannot see well—the odds are not as uneven as you think."

"Why do they not just hole up in their ship?" was my second question.

"They have equipment in the tunnels. Once before they tried retreating into the ship at night. The natives smashed things that could not be repaired—they had to go off world for more."

"You seem to know a lot about them!" flashed the Patrolman.

"You," returned Eet in his most insufferable voice,

155

"are one Celph Hory, ten years with the force. You are a native of Loki, one of four sons, two of whom are dead. You were sent here, not on a routine scout, but to search out the source of a well-sustained rumor that the Guild has made a discovery which will give them superiority in space. You have orders to keep under cover (which you did not carry out well, mainly because your ship had been skillfully sabotaged, something you did not discover until you were in orbit here) and to report back, not revealing your presence to the Guild. Is this not true?"

I heard a breath drawn in sharply. "You read minds." Hory made it close to an accusation.

"I merely follow the instinct bred into me, as you follow yours, Hory. Be glad that I do, or you would have been prisoner until Captain Nactitl gave the order for your burning. He was debating the folly of keeping you any longer an hour ago. I would suggest as speedy a withdrawal as possible. These miners have not come upon what they are seeking, but they are close—"

"You found it!" I broke in. By this time I could pick up not only Eet's mental speech but some of his emotions. He was at his smuggest now, suggesting that once again he had bested those physically stronger and bigger.

"So far they look in the wrong place. However, sooner or later that will occur to them. Nactitl is not in the least stupid, and certainly not to be underrated. He has only failed so far because he did not have the right guide."

The right guide! The ring which Eet had taken, which —which might have drawn him to the source. I wanted to ask questions so badly they choked my throat, buzzed in my head. But if he answered them, then Hory, too, would have that information.

"What have they to find here?" broke in the Patrolman, and I knew he would continue to seek an answer. It all depended now on how much he knew of gems. If I guessed wrongly and he had any training in that field, then my secret was threatened. But again Eet took the lead, giving me a briefing in his reply.

156

"A source of revenue, which also means power." It was very easy to forget at such times he was only a small furred creature. His communication was not that of an equal, but soared only too often into patronizing explanations. "This was a mine of—how many years ago we cannot guess. But I would say the diggings of one of the Forerunner civilizations. Unfortunately for the present-day seekers, they have been picked clean."

"But you said Nactitl was just not looking in the right place—"

"He searches the old diggings. If he looked among the ruins he might find other clues. Unfortunately we cannot linger to investigate on our own. I would suggest that we find your ship," he said to Hory, "and lift as soon as possible. To hide out in this area is unwise. The sniffers are out—"

"Sniffers?"

"The natives; they hunt largely by scent. At any rate the Guild activity here is drawing more and more of them and they have established a ring about the landing field. As yet they are not ready to attack, but they very efficiently serve as a means of confining off-worlder activity to this general vicinity. Even to reach your ship will be something of a problem which will increase materially with every passing moment. But one man alone is not going to change Captain Nactitl's mind and—"

I felt Eet's body stiffen, his head go up and forward.

"What is it?"

"We have less time than I had hoped!" His message flashed to us. "They endeavored to reach your late guard by hand com. When he did not answer they ordered a general alert."

We had only those few instants of warning. The beamer mounted on the sentry post went into stepped-up action, sweeping its light wider and farther. But bright as it was in the open, it still could not penetrate the hollow pools of shadow which were to be found among the ruins. And we had luckily dropped into one of those.

"To the right—" Eet took over direction. "Move out at the next sweep."

"To the left." Hory was equally insistent. "My ship—"

"It will not be that easy," Eet snapped. "We must go right to eventually win left. And we shall have to go deeper into the fringe of the ruins, maybe even out into the open—"

"Do we cross the river?" To my mind that would be the point of greatest vulnerability. I did not see how we could pass that under the fire of an alerted camp.

"For so much favor we may thank whatever gods or powers your species recognizes," Eet returned. "Luckily this representative of your law chose to set down on this bank. But it is necessary to flank their post and to avoid any party coming from their ship to reinforce the guard there. Now—right—"

I had been watching the sweep of the beam and it now touched the point farthest from us. So no prompting from Eet was needed to send me scuttling to the next patch of dark I had already marked as a good hiding place. Hory did not leap with me, but my move must have spurred him to action, for he was little behind me in reaching that new lurking place.

Unfortunately the cover seemed designed to lead us farther and farther from our real goal. Yet we could now hear sounds from over the river and see the flash of beamers, which marked a search party setting out from the ship. One of those beamers was set up to illuminate not only their bridge, but a goodly portion of land on our side, an open field of light I saw no way to avoid.

"Not over, but under—at that next hole." Eet's hind claws dug convulsively into my flesh as I gathered my legs under me, readying for the next dash.

He must mean the next patch of deep shadow, but what his "under, not over" meant I was not to learn until I reached it, or rather was engulfed in it. For it was not merely a lurking place behind a pile of stones, but indeed a hole, into which I tumbled.

I flung out my arms and my fingers scraped rock on three sides. Then Hory landed half on me, sending me teetering toward the fourth. I did not strike any barrier there as I fought for my balance, my feet in their pack coverings skidding on a smooth stone surface. Again I felt about me. Walls not too far away on either side—but open before. And I heard Hory scuffling behind.

"Ahead—" Eet urged.

"How do you know?" I demanded.

"I know." He was confident. "Ahead."

I felt my way along. I was in a passage. Whether it was indeed some runway planned by the builders I did not know. It might have been fashioned by the tumbling of walls. The flooring inclined and I splashed into a pool of water. There was a dank smell which grew thicker as we advanced.

"Where do we travel? Under the river?" I asked.

"No. Though perhaps river water does seep here. Look now to your right."

Ahead was a faint glow which brightened as I slipped and slid on. Through my mind shot a memory of those slime trails within the wreck. Would we find those here also? But at least we could depend upon Eet for a warning—

I came to the site of the glow. There was a square opening in the wall to my right where a block had been removed or had fallen out. And through this improvised window, I looked down into a chamber of some size. Down its center ran a table of the same stone as formed the walls, save that this was not so eroded. And set on it were boxes. They had been metal; now they were pitted and worn, and some had fallen into rusty dust, only their outlines marked on the table. But there was one very near to our window which appeared whole, and in it were stones which gave forth feeble sparks of life. The glow which had drawn my attention did not come from those, but from what lay beside the box. Eet uncurled from my shoulders and passed in a leap through the window to the surface of the table. He raced along it until he came to the ring, thrusting one of his hand-paws through it, using the other to draw it farther up his shoulder like a barbaric armlet.

He made a second leap, back onto the stone ledge of the window, then climbed to my shoulders, stuffing the ring inside my tunic, where it lay, almost too warm for comfort, against my skin.

"What is it?" To my surprise Hory's voice did not come from behind me, but from some distance farther back along the passage. "Where are you? What did you stop for?"

"There is a wall opening here," Eet reported smoothly. "But it is of no service to us. The way ahead, however, is clear."

I was puzzled. I had believed Hory directly on my heels and I had been sure he must have seen what lay in the room. Now it appeared that he had not. But I asked no questions of Eet.

Once more the passage sloped—but now up. It was leading us in the direction we had been aiming for. We took it step by careful step. I listened intently and knew the others must be doing the same.

"There are many loose stones ahead," Eet informed us. "You must move with the greatest care. But it is not too far now before we reach the fringe of the ruins. Beyond that we have yet to avoid the sniffers."

We emerged into heaps of loose rubble. My sight had returned to normal and I saw enough to guess that this material marked the miners' dump. We plotted a path through it with caution. But luckily the higher heaps were between us and the sweeping beam. The activity was now on the cliff side of the river, and at the ruins nearest the tunnel beamers were turning the night to day.

But our luck held as we crept from the edge of the last rubble pile into the brush. This was tangled and thick, but it made a curtain for us.

"They will expect us to make for the Patrol ship," I pointed out to Eet.

"Naturally. But they will expect that to be bait in a trap for both of you. Probably they have already taken steps there—"

"What!" Hory stopped short. "But they could not in-

160

terfere with the ship itself—it is on personal time lock."

"Such trifles might not deter a determined Guild expert," Eet replied. "But Nactitl has not been able to foresee my presence or some other minor mishaps. I tell you, keep on. Once we reach the ship we need not worry about escape off world."

Knowing Eet, I trusted that tone of assurance. Hory probably did not, but he followed as if he had no choice— which in truth he did not, unless he proposed to skulk about the terrain or go into suicidal battle with the Guild.

FOURTEEN

"Sniffers!"

Eet's warning halted me. There was enough light and noise behind us to inform the natives that those of the ship's camp were hunting.

"Where?" Perhaps Hory was now willing to depend upon Eet's senses, if not to accept his advice.

"Left—in the tree."

That was not as tall as the forest giants, but it did tower well above us. And its foliage made so impenetrable a cone of dark that no eyes of ours could sight what might hide there.

"He waits to leap as we pass beneath," Eet informed us. "Swing well away; he will leap but fall short."

This time we were not unarmed. Hory had one of the X-Tee's lasers, I another. To spray about without a definite target, however, would be folly. I held the weapon at ready and started around the tree.

It was like a blow in my face, striking deep into my head, then seeming to center in my ears. I staggered under it and heard Hory cry out in equal torment.

Eet twisted on my shoulders, thrust in his claws to keep his position. I forgot all about any menace from the natives; all I wanted was to be rid of the agony in my head.

"—hand—take Hory's hand—hold—"

Eet's mind voice was almost muffled by the pain in my head. His hand-paws had gone to my ears, gripping them, and I could feel his body resting against my head, an addition to my misery.

"Take Hory's hand!" The command was emphasized

by a sharp twist of my ears. I tried to lift my hand to pull that tormentor from my shoulders, but found that, instead of obeying me, my flesh and muscle were flung around, and my fingers seemed to close of their own accord on warm skin and bone, in a grip riveted past my breaking. The Patrolman, moaning, tried to break away from me, to no effect.

"Now—on!" Again Eet twisted my ears. Dazed from the pain in my head, I stumbled in the direction he aimed me, towing Hory behind.

There was a shrilling from the tree, and something dark fell, not leaped, from it, to lie writhing on the ground. We dimly heard other sounds, a rustling of movement throughout the brush. Things hiding there were now moving past us toward the cliffs.

Only Eet's sharp hold and constant misuse of my ears kept me going. For, as I moved, it was as if I waded through a swift current determined to bear me back toward the ruins and the Guild ship, which I had to fight with all my strength.

It was dark here, but Eet rode me as a man might mount a beast of burden, guiding me by his hold, steering me here and there. And I could only obey those tugs, always drawing Hory along by a grip I could not release.

For years, or so it seemed, that zigzag march lasted. Then I smelled charred vegetation and we came to where the growth was shriveled by rocket blast, or burned off altogether. Before us, standing on its fins, was the Patrol scout ship.

Only a dark bulk—I could not make out a ramp, or any dark hatch open on its side. And I remembered Hory's talk of a time seal. If he could not lift that at will, we had reached our goal but were still barred from safety.

The pull on me, the pain in my head, still existed, but either its force had lessened, or I was now so accustomed to it that the agony had decreased. Eet still kept his grip on my ears, but when I paused before the ship he did not urge me on.

Instead he turned his attention to Hory, though my brain, too, received his imperative command:

"Hory, the time seal—can you denegate it?"

The Patrolman swayed back and forth, tugging feebly against my grip, trying to turn toward the ruins.

"Hory!" This time Eet's demand for attention was as painful to the receptive mind as the torment from behind.

"What—" Not quite a word, more nearly a moan. With his free hand the Patrolman pawed at his head. The laser was gone; he must have dropped it at the attack.

"The seal—on—the—ship—" Eet's words were heavy in impact, like the ancient solid-type projectiles when they struck into flesh. "Deactivate the seal—now—"

Hory turned his head. I could see him only dimly. With his free hand he fumbled at the front of his tunic. All his movements seemed so uncoordinated that one could not believe he could complete any action. He brought out a hand com.

"Code!" Eet kept at him relentlessly. "What—is—the—code?"

As if he could not even be sure of the position of his mouth, Hory raised his hand in a series of jerks. He mumbled. I could understand none of the sounds clearly. And whether, in spite of his clouded mind, he was responding to Eet's order, I had no idea. His arm dropped heavily, to swing by his side. It seemed he had failed.

Then there was a noise from the ship. The hatch opened and the tongue of a narrow landing ramp licked forth, to touch the seared earth only feet away.

"In!" Eet's order rang almost as shrill as one of the sniffers' screams.

I dragged Hory along. The ramp was very narrow and steep, and I had to negotiate it sideways in order to tow the Patrolman. But step by step we climbed the span to enter the hatch.

It was like walking into a soundproofed chamber and slamming the door behind us. Instantly the tumult in my head ended. I leaned against the wall of the compartment just within the hatch, feeling the drip of my own sweat from my chin. My relief was so great it left me weak and shaking.

By the glow of the light which came on as the hatch closed behind us, I could see that Hory was in no better state. His face was greenish-white under the space tan and slick with sweat. He had bitten his lip and drops of blood still gathered there in bubbles, to feed a thin trickle down his chin.

"They—had—a compeller—on us—" He got out each word as if to form it with his savaged lips was a fearsome task. "They—"

Eet had released his hold on my ears and had dropped down to my shoulders once again.

"Better get off planet." If the compeller had affected the mutant, he did not show it. And now it was far easier to follow his suggestion than to undertake any action on my own.

I think Hory was in much the same state. He lurched away from the wall and drew himself through the inner hatch. As we followed I heard the clang of the rewinding ramp, the automatic sealing of the door behind us. Again I felt a wave of relief.

To get at us now they would have to use a super-destruct. And the Guild ship, as well equipped as it might be, could not carry one of those—it was not large enough.

Hory took the lead, pulling up the core ladder of the ship. Then Eet climbed with a speed which left both of us behind. We passed by two levels to enter the control cabin. The Patrolman reached the pilot's swing chair and began to buckle himself in. He moved as one in a dream and I do not think he was really aware of my presence, though he must have been of Eet's.

Patrol scouts are not meant to carry more than one man. But in emergencies there might be exceptions, and there was a second blast-off seat in the rear of the cabin. I got into that and was making fast the straps when Hory leaned forward to press the course tape release.

Eet sprang from somewhere and lay full length along my body.

There was an awakening of lights on the board, a vibration through the ship. Then came the pressure of blast-off. I had known that of the Free Traders and small freighters, which had seemed so much worse than that of liners. But this was a huge hand squeezing me down into darkness.

When I saw dizzily again, the lights on the board no longer played in flashing patterns but were set and steady. Hory lay in his seat, his head forward on his chest. Eet stirred against me. Then his head arose slowly and his beads of eyes met mine.

"We are out—"

"He set a course tape," I said. "To the nearest Patrol mother ship or base, I suppose."

"If he can reach it," Eet observed. "We may have bought time only."

"What do you mean?"

"Just that Nactitl cannot afford to lose us. The Guild are playing for the largest stakes they have yet found— for many of your human centuries. They will not allow the fate of a single Patrol scout to upset their plans."

"They cannot mount a destruct—not on their ship."

"But they may have other devices, just as useful to them. Also, do you yourself want to be delivered to a Patrol base?"

"What do you mean?" I glanced at Hory. If he was conscious he must be able to "hear" Eet's communications.

"He still sleeps," the mutant reassured me. "But we may not have much time, and I do not know how much an unconscious brain can pick up to retain for the future. This is true—what Nactitl seeks he has not yet found. There are only the stones in the storage vault. But they were not mined on that planet, as Nactitl and the Patrol may continue to belive."

"How do you know that? What about those cliff tunnels?"

"They sought something else there, those old ones.

166

No, the cache under the ruins held their fuel supply. But Nactitl will believe they found them in the mines, and so will others. However, the man who *does* eventually find the true source of the stones can make his own luck, if he is clever and discreet. Also—those stones looked dead, did they not?"

"Very dead."

"Your ring stone partly activated them. Just as it can give a boost to any conventional fuel in these ships of yours. You have a bargaining point, but you must use it well. There will be those who would kill you for that ring. And you have more to fear than just the Guild."

His head swiveled around on that exceedingly mobile neck and he looked meaningfully at the Patrolman.

"To stand against the Patrol would require more resources than I have," I answered. The illegality of it did not bother me. The ring was my heritage, and the fact that some musty law made by men I had never seen or heard of might be produced to wrest it from me only raised my anger. I added, "But I will fight for what I now hold."

"Just so." There was satisfaction in Eet's agreement. "You can seem to yield and yet win."

"Win what? A fortune—with everyone sniping at me to get at the secret and tear me down? I want none of that."

Perhaps Hywel Jern, who could have had wealth and yet had settled prudently for comfort, and might have finished out his life in peace had he not been a curious man, had molded me. Or perhaps the need to be free which had kept Vondar Ustle on the move had rubbed off on his assistant.

"You can buy freedom." Eet's thought followed mine easily. "What have you now with Vondar dead? Nothing. Bargain well, as he taught you, when the time comes. You will know what you want most in that hour."

"What *you* want," I countered.

Now his head turned so that he could eye me. "What I want—just so. But our trails run together. I have told you that before. Apart we are weak, together we are strong, a combination to accomplish much if you have the courage—"

"Eet—what are you?"

"A living being," he replied, "with certain gifts which I have placed at your disposal from time to time, and certainly *not* to your disadvantage." Again he read my thoughts and added, "Of course, I have used you, but also you have used me. You would have been dead long since had we not. And to your species, death of the body is an end—do you not believe it so?"

"Not all of us do."

"That is as it may be," he replied ambiguously. "But at any rate, we are together in this life and it is to our mutual advantage to have this pact continue."

I could not deny his logic, though still the suspicion stayed deep in my mind that Eet had plans of his own and would eventually maneuver me into serving them.

"He is waking." Eet looked at Hory. "Tell him to check his speed."

I was no pilot. But I could see there was a red light flashing on the board. That had about it a suggestion of alarm. Hory made a snorting sound and straightened in his web seat, setting it to swinging. He rubbed his hands across his eyes and then leaned forward to look at the board, his attitude that of one alerted to trouble.

"Eet says—look to the speed—" I said.

His hand shot out to thumb a red button under that red flash. The red spark vanished, a yellow one flashed in its place, held steady for a short space, then became red again. Once more Hory tried the button. But this time there was no change in the light. His fingers played a swift pattern over the other buttons and levers, but the signal remained stubbornly red.

"What is the matter?" I asked.

"Traction beam." Hory spit out that explanation as if it were a curse. "They have lifted behind us and slapped a traction on. But a ship of that size, how could they be so equipped?" Still he continued to try his keys. Once the light paled, but only momentarily.

"They can pull us back?"

"They are trying. But they cannot down us—not yet. They can only keep us out of hyper. And they may think they can board—if so they are going to be surprised. But they can keep us tied near that planet."

"Waiting for reinforcements? Why cannot you do the same—call for help?"

"They have a com blanket over us. If they expect reinforcements they were already sure of their coming. I have heard of Guild superships; this must be one of them."

"What do we do then—just wait—?"

"Not if we are wise," Eet cut in. "They do expect aid and it will be of such nature as to take this ship easily. What you stumbled on here, Hory, is a Guild operation of such magnitude that they are willing to throw many of their undercover reserves in—or did you arrive here with a suspicion that that was so?"

"I suppose you have a suggestion?" Hory asked bitingly. "I can maintain my shield but not break their hold—to do that is to lose my own escape force. They could reel us in before I could fire effectively."

Eet did have an answer. "The ring stone, Murdoc—"

"How?" I had felt the action of the ring on my own body, its drawing power across the wastes of space, and on the planet below. But in what way could it be used on this ship to break a traction beam which held so powerful a vessel in bonds?

"Take it down, to the engine room," Eet ordered.

His knowledge was certainly greater than mine, and I continued to wonder where he had gained it. Reading minds seemed easy enough for him, but how he knew uses for the baffling gem I could not understand. Was it all part of Eet's mysterious past, before he had, as he put it, obtained a body to serve him in the present? Was —could Eet have a link with those who had once used the stones for motive power? How long had Eet been a seed, or stone, or that thing Valcyr had swallowed?

Even as I speculated I was unbuckling, preparing to leave my seat. I had learned my confidence well; if Eet

169

thought there was a chance the ring might save us, I was willing to try it.

"What will you do?" Hory asked sharply.

Eeet answered. "Try to augment your power, Patrolman. We are not sure, we can only try."

It was thoughtful of him to say "we," since, as always, I was merely the one to carry out plans hatched in that narrow head of his.

We descended the ladder to the lowest level and made our way to the reactor room. Eet made the same questing movements of nose and head as he had used to steer us through the forest. Then with a quick stretch of his neck, he pointed his nose at a sealed box.

"There, but you must make it fast. Use a weld torch—"

With the air of one humoring madmen, Hory opened a small compartment on the wall and took out the tool Eet had asked for. I brought out the ring slowly. In spite of Eet's suggestion that we needed its aid, I could not be sure of that. And I had the greatest reluctance to release it to Hory. I had come to trust no one in relation to the stone, which had already left a trail of blood, and blood belonging to those who meant the most to me, across several solar systems.

For a moment I thought Eet was wrong. The stone displayed no signs of life; it was as dead as it had been the first time I saw it. Very much against my will I laid it on top of the box as Eet had ordered.

Then slowly, almost protestingly, it did show life. It did not blaze as it had in space, or even as it had in the underground room, when it had rested near its fellows, bringing them in turn to a glow. That blaze had been blue-white; this was duller, yellow. Hory stared at it, his astonishment so great that he made no attempt to use the welder.

"Affix it—quick!" Eet cried. His whip of tail lashed back and forth on my back as if he would so beat me to the task. I reached for the welder, but Hory roused and touched its tip to the ring metal against the box, joining them firmly.

"Look—" But Eet was not to finish that warning. Hory

struck out with a follow through of the weld rod. By the good grace of whatever power might rule space, the lighted end of that improvised weapon did not hit Eet. But the rod swept him from my shoulder and hurled him to the floor with such force that he lay limp and unmoving.

I was so astounded by the attack that I wasted a precious moment in sheer amazement. When I started for Hory that rod swept up again so that the glowing point menaced my eyes. There was such determination to be read on his face I did not doubt he meant to use it were I to jump him.

So I retreated as he advanced, unable to reach for Eet, for Hory thrust at me when I attempted that. Since the compartment in which we stood was small, my back was swiftly at the wall.

"Why?" I asked. He had me spread there, my hands at shoulder height, palms empty and out, the glowing point of the rod weaving a pattern of threat directly before my eyes.

Hory, the rod in one hand, searched in the front of his tunic. What he produced was a more refined example of the tangler the Guild men had used on him. It flicked out from the tube, not to weave my whole body into a helpless cocoon, but to loop about my wrists, bringing them tightly together.

"Why?" he echoed. "Because I now know who you are. You gave yourself away, or that beast of yours did, when he had you bring out the ring. What happened back there? Could you not agree on the Guild's terms? We have been tracing you for months, Murdoc Jern."

"Why? I am no Guildman—"

"Then you are playing a lone hand, which is enough to label you fool. Or do you reckon your beast high enough to support you? You are rather useless without him, are you not?" Hory kicked out and Eet rolled over. I tried desperately to reach him through mind touch, but met nothing. Once before I had believed him dead; now the evidence of my eyes assured me that was true.

"You accuse me of playing some game." I strove to

171

control my rage; anger can betray a man into foolish error. Perhaps I had not learned the proper submergence of emotions my father had believed necessary to make the superior man, but I had had excellent tutoring and put that to the test now. "What do you mean?"

"You are Murdoc Jern and your father was a notorious Guildman." Hory used the blazing rod as if I were a child and he were an instructor about to indicate some pertinent point on a wall projection from a reading tape. "If you are not a full member of the Guild, you have access to his connections. Your father was killed for information he had, probably about"—with the rod Hory indicated the ring—"that. You were on Angkor when it happened. Then you shipped out, having broken with your family. You were on Tanth when your master Vondar Ustle was killed under circumstances which suggest his death had been arranged. What caused that Jern? Did he discover what you were carrying and plan to inform the authorities? Whatever happened, matters did not go as you expected, did they? You did not walk out free with your master's private gem stock to back you. But you did get off world—

"The ship you lifted in is suspect as a part-time Guild transport. They dropped you here, didn't they? And later you fell out with your bosses. You ought to have known you could not stand up to the Guild. Or did you believe that with that beast of yours you could do it? We will get the truth out of you with a reader-helm—"

"When and if you get me to a Patrol base!"

"Oh I think that now there will be no chance of your escaping. You, yourself, obligingly arranged that. But I am forgetting, you are not shipwise, are you? You do not have the 'feel.' We have broken free of the traction and are back on course. Now—" Still facing me with the ready rod, Hory stooped and picked up Eet, a long string of furred body, by the hind legs. "This goes into cold storage. The lab will want to see it. And you shall go into another kind of storage, until you are needed."

He drove me with his heated rod out of the engine compartment, toward the ladder which led to the upper levels. I backed slowly, trying to see any small chance which might work for me. But even though I might be reckless enough to charge him, he need only with pressure of one finger bring that rod to top heat and lay it across my face to discipline me into obedience.

Eet swung, a pitiful pendulum, from Hory's hand. I looked at his body and my hate was no longer hot but cold, clear and deadly in me. And because I did look at Eet at that moment I saw my chance. For Eet came to life, twisting up and around to bury needle-sharp teeth in the hand which held him. And as Hory yelled in pain and surprise I charged.

FIFTEEN

Though I could not use my hands (and I would have used them to some purpose, for my father had had me carefully tutored in those forms of unarmed combat which are useful for a space rover), I did use my head and body as a battering ram, striking Hory hard just below his chest, driving him back against the wall. His breath went out of him in a great gasp. But I could not follow up the small advantage as I wanted; I could only strain to hold him helpless with my weight against his body. And it was a stalemate to which I could see no profitable conclusion.

Eet had played a leading role in the initiation of this fight, but I did not expect any more from him. However, he was not to be counted out, as I discovered. His slim body flew through the air, to land on Hory's bent head, his whip tail lashing my cheek as he passed. He dug in his claws, and caught the Patrolman by the ears as he had me when he steered us away from the cliffs.

Hory screamed and tried to raise his hands to his head, while I wriggled the closer to keep him down and give Eet his chance to win a small victory. Then, regaining some detachment, I backed away, only to charge again, the full force of my shoulder aiming at the base of Hory's throat. Had I been able to deliver that blow as intended, he might have died.

As it was, he made a crowing noise, and when I stood away, he tried to bring his hands up to his throat. But his knees folded under him and he bowed slowly forward. In fact he might have slipped along the ladder and fallen had I not taken his weight, bracing myself, against my thighs.

Eet loosed his hold, leaving bleeding gashes behind, and whipped down Hory's body, using his paws to tear open the Patrolman's tunic and bring forth the tangler. As if he had used one many times before, he turned it on its owner. And in moments Hory was again as neatly packaged as he had been back in the tunnel.

The mutant panted heavily as he drew back on his haunches, holding the tangler between his hand-paws, his attention on the Patrolman. Hory gasped for breath, a dark tinge still in his face. I wondered if my blow had broken some bone, and if I had done worse damage than I had first thought. In spite of the fate he had meant to deal to Eet, and his plans for me, when I had time to think without the heat of rage blinding me, I did not want to kill him. I have killed to defend myself, as I did on Tanth, but never willingly—few men do. And to kill with one's hands is also another matter. Hory was following orders, with, as he believed, law behind him—though sometimes right and law are not one and the same thing. I respect the Patrol and have a healthy fear of them. But that does not mean I tamely submit to a decree which may not fit with justice. On the frontiers, of necessity, the law must be more flexible than it is on long-settled worlds. And it seemed to me, from what Hory had said, that I had been summarily judged and sentenced without a chance to defend myself.

"Your hands—" Eet had frisked up the ladder and was now at my shoulder level.

I held out my bound wrists and his sharp teeth made short work of clipping through those strands. Freed, I knelt and settled Hory back against the wall, pressing in and out on his rib carriage until he was breathing less painfully and the dark shade had faded from his face.

"You—can—not— Our—course—is locked—" he half whispered. "Take us—to—base."

His satisfaction at that was plain to read. And perhaps he was right. If a course tape had been locked in the auto-pilot, there was nothing we could do to alter it, and our freedom would last just as long as it took us to reach our destination. It would seem that Hory, bound and in our power as he was, still held the victory.

He smiled, perhaps guessing from some change in my expression that I knew that. After all, I was no pilot, and if there was any way of confuting a course tape, I did not know it. Nor, I was sure, did Eet. -

"Bring him—" Eet indicated Hory and the ladder.

"I cannot help you," Hory said. "Once the tape is locked in—that is that."

"So?" Eet swung his head, keeping his eyes on a level with Hory's as I boosted the Patrolman to his feet. "We shall see."

The mutant's confidence did not appear to ruffle Hory. However, he did not fight me as I urged him up the ladder. He could have made it nearly impossible to climb; instead, he seemed to do so willingly enough, allowing me to steady him where he could not use his hands. The lesser gravity in the ship was an aid and I made the most of that.

I think Hory was prepared to savor our dismay when we discovered how right he was and that we could do nothing to halt or change the flight of the ship.

To me the control board meant nothing. But Eet sped across the cabin, leaped to Hory's seat, and from that to the edge of the panel, his head flicking from right to left and back again as if he were searching. Whatever he sought he did not find. Instead he drew back again to the seat, hunching up, his neck pulled in to his body, his eyes staring. His mind was tightly closed, but I knew he was thinking.

Hory laughed. "Your superbeast is baffled, Jern. I told you—make your submission and—"

"Trust the Patrol?" I asked. Perhaps I had come to depend too much on the near-miracles which Eet had achieved. It certainly looked as if Hory was right and we were his prisoners, instead of the situation being reversed.

"Full cooperation will mitigate your sentence," he returned.

"I have not been tried, *or* sentenced, yet," I parried. "And your charges, or those you stated, are very vague. I inherited the ring from my father. I defended myself from a quite unpleasant death on Tanth, and I paid my own passage off that misformed planet. You yourself saw that I was *not* cooperating with the Guild back there. So—of just what am I guilty? It seems to me that I have in fact been cooperating with the Patrol, in your person, right along—seeing as how Eet got us away from that tunnel and my ring broke the traction beam—"

Hory still smiled and there was nothing friendly in that stretching of lips. "When you were on Tanth, Jern, did you ever hear the folk-saying they have—'He who does a demon a service is thereby a demon's servant'? What you have in that ring, if it is what rumor claims it to be, is not for the owning of any one man. We have our orders to destroy it and its owner—if that seems necessary."

"So going beyond the law?"

"There are times when the law must be broken if the race or species is to survive—"

"Now that," Eet's voice rang in our heads, "is a dangerous concept. Either the law exists, or it does not. Murdoc believes that on some occasions the law can be bent, or bypassed for the protection of what seems to be right. And you, Hory, who are pledged to the upholding of the strict letter of the law, now say that it can be broken because of expediency. It would seem that the laws of your species are not held in high respect."

"What do you—" Hory turned on Eet a blast of hate which even I could feel. I moved quickly between him and the furred body now in the pilot's seat.

"What do I, an animal, know about the affairs of humans?" Eet finished for him. "Only what I learn from your thoughts. You do not want to deem me more than 'beast,' do you, Hory? Now I wonder what there is within you that holds you to that point of view, even though you know it is wrong. Or is it all a part of not wishing to admit that you can be wrong in other ways also? You seem to put"—Eet paused to survey the Patrolman closely —"an extraordinary valuation of your own actions."

177

Hory's face flushed; his lips were tight-set. I wished at that moment I could read his thoughts as well as Eet did. If Eet found them threatening, he did not comment on that, but now struck off on another track.

"If *my* species is to survive, and *I* think that a necessary thing, steps must be taken here and now. You are probably right, Hory, in believing that this ship cannot be turned from its present course. But are you so sure that that cannot be reversed?"

I saw the startled expression on Hory's face. His mind must have been easy for Eet to read.

"Thank you." Satisfaction was plain in Eet's reply. "So that is the way of it!" He leaped again to the edge of the control board and flexed his hand-paws over its surface as one might do preparatory to making some delicate and demanding adjustments on a complicated piece of machinery.

"No!" Hory lunged for him, but he came up against me and did not reach the board. I struck once with the edge of my hand, one of the tricks of personal combat which I had been taught. He went down and out an instant after the blow landed.

I dragged him to the passenger's seat, heaved him up, and buckled him in. Then I turned back to Eet, who was still studying the board, his head darting from side to side, his paws above but not yet touching any of the buttons or levers.

"A pretty problem," he observed. "The result will be complicated by the booster power of the stone. It can be reversed, yes. I read that in his mind when I startled him by such a suggestion. Such a shock will often uncover necessary information. But at our present speed, we shall probably not land near where we took off."

"And what can we gain by returning? Oh," I said, answering my own question, "we cannot alter course until we land again. But I am no pilot. I cannot lift this ship off planet even if we are able to set a second course."

"A fact to consider later, when the time comes to put it to test," was Eet's comment. "But have you any wish

178

to continue this present voyage under the circumstances?"

"What about the Guild ship? It could be on our trail again if we return—"

"Consider the facts—will they be expecting our return? I do not believe that anyone, even someone as shrewd as Captain Nactitl, might foresee that. And if we can set down some distance from their camp, we shall win time. Time is the weapon we need most."

Eet was right, as he always was: I did not want to finish out the voyage on Hory's tape. Even if I were not already under charges, taking over this ship would place me so deeply in the ill graces of the Patrol that I could have small defense.

"Thus and thus and thus—" Having completed his study of the board, Eet made his choices with lightning rapidity. And I was not shipwise enough to know if he had chosen successfully. I watched lights change, fade, others take their places, and hoped fervently that Eet knew what he was doing.

"Now what?" I asked as he scrambled from the edge of the board back into the pilot's seat.

"Since we have only waiting left, I would suggest food—drink—"

He was so right. Now that he mentioned it, the E-ration I had consumed in the tunnel was long behind me and I had nothing but an aching and empty void for a middle. I inspected Hory's lashings. He was still unconscious, but his breathing was regular. Then I went below, accompanied by Eet, who could take the ladder with far more speed than I could. We found a small galley with—to me—a luxurious supply of rations, and had a feast. At that moment it was equal to a Llalation banquet and I savored every mouthful with relish.

Eet shared my food, even if it were not the end product of a hunt. It was when we were both full that I turned again to consider the future.

"I cannot pilot us off world," I said again. "We may be planet-bound on a world which certainly would not be my choice to colonize. If the Guild ship follows us in,

179

they will be able to mark our landing and will be after us. And I do not know enough about this ship to use its weapons. Though I suppose, if it is a matter of *his* destruction, we could trust Hory enough to man the defenses, whatever they may be."

"Especially, you are thinking, since I can keep reading his mind and will be alert for the moment when he may try to turn those same weapons against us." Eet carefully washed each finger with a dark-red tongue, holding it well out from its fellows to be lapped around. "They will *not* be expecting us. As for getting off world again, that will come in due time. Do not seek out shadows in the future; you will discover oftentimes that the sun of tomorrow will dispatch them. I would suggest sleep now. That eases the body, rests the brain, and one awakes better prepared to face the inevitable."

He jumped from the swing table and pattered to the door.

"This way—to a bunk—" Pointing with his nose, he indicated a door directly across the level landing. "Do not worry—there is an alarm which will rouse you when we do enter atmosphere once more."

I pushed the door aside. There was a bunk and I threw myself on it, suddenly as tired as I had been hungry. I felt Eet leap to my side and curl up with his head on my shoulder. But his mind was sealed and his eyes closed. There was nothing to do but yield to the demands of my overtired body and follow him into slumber.

I was jerked out of that blissful state by a strident buzzing far too close to my ear. When I looked blearily around I saw Eet sitting up, combing his whiskers between his fingers.

"Re-entry alarm," he informed me.

"Are you sure?" I sat up on the bunk and ran my hands through my hair, but not with the neat results of Eet's personal grooming. It had been far too long since I had had a change of clothing, a bath, a chance to feel really clean. On my hands and body, the pink patches of new skin were fading. It should not be long before my piebald state was past and I would bear none of the stigma of the disease which had taken me from the *Vestris.*

"Back where we started from, yes." Eet did sound sure, though I could not share his complete confidence, and would not until I was able to look outside.

"Might as well strap down right here," he continued.

"But the ship—"

"Is on full automatic. And what could you do if it were not?"

Eet was right, but I would have felt less shaky had Hory been riding in the pilot's seat. It is very true that the autopilots have been refined and refined until they probably are more reliable than humans. But there is always the unusual emergency when a human reflex may save what a machine cannot. And, though the engines of a space ship practically run themselves, no ship ever lifts without pilot, engineer, and those other crewmen whose duties in the past once kept their hands ever hovering over controls.

"You fear your machines, do you not?" As I buckled down on the bunk Eet stretched out beside me. He seemed prepared to carry on a conversation at a time when I was in no mood for light talk.

"Why, I suppose some of us do. I am no techneer. Machines are mysteries as far as I am concerned." Too much of a mystery. I wished I had had some instruction in spacing.

But my thoughts and Eet's answer, if he made one, were blanked out in the discomfort of orbiting before planet-fall. And I found that to be twice as great as what I had experienced before. My estimation of Hory arose. If he had constantly to take this sort of thing he was indeed tough. My last stab of fear concerned our actual touch-down. What if the automatic controls did not pick a suitable spot on which to fin in and we were swallowed up in some lake, or tipped over at set-down. Not that there was one thing I could do to prevent either that or any other catastrophe which might arise.

Then I opened my eyes, with the thumping pain of a

sun-sized headache behind them, felt the grip of planet-side gravity, and knew that we had made it. Since the floor of the cabin appeared to be level, we had had a suitable landing, too.

Eet crawled out from beneath the strap which had gone across my chest and his body. His quick recovery from the strains which always held me in thrall was irritating. I had thought him dead after that violent blow he had taken from the rod. But from the time he had turned to bite the hand which held him, he had shown no sign of nursing even a bruise.

"—see where we are—" He was already going out the cabin door. And in the silent ship I could hear the scraping of his claws as he climbed the ladder. I followed at a far more moderate pace, stopping on the way to pick up a tube of restorative from the rack in the gallery. Hory would need that and we would need him —at least until we learned more about where we were and what might be ahead of us.

The Patrolman's eyes were open, fixed on Eet in a stare which suggested he did not in the least want to see the mutant. And Eet was in Hory's lawful place, the pilot's seat. For the first time since I had known him, my companion appeared truly baffled.

As always the control board was rigged with an outside visa-screen. But the button which activated that was now well above Eet's reach, meant to be close to the hand of a human pilot reclining in that swing chair.

Eet had scrambled up as high as he could climb, his neck stretched to an amazing length. But his nose was still not within touching distance of that button. I crossed over to push it.

The screen produced a picture. We seemed to be facing a cliff—and it was too close to have reassured me had I seen it before we landed. Insofar as I could compare it in memory, it was of the same yellow-gray shade as that which had been tunneled by the long-ago miners. But this had no breaks in its surface.

For the first time Hory spoke. "Put on the sweep— that lever there." Bound as he was, he had to indicate with his chin, using it as a pointer. I dutifully pressed that second button.

The cliff face now appeared to travel past us at a slow rate. Then we saw what must lie to the left, open sky with only the tops of greenery showing.

"Depress," ordered Hory almost savagely. "Depress the lever. We want ground level."

There was almost a sensation of falling as our field of vision descended rapidly. The tops of the growth became visible as the crowns of large bushes. There was the usual smoke and fumes left by the deter rockets, a strip of seared ground between the ship and that shriveled wall of green. Nowhere did I see the giant trees which had caught the LB in for the forest.

Neither were there any ruins, nor the wreckage of the ancient ship, nor, what I had dreaded the most, the spire of the Guild vessel. As the visa-screen continued to reveal the land about us, it looked very much as if we were in a wilderness. And how far we were from the mining camp was anyone's guess.

"Not too far." Eet climbed up on the webbing to watch the sweep across the countryside. "There are ways of locating a ship, especially on a planet where there is no interference in the way of ordinary electronic broadcasting. He has already thought of that—" The mutant indicated Hory.

I turned to the Patrolman. "What about it? We are back on that planet, I know this vegetation. Can you discover the Guild ship or camp for us?"

"Why should I?" He was not struggling against his bonds, but lying at his ease, as if action was no concern of his. "Why should I put myself into your friends' hands? You have a problem now, have you not, Jern? Take off on the tape set in the autopilot and you will reach my base. Stay here—and sooner or later your friends will come. Then you had better try to make a deal. Perhaps you can use me as a bargaining point."

"You have given me little reason to want to do anything else," I retorted. "But those are not my friends, and I am not about to make any bargain with them."

Almost I was tempted to let him believe that his supposition was the truth. But why play murky games when I might well need his cooperation in the future? The ship would take off on a tape, without the need for a human pilot. But whether he had a supply of such tapes on board, whether I could affix and use another, whether I could be sure my choice would not merely take me to another Patrol post, that I must find out. And time to learn might be running out—they might already be tracing us.

I—we—needed Hory, yet we must not make too much of that need lest he play upon it. So I had to convince him that we must cooperate, if only for a short period of truce.

"Do you know what they hunt back there?" I tried a different track.

"It is easy enough to guess. They try to find where those stones were mined."

"Which—" I said slowly, "Eet has discovered, though they have not."

I feared some denial from Eet, but he made no attempt at communication. The mutant was still watching the screen as if the picture on it was the most important thing in the world. I was feeling my way, but it heartened me a little that he had not promptly protested my assertion concerning his knowledge.

"Where is it then—?"

Hory must have known I would not answer that. The screen now showed a wider break in the growth. Beyond the ground our descent had scorched was a slope of yellow sand, of so bright and sharp a color as I had not seen elsewhere on this dusky world. That provided a beach for a lake. The water here was not slime-ringed, murky, and suggestive of evil below its surface; it had not been born of any dying flood. This was as brightly green as the sand was yellow, so vividly colored both they might have been gems set in dingy metal.

"It is the nature of these stones"—I made a lecture of my explanation, supplying nuggets of truth in a vast muffling of words—"that they seek their own kind. One

184

can actually draw you to another. *If* you will yield to the pull of the one you have. Eet took the ring just before the Guild ship landed. We had been following such a pull, and he continued to follow it. He found the source of the attraction—"

Eet gave no sign he heard my words. He was still watching the screen in complete absorption. Suddenly he made one of the few vocal sounds I had ever heard from him. His lips parted to show his teeth, cruelly sharp, and he was hissing. Startled, I looked at the view on the visa-plate.

SIXTEEN

The viewer swept on. What we now saw must be on the other side of the ship. And if the rest of the landscape had been free of any signs that intelligence had ever been there, that was now changed.

An arm of the lake made a narrow inlet. Set in the middle of that was a platform of stone blocks. It was ringed by a low parapet, on which stood stone pillars in the form of heads. Each differed from its fellows so much as to suggest that if they did not resemble imagined gods, they had been fashioned to portray very unlike species. But the oddest thing was not their general appearance, but that from those set at the four corners there curled trails of greenish smoke, almost the shade of the water washing below. It would seem that those heads were hollow and housed fires.

Yet, save for that smoke, there was no sign of any life on the stone surface of the platform. We could see most of it, and unless someone crawled belly-flat below that low parapet, the place was deserted. Eet continued to hiss, his back fur rising in a ridge from nape to root of tail.

I studied those heads, trying to discover in any one of them some small resemblance to something I had seen before on any of the worlds I had visited. And, in the fourth from the nearest smoking one, I thought that I did.

"Deenal!" I must have spoken that word aloud as I recalled the museum on Iona where Vondar had been invited to a private showing of a treasure from remote space. There had been a massive armlet, too large to fit any human arm, and it had borne such a face in high relief. Old, from one of the prehuman space civilizations, named for a legend retold by the Zacathans—that was Deenal. And about it we knew very little indeed.

Yet that was the only one—I counted the heads—out of twelve that I had any clue to. And each undoubtedly represented a different race. Was this a monument to some long-vanished confederation or empire in which many species and races had been united?

We have nonhuman (as we reckon "human") allies and partners, too. There are the reptilian Zacathans, the avian-evolved Trystians, the strange Wyverns, others—a score of them. One or two are deadly strangers with whom our kind has only wary contact. And among those aliens who are seemingly humanoid, there are many divisions and mutations. A man in a lifetime of roving may not even see or hear of them all.

But Eet's reaction to this place was so astounding (his hissing signs of hostility continued), that I asked:

"What is it? That smoke—is there someone there?"

Eet voiced a last hiss. Then he shook his head, almost as if he were coming out of a state of deep preoccupation.

"Storrff—"

It was no sound, nor any word I recognized. Then he corrected himself hurriedly, as if afraid he might have been revealing too much in shock.

"It does not matter. This is an old dead place, of no value—" He could have been reassuring himself more than us.

"The smoke." I brought him back to the important point.

"The sniffers—they take what they do not understand to make of it a new god cult." He appeared sure of that. "They must have fled when we landed."

"Storrff—" Hory voiced that word which Eet had planted in our minds. "Who or what is Storrff?"

But Eet had himself under complete control. "Nothing which has mattered for some thousands of your planet years. This is a place long dead and forgotten."

But not to you, I thought. Since he did not answer

that, I knew it was another of those subjects which he refused to discuss. And the mystery of Eet deepened by a fraction more. Whether the Storrff were represented by one of those heads, or whether this place itself was Storrff, he was not going to explain. But I knew that he recognized it or some part of it, and not pleasantly.

Already the screen was sliding past, returning to our first view of the cliff wall. Eet climbed down the webbing.

"The ring—" He was making for the ladder.

"Why?"

But it seemed that was another subject on which he was not going to be too informative. I turned back to Hory with the restorative. I broke off its cap and held it to his mouth while he sucked deeply at its contents. Must we keep him prisoner? Perhaps for the time being. When he had finished I left him tied in the seat to follow Eet.

The ring was no longer affixed to the top of the box. There was a spot of raw metal where it had been. Eet stood at the wall on the other side of the cabin, his forefeet braced against that surface, staring up at a spot too far above his head for him to reach.

There clung the ring as tightly as if welded. But it was not a cementing of the band which held it so. Instead the stone was tight to the metal. And when I tried to loosen it, I had to exert all my strength to pull it free of the surface. All the while it blazed.

"That platform in the inlet—" I spoke my thought aloud.

"Just so." Eet climbed up me. "And let us now see where and why."

I stopped by the arms rack inside the hatch, the ring, in my palm, jerking my left arm across my body at a painful angle. A laser in my hand would give me more confidence than I had felt earlier.

The ramp cranked out and down and we exited into bright sunlight, my hand pulled away from me. The charred ground was hot under my lightly-covered feet, so that I leaped across it. At the foot of the cliff I turned toward the inlet, allowing the ring to pull me.

"Not a cliff mine." I still wondered about that.

"The stone is not from this world." Eet was positive. "But—there is that out there"—he indicated the platform—"which has more draw than the cache in the ruins. Look at the ring!"

Even in the sunlight its fire blazed. And the heat from it was enough to burn my hand, growing ever more uncomfortable, though I dared not loose my hold on it lest it indeed fly through the air, not to be found again.

I plowed through sand which engulfed my feet above the ankles. It was a thin, powdery stuff into which I sank in a way I did not like. Then I came to the water's edge. In spite of its brilliant color, it was not transparent, but opaque, and I had no idea of its depth. The ring actually jerked me forward and I had to fight against wading in. Nor could I see any way of climbing up to the platform, since it would be well above the head of one in the water and there was no break in its wall.

Had I followed the pull instead of fighting it until I wavered back and forth on the bank, I might have fallen straight into one of the traps of this planet. Only the trap became impatient and reached for me. The emerald surface broke in a great shower of water, and a head which was three-quarters mouth gaped in a hideous display of fangs and avid hunger.

I thumbed the laser as I stumbled back into the thick sand. The beam shot straight into that exposed maw, and the creature turned and twisted frenziedly though it uttered no cry. It was armored in thick scales and, I believed, by chance alone, I had struck its most vulnerable point. Around it the water was beaten into green froth by its struggles and it was still writhing as it sank. Then it arose partly to the surface, drifting from between me and the platform.

Moments later the body began to jerk from side to side and I caught dim glimpses of things which tore at it, devouring the eater in turn. But I was duly warned against trying to cross that strip of inlet, narrow as it was.

"The sniffers—" I remembered Eet's report. "If they use this as a temple, how do they reach it?" Of course they could be immune to the water lurkers, but that I did not accept too readily.

"We have not seen the other side," Eet returned. "We might do well to explore in that direction."

The pull of the ring was a force against which I had continually to fight as I walked along the beach, first paralleling the platform and then away from it. When we reached the end of the water and I could see the other side, Eet was proven right as he had been so many times before.

Lying on the sand was a collection of saplings and poles, tied and woven together with twisted ropes. Properly moved into place, it could span between beach and platform, though it would then be at a sharp slope.

The ring pulled me on, and it seemed to me that its tug was stronger, as if it grew impatient, redoubling its demand on me. I found myself running, or trying to run, through the sand, though it was hard to keep my feet, my left hand, holding the ring so tightly my fingers cramped, straight out, across my body, pointing to the platform.

When I reached the bridge I was caught in a dilemma. To let go of the ring, to holster the laser, both actions might mean disaster. Yet I was not sure I could shift the bridge without using both hands and all my strength. The wood lengths from which it had been made were bleached white and might be lighter than they looked—but—

Carefully, fighting until I was sweating as if I had been in another brawl with Hory, I forced the ring back to my chest, unsealed a slip of the coverall, and clapped the band inside. Within my clothing it pushed out the fabric, but that was tough and would hold.

The laser went into my belt, and I hurried to deal with the bridge. It was unwieldy, but my hopes that it was light were realized. I got it up and swung it around, so that the other end dropped on the top of the wall. And I had no sooner done that than the seal on the breast of my coverall burst open. Not the fabric, but the fastener had yielded to the struggling of the ring.

My grab missed the band. With the stone flashing in triumph, it flew out toward the platform. Now I must follow.

I made that trip on my hands and knees, Eet running as a dark streak ahead. And I felt particularly vulnerable as I climbed. For the span swung alarmingly under my weight and I thought that at any moment it would slide from its hold on the upper wall and hurl me into the water.

There was also the possibility that the sniffers might return. And I had no wish to conduct a running battle up or down this very precarious passage. But at last I was able to put out a hand and rest it on solid and unyielding stone, pull myself to the dubious safety of the wall, and then jump to the platform.

The smoke from the nearest head trailed about me, and I sneezed at its odor. Then I thought, for a second or two, that there was a fifth fire lit in the center of the platform, though this did not smoke. Eet was warily circling that blaze—which was no fire after all, but the stone, in such furious display of energy as I had never seen.

"Keep off!" Eet's warning stopped me. "It is too hot to handle. It is trying to reach what calls it so strongly. And it will either destroy itself now, or reach that which it seeks. But it is beyond our control."

I knelt to see the better. Beyond our control? It had always been that. We had set it to our service in the ship, but how easily it had broken free. And all other times we—or I—had obeyed it and not it me.

Eet was right. The warmth that came from it was now a seething furnace heat. There was a raw radiance which hurt my eyes, a thrust of heat that drove me back and back, until I crouched against the wall beneath one of the smoking heads.

The mutant was probably right in believing that this unendurable burst of energy fought to destroy the stone,

191

burn it to one of those cinders. But if it sought death, it was going in a blaze of glory.

I had to shield not only my eyes but my face against the fury. Eet was not with me. I hoped he was safe on the other side of that inferno.

"Just so," he let me know. "It is still trying to cut through."

I did not try to witness the struggle. The bursting light would have blinded me. Even though I shut my eyes, held my hands tightly across them, and turned my face to the wall, I could feel the effects of the holocaust. Could I bear it much longer? If the heat increased I might be seriously burned, or forced into the lake. Between one fate and the other there was little choice. Then—that lashing heat was gone! The stone had died—

Pushing around, I got to my feet. I did not take my hands from my face and open my eyes until I stood upright. Then I looked away, dreading to face what must lie in front of me.

When I did, I fully expected to see a charred cinder. But what was there was an opening in the platform, a perfect square, as if some door had been burned away. And the light from below was not exactly faded, but was pulsating in a less strident and eye-destroying way.

Eet had already reached the hole. I saw his head shoot out and down as he stretched his neck to its greatest extent to view what lay there. But I went more cautiously, testing each block I stepped upon. That hole bore a likeness to a trap door and I had no wish to be caught in such.

The surface seemed solid enough, and with a couple of hesitant strides I joined my companion to look into the interior. The glowing stone lay on a coffer such as the one we had seen in the derelict ship. But the stones in this were very much alive, more so even than those in the cache of the ruins. And their light, coming through a slit, gave us an excellent view of the vault.

It would seem that the platform was only the outer shell of a room, perhaps a storeroom like that of the ruins. There were many boxes in orderly piles along its walls, and none of them had been affected by time. All were tightly sealed, showing not even hair-thin marks of an opening.

Only after I had studied them for a long moment did their general size and shape make me uneasy. There was something about them—long, narrow, not too deep. What was it—?

"Can you not see?" asked Eet. "These did not give their dead to the fire; they hid them away in boxes, as if they could lock them from the earth and the changes of time!" His contempt was cold.

"But those stones—if this is a tomb, why leave the stones here?"

"Do not many races bury treasures with their dead, that those no longer with them may carry into the Final Dark what they esteemed most in the days of their strength?"

"Primitive peoples, yes," I conceded. But that a race which had achieved space flight would do so—no. And now I noted something else. While many of those boxes did bear too close a resemblence to coffins to dismiss Eet's explanation as fantasy, there were others of different dimensions.

Eet interrupted my thoughts. "Look about you!" His head shot up and turned from side to side, the nose pointing at those rows of heads. "Different species, perhaps different shapes for bodies. This was a composite tomb, made to hold more than one people—"

"Yet all following a single burial ceremony?" I countered. For even among the same species there are different modes of paying honor and bidding farewell to the dead. And to find one vault holding so many burials, seemingly united—

"It might be so," Eet answered. "Let us assume that a composite garrison, even a single ship's company, were marooned here. That there was no chance for their eventual return home. Yet, they would hope that in the future there might come those to seek out their final resting place."

My mind took an imaginative leap. "And the stones

were then left as payment for their return to their proper worlds, or for the type of funeral they desired?"

"Just so. Those would do as burial fees."

How long had they waited? Did the worlds which had given them birth still exist? Or did these planets now lie barren under dying suns half the galaxy away? Why had the builders of this place remained here? Had their empire broken apart in some vast and sudden war? Had the relief ships never come? Had the ship fallen at the ruins been their last hope, destroyed before their eyes in some mechanical or natural catastrophe? And the derelict we had found drifting—had that been a relief ship they had awaited? When it did not arrive had they surrendered to the fact of no escape and built this vault to tell their story to the future?

I glanced from wall to wall of that tomb. There was no message left there for our reading. Then I looked once more at the heads of the parapet. These, seen close up, were eroded to some extent, but they had not been as badly aged as the ruins by the cliff. Were they the actual portraits of those resting below, or did they only represent types of races?

Six were definitely nonhuman. Of those, one, I believed, was insectile, at least two vaguely reptilian, one batrachian. The rest were humanoid enough to pass as kin to my own species. Two were as manlike as the space rovers of my own day. There were twelve of them—but what had brought such a mixture to this planet?

I turned to Eet. "This *must* be the source of the stones—and these came to mine them."

"Leaving the galleries picked so clean? That ring did not lead to them. I do not believe that could be true. This may have been a way station for such a shipment. Or it may have had a purpose we cannot conceive of now. But—the fact remains that we do have here a cache of live stones. Enough, as that Patrolman would point out, probably to disrupt the economy of any government. The man or men who take that box and are able to hold it will rule space—for as long as they can keep the stones."

I came back to the vault opening. "The light—it is

194

beginning to die. Perhaps the stones are also—" It was decidedly less light in the crypt.

Eet crossed the platform in a couple of his bounds, leaping now to the parapet. Only for a second did he so face the ship, his whole stance suggesting he was alert to what I could neither see nor hear. Then he was back at the same speed.

"Down!" He dashed against me, his impetus striking me almost waist-high. "Down!"

I did drop, my feet going over the edge of the opening. Then I swung by my hands and landed with a jar on the floor, scraping against the side of the box which held the stones. Though the light they emitted was now no more than a small and flickering fire, it was enough to show me safe footing.

I glanced up just in time to see a spear of light flash across the opening, hardly above the level of the parapet. Laser—but not a hand one! That was from the barrel of a cutter, and it must have been fired from the ship!

Eet climbed a pile of those boxes. He was crouched now well away from the hole, yet near the wall facing the ship, his head laid to the stone blocks as if through them he could still hear something.

I put my hand on the ring. There was warmth in it, and a gleam to the stone, but as far as I could see, it no longer threatened any would-be wearer. And, to my surprise, it did not adhere to the box, but came away easily. For safekeeping I put it into the front of my coverall, making sure the seam was tightly sealed.

Again I looked to Eet. The glow was further reduced, but not entirely gone. I could see him well enough.

"Hory?" I asked.

"Just so. It would seem he had resources we did not know about. Somehow he loosed himself. He has now tried to kill us and failed, so he will search for another and more effective form of attack."

"Go off world—bring in the Patrol?"

"Not yet. We have hurt his pride sorely by what we have done to him. There was more to his being here, I believe, than we—or I—first read in his mind. He may have had an inner shield. Also, he believes if we are left here we shall of necessity join forces with the Guild and perhaps be beyond reach before he can return. No, he wants the ring—and our deaths—before he goes."

"Well, we may not be dead—but how will we get out of here?" To try to climb again to the platform would expose us to Hory's beam. He need only wait; time was now on his side.

"Not altogether," Eet informed me. "If the Guild left men here, and we can safely conclude that they did, they will have monitored our planeting. And they will send to see who landed. Remember, they picked up Hory the first time. Almost too easily. Now I wonder why."

I brushed aside Eet's speculations about the past. "We may be half a continent away from their camp."

"But they must have some form of small aircraft. It would be necessary for their explorations. Yes, they will come—and I do not think we are as far from their base as you suggest. The ruins were once part of a settlement of some size. This tomb would not be located too distant from that."

"Always supposing it is a tomb. So we have to sit here and wait for the Guild to come after Hory. But how will we be any better off then?"

"We shall not, if we do so wait," Eet answered calmly.

"Then how do we get out—just by wishing?" I asked. "If we top that hole, he burns me—though you might be able to make it."

Eet still held his listening position against the wall. "Just so. An interesting problem, is it not?"

"*Interesting!*" I curbed my temper. I could think of several things to call the present situation, all of them more forceful than "interesting."

SEVENTEEN

My hand kept returning to the ring beneath my coverall.
It had led us on a wild chase, probably to our deaths—
where we would lie in company. I glanced around the
vault. The light was low, and shadows crept toward
us from the rows of ominous boxes. Behind those was
only the heavy masonry of the walls. Even if we were
able to cut through on the opposite side from the ship so
that Hory might not sight our going, we would still have
the water to cross.

The ring. It had saved me and Eet before, though
perhaps that was only incidental to its seeking for its
kind. Could it do anything to get us out of here? Hory
wanted it—wanted it badly—

I glanced at Eet, who was now a barely discernible
blot against the wall.

"Could you reach Hory's mind from this distance?"

"If there was a reason—I think so. His has—at least
on the surface—a relatively simple pattern—like yours."

"How much influence could you bring to bear on him
under contact?"

"Very little. Such a tie needs cooperation to be successful. The Patrolman does not trust me, nor would he open
his mind to me now. It would be necessary to break
down active resistance. I could not hold him in any
thrall."

"But—you could me?" I did not know just what I
fished for. I was one feeling his way through the dark
by touch alone. If I chose rightly it meant life; if I
failed—well—we might not be worse off than at present.

"If you surrendered your full will. But that is not in

197

you. There is a stubborn core in your species which would resist any take-over. Whether you wished to co-operate or not, I would have a struggle on my hands."

"But Hory does not know that. All he knows is that you communicate mentally. He knows, though he will not admit it, that you are not an animal. Suppose he were led to believe that you have been controlling me all along, that I am only hands and feet to serve you. Suppose I acted that part now, got out there saying you were dead, I was free and wanted nothing more than to get back with him—bringing the ring?"

"And just how are you going to make that clear to him?" Eet inquired. He left the wall, flowed over the boxes to hunch before me, his eyes level with mine. "If you emerge on the platform he will burn you instantly."

"Can you die spectacularly in a way he can see?" I countered.

There was amusement rather than any direct answer. "Clutching my throat and flopping about?" he asked after a moment. "But with a laser you cannot perform so. I would be scorched fur and a dead body instantly. However, always supposing we *could* convince Hory I had made my exit permanently—what then?"

"I would emerge, dazed, cowed, ready to be taken prisoner—"

"While I would later come to your rescue? Do you remember that we played somewhat similar roles before? No, I do not believe Hory is so gullible. Do not underestimate him. He may be more than he seems."

"What do you mean?"

"I believe he has a mind shield—that I have read only surface thoughts—perhaps what he was programed to reveal. Did not you yourself once say 'Do not underrate your opponents'? However, your suggestion has some points worth considering. Suppose you were the one to meet his laser beam?"

"But—he hates you. Would he treat with you?"

"Just so—a question. However, there is an implanted feeling in your race that size and superior muscularity count much. Hory hates me as a freak, a thing which

198

belies his superiority. Therefore, he *must* deal with me—for his own emotional satisfaction—not by a flash of fire, but rather by delivering me to his superiors in triumph. So far we have bested him and that rankles. I wish we knew more." Eet hesitated. "He is a puzzle. And he is also intelligent enough to know that time is his enemy. Do you think he has not already figured out a Guild detachment may be on its way here?

"But they could not shake him out of his ship. Only—he needs the ring as a booster to take off. He wants the ring, and he would like me—you are merely incidental."

"Thank you!" But Eet's dissection of the problem was not irritating—it was true. "So I die—"

"As conspicuously as possible. I will then endeavor to take over the noble mind of Hory, promising him the sun, any vagrant moon, and, of course, the stars, all via the help of the ring. I think he will use a stun beam on me—"

"But—"

"Oh, I do not think that weapon will be as effective as he thinks it is. I shall be transported to the ship, doubtless installed in a cage, and Hory will see his way clear to departing."

"Leaving me here? How—"

Again amusement from Eet. "I said I could not control Hory without his assistance. But there is one time when that assistance, unconsciously, may be mine for a short period. When he thinks I am totally in his power, he will then, by our hope, relax his guard. I do not need to advise you that period will be short. I am his shocked and docile prisoner, you are dead. He has full control—"

"And if the stunner really works on you?"

"Do you want to await death here?" Eet countered. "What one can say this or that sore stroke will not fall on his shoulders, aimed by the strong arm of fortune? Do you wish to sit here waiting for the Guild, or perhaps for Hory to switch on whatever heavy armament his ship affords and burn us to the bare rocks, setting even those to bubbling around our roasted ears? What I have learned of your minds suggests I have a good chance for what

I propose to do. Esper powers are not used much and to mechanical devices such as cages there are always keys."

Perhaps my partnership with Eet had made me particularly susceptible to his self-confidence, or perhaps I merely wanted to believe that his plan could work because I could not turn up a better. But I made tacit agreement when I asked:

"And how do I die by laser beam without being crisped in the process? That is a weapon one does not dodge, or survive. And Hory will not be aiming over my head, or any place except where it will do him the most good and me the least!"

It was now twilight in the vault and I could see Eet but not too clearly. If he had a plausible answer I was willing to agree that in this partnership he was the senior.

"I can give you five, perhaps ten heartbeats—" he answered slowly.

"To do what? Act as if I were going to jump in the lake? And how—"

"I can expend a little power over Hory, confusing his sight. He will aim at what he thinks is his target. But that will not be you."

"Are you sure?" My skin crawled. Death by fire is something no one of my kind faces with equanimity.

"I am sure."

"What if he comes to view the remains?"

"I can again confuse his sight—for a short period." After a long moment's pause he spoke more briskly: "Now —we make sure of a future bargaining point—"

"Bargaining point?" My imagination was still occupied with several unpleasant possible future happenings.

"The cache of stones here. I do not think that without the ring they will be visible."

"The ring." I took it out. "You will take the ring, and leave the stones here as bait to draw him back?"

Eet appeared to consider that. "If he had more time perhaps. But I think not now. Give me the ring.

These—we do not want them in sight, if and when he comes to pick me up."

It was my muscle which dragged the box from below the opening and concealed it back behind one of the rows of coffins.

"Now!" Eet sat on a box. "He will not fire until you are out in the open, making a dash for the parapet. The laser may beam close enough so that you will feel its heat. The rest is up to you."

My good sense belabored me as I climbed up, reached out to grasp the edges of the opening. If—if—and if again—

Eet popped out, running, heading for the parapet. I had only an instant and then I fell, a searing, biting pain along my side—a pain so intense that I was aware of nothing else for a second. I could smell my clothes smoldering. Then Eet was back with me, pulling at my coverall as if to urge me up and on, though in reality putting out those lickings of fire.

His mind was closed to me, and I knew he was on the defensive, waiting for a second attack from our common enemy. Suddenly he stiffened, fell over, and lay still, though his eyes were open and I could see the fluttering of his breathing along his side. Hory had used a stunner even as Eet had foreseen, but how effectively? And I could not query Eet as to that.

Around one of his forelegs was the ring. Perhaps his pawing at my smoldering clothing might have been translated by the watcher into a hunt for that. Now we lay still, I belly down, my head turned toward Eet, he flattened out, his legs stiff. Where was Hory?

It seemed to me that we lay there for hours. Since we must be under observation from the ship, there was no chance to move. I had gone down at the touch of that searing beam, not in a planned fall, and my right leg, half doubled under my body, began to cramp. I would be in no shape to carry on battle should Hory decide I was not safely dead. In fact he would be a fool not to crisp us now as we lay.

Except that Eet was sure the Patrolman wanted him.

201

And he had contrived to collapse so close to me that now a sweeping beam aimed from the ship could not remove one of us without killing the other into the bargain.

I could not raise my head to watch the shore line or the span, both hidden by the parapet. Winged things came out of nowhere to buzz about us, crawl across my flesh. And I had to lie and take their attention with no show of life. In that period it was driven home to me again that a man's hardest ordeal is waiting.

Then I heard a crackling. Someone, or something, was climbing the span from the shore, the frail structure creaking and crackling under the weight. A many-legged thing crawled across my cheek and I shrank from its touch, so that it seemed my very skin must shrivel.

My field of vision was so limited! I was not even facing the direction where booted feet would be visible as they crossed the parapet. I heard the metallic click of the sole plates of space footgear on the stone.

Now—would Hory finish the job by simply turning a hand laser on me? Or would the illusion Eet promised hold long enough to deceive him? Perhaps Eet was truly stunned, unable to provide such cover.

Those few moments were the longest of my life. I think had I come out of them with the touch of old age upon me I would not have been surprised.

The boots came into my restricted line of vision. The crawling thing on my face now rested across my nose. A hand reached down and I saw the sleeve of a uniform. Fingers closed on Eet, swung him aloft out of my sight. I waited for a burning flash.

But (and for an instant I could not believe it) the boots turned, were gone. I was not yet safe; he could pause before he climbed the parapet and fire at me again.

I heard the scrape of his boot plates die away and listened once more to the creak of the span. He had only to pull that down or burn it to make me a prisoner.

How long before I dared move? The need to do that became a growing agony in me. I lay and endured as best I could. What came at last was enough to fill me with despair—the clatter of a ship's ramp being rolled in. Hory was back in his fortress and he had activated the sealing of the ship. Preparing to take off?

I waited no longer, struggling against the stiffness and pain in my body, rolling into the shadow of the parapet. Then I pulled along to reach the span. It was still in place; Hory had not stopped to destroy it. Perhaps he intended to return and investigate what lay here after he had made sure of Eet and the ring.

Half sliding, at a speed which left splinters in my hands, for I lay almost flat on that fragile link with land and allowed its slope to carry me to the beach, I reached the sand. Once ashore, I sprinted for the underbrush, expecting at any instant to be enveloped by fire.

The very uncertainty of what might be happening, or Hory's next move, was as hard to take as if I were under physical attack. I must rely entirely on Eet. And whether at this moment he was a helpless captive I did not know. But I could not expect more than the worst.

There was one fairly safe place if I could reach it—directly under the fins of the ship. Always supposing Hory did not choose that particular moment to press the off button and crisp my cowering body by rocket blast. Throwing all caution to the winds, I dashed straight for the ship and somehow reached that hiding place. My side was ablaze with pain. The laser had not really caught me—I would have been dead if it had—but it had passed close enough to burn away the fabric and leave a red brand on my ribs.

So far I had managed to keep alive. But now what? The ship was sealed, Eet imprisoned in it, and Hory the master of the situation. Would he lift off world? Or could his curiosity be so aroused by the vault that he would make another visit to it? The ring! What if he used the ring even as we had done and followed its guide? But would he be so incautious—

"Murdoc!"

Eet's summons was as demanding as a shout from an aroused sentry.

"Here!"

"He is now under my control—for how long—" Eet's thread of communication broke. I waited, tense. Dare I beam to him where I was and how helplessly outside the sealed ship? If his control had slipped, then perhaps Hory would be able to pick that up too. I knew too little about his own powers.

Then I saw the loops set in the fin, surely meant to be hand- and footholds, leading up to the body of the ship. But would they bring me to any hatch? They might be for the convenience of workmen only. That they might— a thin chance—be indeed a way in, made me move.

My seared side hurt so badly as I racked it by my struggles that only will power kept me going. I reached the top of the fin. My ladder did not end there as I feared it would. The holds were now smaller, less easy to negotiate, but beyond them was the outline of a hatch.

I took a chance— "Eet!" I am sure my summons was as strident as the one he had roused me with, because I knew this to be my last chance. "A hatch—lower—can you activate the opening?"

I knew that I was asking the impossible. But still I made my way toward it, clung to the side of the ship as sweat poured down my face and arms, threatening my hold on those slippery loops.

But the crack around the sealing was more pronounced. It was giving. I loosed one hand and beat upon it with all my strength. Whether that small expenditure of effort did hasten the process, or whether the controls suddenly loosened, I had no way of knowing, but the whole plate fell away.

What I crawled into was a much larger space than the upper hatch into which the ramp led. And it was occupied, almost to the full extent of the area, by a one-man flitter—a scout intended for exploration use.

I had found not only a door in but a possible escape out. Before I crawled over and around the machine to the inner hatch, I got out of the flitter one of its store of emergency tools, a bar for testing the composition of ground, and wedged it with all the strength I could to hold the hatch open. Now, even if Hory tried to take off, the ship would not rise. That hatch would have to be closed and he must do it by hand. The protection alarms of the ship would see to that.

The inner hatch had no latch, and it gave easily. I was out in a corridor. I had a laser, and I had also taken an aid kit from the flitter. Now I leaned back against the wall to open that. I brought out a tube of plasta-heal and plastered its contents liberally over my ribs. That almost instantly-hardening crust banished pain and began the healing, giving me renewed strength and mobility.

Then, feeling far more able to tackle what might await me above, I slipped along the ladder. Had I had more than a passenger's knowledge of the ship I might have found a more secretive way from level to level, but I did not. So I had to go openly, up to the control cabin, where I was sure I would find both Eet and Hory.

I did not attempt to touch minds with Eet again. If my last appeal to him had alerted the Patrolman, then Hory would guess I was in the ship and would be readying traps for me.

One small advantage I had. My feet had nearly worn through those covering which had been the linings of the space boots. The material was tough but it had become very thin. The lack of boots now gave me silence as I took the core ladder one hesitant step at a time, listening ever for either a betraying noise from above, or the sound of engines.

I had advanced to the level which held the galley. As yet I had heard nothing, nor had I had any message from Eet. The silence which covered my advance now seemed ominous to me. Perfect confidence on Hory's part could keep him waiting for me. And since I would emerge from a well in the floor there, he would have me at his mercy when I reached my goal.

Now I had only those last few steps. I flattened myself against the ladder, tried to make of my body one giant ear, listening, listening.

"I know you are down there—" Hory's voice. But it sounded thin, strained, almost desperate, as if its owner was in such a vice of tension as to be on the raw edge of breaking. What could have reduced him to such a state?

"I know you are there! I am waiting—"

To burn my head off, I deduced. And then Eet broke in, but he was not addressing me.

"It is no use, you cannot kill him."

"You—you—" Hory's voice arose in an eerie shriek. "I'll burn you!"

I heard the crackle of a laser beam and cringed against the ladder. Then I found myself climbing without my mind ordering my hands and feet into action. There was ozone in the air and I saw, shooting across the mouth of the well, flashes of light.

Eet once more: "Your fear is self-defeating, as I have shown you." He seemed very calm. "Why not be sensible? You are not unintelligent. Do you not see that a temporary alliance is going to be the only solution? Look up at that screen—look!"

I heard an inarticulate exclamation from Hory. And then Eet spoke to me.

"Up!"

I took the last two steps with a rush, remained half crouched, my laser ready. But I did not need that. Hory stood, his back to me, a laser in his hand, but that hand had fallen to his side. He was staring at the visa-screen and I saw over his shoulder what held him oblivious.

Across the inlet, facing the platform of the vault, a square of gleaming metal pushed out of the brush, advancing onto the sand at a crawl. I do not know what type of machinery it hid, but there was a small port open at its top. And I thought that whatever lurked behind it was certainly a deadly promise.

How well protected this ship might be I could not tell, but there are some weapons which it might not be able to withstand. A quick lift could be our only hope. But—the bar I had left in the hatch—an anchor keeping us grounded.

"Eet—" I paid no attention to Hory. "I have to unstopper a hatch—so we can lift—"

I half threw myself into the well, skidding down the

ladder in a progress which was a series of falls I delayed from level to level by grabs at the rails. Then I slammed along the corridor at the bottom, wedged past the flitter once more. I had done my work of locking the hatch open almost too well. Though I jerked at the bar, I finally had to use the butt of the laser to pound it loose. At last it fell with a clang. I pulled at the far too slowly moving door, brought it shut, dogged it down as fast as I could.

Panting, I started back up the ladder. Would Hory's solution be the same? If so, I would have to reach a shock cushion before we lifted. Also—what was going on in the control cabin?

My ascent was not as speedy as the descent had been, but I wasted no time in making it. And I half expected to be greeted by a laser blast, or at least threatened into submission.

But Hory stood with both hands on controls, not those of the pilot, but another set to one side. A beam flashed out from the ship. The visa-screen allowed us to follow its track as it struck across the platform. But it was mounted on a higher course now, to hit directly on that wall of metal moving slowly out of the brush.

There was no resulting glow of the sort that would have followed such an impact on any surface I knew. It was almost as if the shield simply absorbed the ray Hory hurled at it.

I glanced from the screen to look for Eet. There was a burned-out, melted-down mass of wiring to one side of the passenger webbing. But if that had caged the mutant, it had not done so for long. Now he clung to the pilot's seat, swinging back and forth, as intent upon the screen as Hory.

A second or two later, and the ship rocked as if a giant fist had beat upon it. Not from the direction of that advancing shield, but from behind. We had been intent upon one enemy and lowered our guard to another. There was no time to assess the nature of that second, only to feel what attack it launched. I kept my feet by grabbing at the back of the seat. Hory crashed against the bank of buttons he tended, caromed off to the floor. Lights flickered and ran wild across both boards.

Eet sprang from his hold to the edge of the board. We were slightly aslant, enough to make it noticeable that we had been rocked from a straight three-fin stand. Another such blow would send us over, to lie as helpless as a sea dweller stranded ashore.

"Cushions!" Eet's warning rang in my head. "Blast off—!"

I caught at Hory, pulled him over against the pilot's chair so that we both lay half across the webbing. The quiver of the ship's awaking was about us. I saw Eet's paws playing across the board, his long body seemingly plastered to that. Then we did indeed blast off—into a nothingness of mind.

EIGHTEEN

There was the sickly taste of blood in my mouth, a lack of clarity in my mind—

"Murdoc!"

I tried to raise my head. Under me, for I lay on a smooth surface, a vibration reached into my body, bringing into life every ache and pain I had. I rolled, brought up against a wall, clawed above me for support, and at last got to my feet.

Fighting against dizziness, I stared slowly about. Eet still clung to the edge of the control board. And drawing himself aloft, even as I had done, was Hory, blood trickling from a gash along his jaw, his movements discordant and fumbling.

I turned to Eet. "We upped ship?"

"After a fashion." Seemingly he was not so affected by the force of the take-off.

"Back on the sealed course again—" I could remember better now.

Hory shook his head as if trying to clear it from some bewildering fog. He looked at me, but in an unfocused way, as if he did not really see me. Or, if he did, my presence had no meaning for him. He put out a hand to catch at the pilot's seat, pulled himself laboriously into that, and relaxed in its embrace.

"We are on course." His voice was drained and weak. "Back where we were. Next set down will be at the Patrol base—or do you want to reverse again?"

He did not turn his head to look at me as he spoke. If the active combativeness had gone out of him, there was still a core of determination to be read in his tone as his voice grew stronger and steadied.

"The Guild are in control down there." I did not know what I wanted, save to keep from sudden and painful death, a fate which had dogged me far too long. Perhaps some men savor such spice in their lives, but it was not to my taste. I was so tired I wanted nothing but peace. And a way out—with neither the Guild nor the Patrol snapping at my heels. The only obstacle to that was that neither organization was one to relinquish easily what it desired. In that moment I damned the day I had first laid eyes on the zero stone. Yet when I looked to Eet and saw he wore the ring about his forelimb, something about it drew and held my eyes. And I do not think I could have hurled it from me had it lain within my grasp. I was as tied to it now as if I were bound by a tangle cord.

"To no purpose—" That was Eet. For a moment I did not understand him, so far had my thoughts ranged. "Look—"

His paws moved and on the visa-screen appeared a picture.

"This registered as we took off," he explained. "It remained."

I saw the platform of the heads approaching sharply, as if we had crossed above it. And I remembered the ship had been slightly aslant.

"The tail flames of the rockets"—Eet used his instructor's voice—"must have swept across it."

He did not enlarge on that but I understood. The flames—could they have resealed, or cleaned out the crypt? If sealed, then the cache of the best stones was once more hidden. And we were the only ones who knew of their existence! A bargaining point? The stones we had seen in the room of the ruins had been close to exhaustion, those in the vault fresh. They were probably the cream of those owned by the ones who had established the tomb. If the Guild depended upon those from the ruins, they could still be defeated by whoever had the others.

I knew that Eet was reading my mind. But he remained silent, so that Hory could not share my realization of that small superiority. The mutant continued to watch the visa-screen until it went blank.

"They are not going to find what they want," he said to Hory.

The Patrolman lay in the webbing as one exhausted. The blood on his cheek was clotting. His eyes were half closed.

"You have not won either," he said, his words slurred.

"We never wanted to win anything," I responded, "except our own freedom."

Then I felt a sudden strange sensation, a sharpening of contact— Eet's thoughts? NO! For the first time I touched, not Eet, in such communication, but another human brain directly.

I tried to break away. It had been hard at first to accept that Eet could so invade my mind at will. But somehow I had been able to stand it because he was alien. This was far different. I was being pushed against my will into a raging torrent which whirled me on and on. And even to this day I can find no proper words to express what happened. I learned what—who—Hory really was—as no man should ever know one of his fellows. It is too harsh a stripping, that. And he must have learned the same of me. I knew that he meant to bring me to his form of justice, that he looked upon me with scorn because of my association with Eet. I could see— and see—and see— And that enforced sharing went on forever and ever. I saw Hory not only as he was now, but as he had been back and back down a trail of years —all of which had formed him into the man he now was—just as he must also see me—

I fought vainly against the power which made me see so, for I feared I would be utterly lost in that other mind, that Hory was becoming me, and I Hory. And we would be so firmly welded together in the end that there would be no Hory and Jern, but some unnatural whirling mass fighting itself—trapped so—

Then I was released and flew out of the mind stream as if some whirlpool had thrust me off and out. I lay retching on the floor, aware again that I had a body, an

211

identity of my own. I heard noises from the pilot's chair which suggested my sickness was shared, even as we had shared other things—too many of them.

Somehow I got to my hands and knees and crawled to the wall again, once more pulled myself up by holding to the equipment here. I faced around slowly to stare at Hory, while he looked back at me, dully, with a kind of shrinking.

Beyond him, on the floor, lay a small flaccid body—Eet!

Keeping hold on the wall, for without that support I was now helpless to move, I edged along until I passed Hory to stand above the mutant. Then I let go, fell to the floor rather than knelt, to gather up Eet's body and hold it tight against me. That same emotion which had moved me when Hory had tried to kill Eet in the engine room flooded through me once more. It strengthened me, shaking me completely out of my daze.

Eet had done that—had made us free of one another's minds. And he had done it for a purpose. I cradled Eet's too-limp body, smoothing his wiry fur, trying to discover some indication he still lived.

"You know," I said to Hory, "why—"

"I know—" His words came with long pauses between them. "Is—he—dead?"

I stroked and smoothed, tried to feel some light breathing, the pound of a heartbeat, but to no purpose. Even so, I could not allow myself to believe the worst.

However, I did not try to reach Eet's mind. Now I shrank painfully from such contact. I had wounds which must heal, the strangest wounds any of my species may ever have borne.

"The—aid—kit—" Hory's right hand rose, shaking badly. Yet he managed to point to a compartment in the far wall. "A stimulant—"

Perhaps. But how well medication intended for our breed would serve Eet I did not know. I worked up to my feet again, holding the mutant tightly to me, and began that long journey around the cabin. One-handed, I fumbled with the latch, snapped open the cubby. There was a box—in it a capsule. And that was slippery between my fingers, so I had to use care to bring it forth. One-handed, I could not crush it.

Holding it and Eet, I retraced my steps, bracing myself erect by one shoulder against the wall, back to Hory. I held out the capsule. He took it from me with trembling fingers while I steadied Eet's body. Hory broke the capsule under that pointed nose, released the fumes of the volatile gas. His hands fell back into his lap, as if even that small exertion had completely exhausted him.

Eet sneezed, gasped. His eyes opened and his head moved feebly as it turned so he could see who held him. He did not try to leave my hands.

Once more I gathered him close to me, so that the head, raised a little as if to welcome such contact, now rested on my shoulder close to my chin.

"He is alive," Hory whispered. "But he—did—that—"

"Yes."

"Because we must know—and knowing—" The Patrolman hesitated until I prompted:

"And knowing—what? You are wedded to your purposes. But you must know now that mine were not as you believed."

"Yes. But—I have my duty."

He gazed at me, but again as if he did not see me for what I was, but rather beyond, into some future.

"We are not meant—" He continued after a pause, "to know our own kind in that way. I do not want to see you now, it makes me—sick—" His mouth worked as if he were about to be physically ill.

My stomach churned in sympathy. He was right. To look at him and remember— Man is not vile—most men—nor depraved, nor monstrous. But neither is he meant to violate another as we had done. Having Eet as a conductor between our minds was one thing; to be directly joined—never again!

"It was meant that we might understand. Words can be screens—we needed free minds," I said. Were he to retreat now into a denial, an attempt to be as we were

213

before, he would negate all Eet had done to save us. That I dared not allow.

"Yes. You—are—not as we thought." He appeared to make that concession against his will. "But—I have my orders—"

"We can bargain." I repeated Eet's earlier suggestion. "I have something to offer—a cache, untouched, of the stones. Did you read that also?" That was my one fear. That when my thoughts had been laid bare to him, he had uncovered all I needed, for the sake of the future, to hide.

"Not that." He turned his head away. Looking at me bothered him. "But—the Guild—"

"Does not know of this one. Nor shall they find it." I could not be sure of that, I could only hope. However, I thought I had a right to argue.

"What do you want in return?"

I made my first offer as I did because there is no reason why one should not begin at the highest point, as every trader knows. "Freedom—to begin with. After that—well, I am a masterless man with Vondar Ustle gone—in a way he died for this. I want a ship—"

"Ship?" Hory repeated the word as if it were new to him. "You—a ship—?"

"Because I am no pilot?" I chose thus to interpret his surprise. "True, but pilots can be hired. I want payment —our freedom and credits enough to buy a ship. In return—the position of the cache. It seems to me the price is low—"

"I am not authorized to make any such bargains—"

"No?" And then I repeated two words, drawing them out of the time when we had been one.

He turned his head laboriously to look at me again, his face very cold and set.

"True—you know that also. So—" He added nothing, but closed his eyes.

I felt a soft bump against my chin as Eet moved his head, almost as if he nodded approval. Eet had been suspicious of Hory. He had reported a shield—had he suspected what might lie below that? Known that this was no simple scout but a Double Star Commander, sent on a special mission? Or had only suspicion been his before he hurled us mind to mind?

A Double Star, one of those whose word could be accepted at once in an agreement. If Hory did now so agree, we were safe.

"We get all the stones," he said. "That ring also."

My fingers had found the ring on Eet's limb; now they closed about it tightly. Not that! But Eet's head once more bumped my chin. He dared not use mind reach intelligible to Hory, but he was trying in this way to communicate. Without the ring—I could not—

I saw Hory's eyes glitter in rising triumph, and knew that he believed he had found my weak point and would thus regain control of the situation and us. In that moment I had the strength for our last battle of wills.

"The ring also—after an agreement is taped."

Hory hitched himself up, reached to the control board. He used his forefinger to release a print seal, bring out a treaty com. There was no mistaking its white and gold casing. And its very presence here told me of his importance among his command.

Now he held it to his lips. But he wet those with the tip of his tongue and hesitated a long moment before he began to dictate:

"In the name of the Council, the Four Confederacies, the Twelve Systems, the Inner and Outer Planets," he recited formally, as he must have done many times before, it came so easily to him, "this agreement shall hold by planet law and star law." He added figures which held no meaning for me but must have been an identification code. Once more he switched to words:

"Murdoc Jern, status, assistant gem buyer, late apprentice to Vondar Ustle, deceased, is hereby declared free of all charges made against him—"

"Erroneously," I prompted as he paused for breath.

"Erroneously," he agreed, not looking at me, but at the com in his hand. "In addition, free of all charges is one Eet, an alien mutant, now in association with Jern."

So now it was officially recognized that Eet was no

215

animal but an intelligent entity coming under the protection of laws made for the defense of such.

"In return, Murdoc Jern agrees to release to the custody of the Patrol certain information, classified"—once more he rattled off a series of code numbers—"which is his. Accepted, sealed, coded by—" and he unemotionally gave that name which was not Hory, and certainly not on a roster of scouts.

"You have forgotten," I broke in sharply. "The bargain is also for compensation—"

For a moment I thought he would refuse even now. His eyes caught mine and I read in them a cold enmity which I knew would exist on his side for all time. He had been humbled here as he thought I had not, or rather he felt a humbling, though I had not in any way triumphed over him. For our embroilment had been mutual and if he felt invaded, was I any the less violated? Now I added:

"Was it any worse for you than for me?"

"Yes!" He made of that an oath. "I am who I am."

I supposed he meant his Double Star, his training, the fact that in the service he was above and beyond some regulations. But if he was a man who had climbed to that post, and the Patrol was as incorruptible as it claimed to be, then also he must be a man of some breadth of mind. I hoped that was true.

Yes, he had said, but now his eyes changed. There was still hatred for me in them, but perhaps he was a bigger man than he had been only moments earlier.

"No—perhaps it was not—" He was just.

"And there was to be compensation." I pressed my point. "After all whether you accept it or not, we have been battle comrades—"

"To save yourselves!" was his quick retort.

"No more than yourself."

"Very well." Once more he raised the treaty com. "Murdoc Jern is to receive compensation in connection with his information, this to be set by a star court, not to fall below ten thousand credits, nor rise above fifteen."

Ten thousand credits—enough for a small ship of the

older type. Again Eet's head moved. My comrade found that acceptable.

"Agreed to by Murdoc Jern." He held out the com and I bent my head to speak into it.

"I, Murdoc Jern, accept and agree—"

"The alien, Eet—" For the first time during this ceremony Hory was at a loss. How could a creature without vocal communication agree on an oral recording?

Eet moved. He swung his head toward the com and from his lips issued a weird sound, part the mew of a cat, yet holding some of the Basic "yes."

"So be it recorded." Hory's tone had the solemnity of a thumb seal pressed by some planet ruler before his court.

"Now"—he reached for another taper, taken from the same recess as the treaty com—"to your part."

I held it before my lips. "I, Murdoc Jern, do hereby surrender"—might as well get the worst done first—"into the hands of a duly registered member of the Patrol a ring set with an unknown stone, the gem having unusual and as yet unexplored possibilities. In addition I do hereby state that there are two caches of similar stones on a planet unknown to me by name. These can be found as follows—" And I launched into descriptions of the cache in the ruins and that of the vault.

The knowledge that he had been so close to both and had not realized it must have been bitter to Hory. But he did not reveal his feelings. Now that his true identity was known he was a different man, one lacking the more emotional reactions of Hory the scout. When I had described both caches and their locations to the best of my ability, I handed the tape mike back. He took it from me as if he feared to touch my fingers, as if I were unclean.

"There is a passenger cabin to the left of the galley," he said remotely, not ordering me to it, but making his desire plain. And I wanted his company no more than he wanted mine.

I descended the ladder wearily, Eet riding in his old place on my shoulders. But before we had gone the mutant had shaken the ring loose, to leave it lying on the edge of the control board. I did not want to look at it again. Perhaps Hory locked it away with the tapes—I did not want to know.

The passenger cabin was small and bare. I lay down on the bunk. But though my body ached for rest I could not quiet my mind. I had given up the ring, the small knowledge I had of the caches. In return I had our freedom and enough to buy a ship—

Buy a ship? Why—why had I asked for that? I was no pilot, I had no reason to want a ship of my own. But ten thousand credits could be used—

"To buy a ship!" Eet answered.

"But I do not want—or need—and cannot use a ship!"

"You will—all three." His reply was assured. "Do you think I went close to ending my being to earn us anything else? We shall have a ship—"

I was too tired to argue. "To what purpose?"

"That shall be discussed at the proper time."

"But—who is to pilot it?"

"Do not dwell so much on the skills you have not; consider rather those you have. There is something else—look within the inner pocket where you carry what is left of your gems."

It had been so long since I had thought of that poor store, a most meager base for the future, that I could not guess what he meant. I fingered that inner pouch and the stones in it moved under my touch. I loosed the seal to turn out the sorry collection. Among them was—I snatched at it and between thumb and forefinger I held a zero stone in its lifeless phase.

"But—!"

Eet read my thought. "You have broken no oath. You surrendered exactly what you promised—the ring and the location of the caches. If another has seen to a better bargain for you—accept it without question."

Hory—above—could he tune in on our exchange? Would he now know what I had?

Eet was plainly alert to the same danger. "He sleeps. He was close to the end of his strength though he did

218

not reveal that to you. But do not mention this again. Not until we are free."

I dropped the stone among the others—all the bits from my wanderings. To the uninitiated it would certainly seem worth no more than, perhaps not as much as, the rest. Eet's cleverness needed no comment.

Then I, too, surrendered to sleep. And sleep I did, off and on for much of the rest of the voyage. But at times Eet and I talked together. Not of the stones, but rather of other worlds, and I reviewed my gem knowledge. I had none of Vondar's prestige, but I knew his methods of trade. And were I to have a ship, there was no reason why I could not continue on my own. Eet encouraged me in such speculations, leading me on to discuss my chances. I was glad to turn my thoughts from the past, and perhaps it gave me some pleasure to play the informant and instructor. For this was one field in which Eet lagged behind.

But there came a time when I was interrupted by a sharp order over the ship's com. We were nearing the base port, it was necessary to strap down for landing. And Hory continued, saying that I would find my cabin a temporary prison until he could make the proper arrangements. I would have protested, but Eet's head counseled discretion.

The mutant had a listening attitude after we set down. And I heard the clang of boot plates on the ladder, passing my cabin. Eet became communicative when their echoes died away.

"He is out of the ship. And he will carry out his part of the bargain. He takes with him the ring, to put it in safekeeping—as I had hoped. Now it will not betray you should you pass near it with the other stone."

"Why did it not do that in the cabin?"

"It did. But at that time you were too occupied otherwise to notice. Get free of these Patrolmen as fast as you can. Then we shall be about our own business—"

"That being?"

Eet was amused. "Gem hunting—what else? I told you that world was not the source of the stones. The Guild and the Patrol will believe so for some time. They will search, they will mine. But they shall not find what they seek. We have only sniffed out the first few steps on a long cold trail. But we have what will serve us as a guide."

"You mean—we are to keep on hunting the zero stones? But how? Space is very wide—there are many worlds—"

"Which makes our quest only the more worth the trying. I tell you—we are meant to do this thing."

"Eet—who—what are you? Did you—were you of the people who owned the stones?"

"I am Eet," he replied with his old arrogance. "That is all that means aught in this life. But if it troubles you—no, I was not of those who used the stones."

"But you know much of them—"

He interrupted me. "The Patrolman is returning; he brings others. They are angry, but they will hold by Hory's bargain. However, walk softly. They would be only too pleased to have some reason to pull you down."

I faced the door as it opened. Hory stood there, with him another, wearing a uniform with signs of high rank. Both men watched me with cold and wary eyes, their antagonism like a blow. Eet was very right, they would like nothing better than to get me by some infraction. I must walk as warily as in a quaking swamp.

"You will come with us. The bargain will be kept." The officer with Hory spoke as if it hurt him. "But for your own protection you will be in maximum security while you are here."

There was a spark in Hory's eyes. "We can keep you safe. The arm of the Guild is long, it can reach far, but *not* into a Patrol base."

So he made clear his thoughts. I had had two enemies. I might have now dealt successfully with one, but there was still the second. My hand wanted to cup over the stones in my inner pocket. Would the zero stone only lead me further and further into danger? I remembered my father and Vondar—and the legendary might of the Guild.

However, who may seize upon time and hold it fast, not allowing the moments to slip by him? I had said I was not a gambler. But Fortune appeared determined to make me one. With Eet warm and heavy about my shoulders, and the future, misty and threatened as it was, before me, I left the cabin to walk into a new slice of life.

Perhaps I went better armed and armored than I had once been; the sum of a man's knowledge may change from day to day, and experience is both sword and buckler. As long as Eet and I walked the same road, free under the stars, then could the present be savored, and let the future take care for itself— After all, what man can influence that knowingly?

I found it enough to have this hour, this day, this small moment, as a victory over odds which I now marveled at our facing. Perhaps I was true son to Hywel Jern in spirit if not body. And still I could cup hand at my will across a zero stone. The door of the cabin was open. So was that of life, and I had not yet found its limit.

ANDRE NORTON, one of Ace Books' most respected and prolific authors—with over forty books and millions of copies in print—is world renowned for her uncanny ability to create tightly plotted action stories based on her extensive readings in travel, archeology, anthropology, natural history, folklore and psycho-esper research. With classic understatement, belied by the enthusiastic critical reception of all her books, she has described herself as ". . . rather a very staid teller of old fashioned stories . . ."

Miss Norton began her literary career as an editor for her high school paper and quickly progressed to writing, publishing her first book before the age of twenty-one. After graduating from Western University, and working for the Library of Congress for a number of years, she began her writing career in earnest, consistently producing science fiction novels of the highest quality.

Miss Norton presently resides in Florida under the careful management of her feline associates.

ANDRE NORTON

"Nobody can top Miss Norton when it comes to swashbuckling science fiction adventure stories." —*St. Louis Globe-Democrat*

07897	**Breed to Come**	$1.95
14236	**The Defiant Agents**	$1.95
22376	**The Eye of the Monster**	$1.95
24621	**Forerunner Foray**	$2.25
66835	**Plague Ship**	$1.95
78194	**Star Hunter / Voodoo Planet**	$1.95
81253	**The Time Traders**	$1.95

Available wherever paperbacks are sold or use this coupon.